CORPSE ROAD

DAVID J. GATWARD

WEIRDSTONE PUBLISHING

Corpse Road
By
David J. Gatward

Copyright © 2020 by David J. Gatward
All rights reserved.

 Created with Vellum

To everyone at Team Space Team: thanks for the awesome support, shizznods!

Grimm: nickname for a dour and forbidding individual, from Old High German grim [meaning] 'stern', 'severe'. From a Germanic personal name, grima, [meaning] 'mask'.
(*www.ancestory.co.uk*)

Corpse Road: Ancient path used by mourners to carry their dead to the nearest church. Also known as burial roads, coffin roads, and lych ways.

Now it is the time of night
That the graves all gaping wide,
Every one lets forth his sprite,
In the church-way paths to glide.

(*A Midsummer Night's Dream*)

CHAPTER ONE

HE HAD HUNTED BEFORE, BUT TONIGHT WOULD BE HIS first kill.

It was all down to the planning, the training, the preparation. Like his favourite hard-as-hell heroes in the SAS always said: train hard, fight easy. And he had trained hard for this, not just physically, but mentally. Everything he'd been doing had come down to what he was about to do and it felt so, so good! The excitement was so much that he could feel it in his fingertips, taste the adrenaline at the back of his tongue. But he forced all that down, breathed deep, kept himself calm.

A successful operation was all down to the seven 'P's: perfect prior planning prevents piss poor performance. And he'd planned this so well, and in such detail, that it almost made him laugh at how easy it was going to be and how surprised his prey would be when he finally pounced. But now was not the time for laughter. That would come later, of that he was absolutely sure. Because this was going to be fun, wasn't it? Exciting, yes, but fun, too. And the others who understood him, they would see how much fun it had been, how much more fun there was to come, and they would laugh along with him. Perhaps they would even be inspired? Now wouldn't that be an outcome, he thought. His deeds inspiring others to carry out their own acts of retribution? Yes, that would be the ultimate goal of this, not just to follow in the footsteps of his heroes, but to become a hero himself and to encourage others to follow. He would be the spark to light the fire which would set the world aflame! And then society would have to take notice, wouldn't it?

As any good soldier would do, he'd done a close-quarter recce, or CQR, of the site a couple of days ago. He knew the area well, that was true, but it was always best to do things by the book. And he had read all of the books, hadn't he? Everything from Bravo Two Zero to The SAS Survival Handbook. He knew it all—what to do, how to do it, even the right acronyms. And his equipment was the best, because he'd researched it, tested it, looked after it.

Lying inside his waterproof and breathable bivvy-bag, and on top of a self-inflating camping mat, not even a rainstorm would be able to stop what he was there to do. He had worked hard at making sure that the only way anyone would ever find it was if they accidentally stumbled into it. The hide he had fashioned around him, from bracken and heather and anything else close to hand, was made in such a way as to be almost invisible, even up close. And its location made that almost an impossibility. He'd even found it difficult to find the hide himself when he'd come back to it earlier, having been out to prepare the site the evening before. There had been a moment of panic where he'd wondered if he had been too careful. But then the relief at finding the hide had washed over him and he'd felt almost godlike, invincible, immortal.

He checked his watch, then went back to staring down his scope, which was attached to his rifle, a bolt-action Accuracy International model and his pride and joy. It had certainly cost enough, hadn't it? But then, you get what you pay for, and like every other bit of his equipment, from the rifle to his knife to the boots on his feet, he'd bought the absolute best. No army surplus here, no way. He was tempted to fire off a few tester shots, just in case, but there was no need. He had zeroed everything in already and was very happy indeed with his grouping at this range.

A yawn broke his concentration and then his stomach rumbled. Hot food wasn't an option, not on an operation such as this, where stealth was paramount. So, a cold boil-in-the-bag it was, and he tore open a pouch and tucked in. The food tasted so good, all the better he was sure because of where he was eating it, not just outdoors, but on an operation which would change his life forever.

Food over, he carefully stashed everything away then ran through in his mind what he was there to do, at the same time checking that he had all of his equipment to hand, which of course he did, and that just made him smile even more, his cheeks starting to ache from it.

Now it was just a waiting game and that gave him more than enough time to post something out to his followers on the dark web, to let them know that what he'd been promising for so long was no longer just a promise, but an actual event unfolding before him. He was taking action, not just for him, for the wrongs he'd suffered, but for all those others like him, and for how they'd suffered, too. Because that's what it was, wasn't it—suffering? No one really understood, but they would, after tonight, of that he would make absolutely sure.

Others had laid the road before him, that was true, and the inspiration he'd drawn from their actions, their sacrifice, he would never be able to truly quantify. But the rebellion had already begun and he was going to make absolutely sure that it continued. All hail the Supreme Gentleman!

It was time for retribution, time to exact revenge on the society that had denied him—and so many others like him— what was rightfully his. If anything, he was the victim. They all were! And society needed to understand that. That's what this was all about, why he'd spent so much time, so much money, on getting ready for this moment. Right down to seeking out his prey and leading her to the slaughter.

A few moments later, his prey wandered into view, and right there and then he had never in his life felt so alive or so powerful.

CHAPTER TWO

At thirty-seven years old, and not exactly in the best of shape, Kirsty Emily Jackson was, for the first time in her life, pitching a tent. Okay, so this wasn't strictly true; she'd had a practice go on the day she bought it a couple of months ago, but had decided that wrestling in the back garden with a seemingly sentient being created from sheets of waterproof nylon and thin aluminium poles didn't really count, not least because she hadn't then gone on to actually sleep in it. No. Because instead, she'd hidden it away in the loft with the rest of her secretly purchased kit so that Daryl wouldn't find it.

Dear God, that bastard of a man . . .

The fleeting thought of Daryl, and what he would have done if he'd found the tent and everything else, sent an icy shudder racing through Kirsty's body so violent that she actually dropped one of the poles. The elastic thread holding it together caused its individual sections to spring back and clatter together, whipping her painfully across the ankle and making her yelp. As she rubbed at where the pole had struck, flashbacks hammered into her with the ferocity of a hail of Hellfire missiles, her mind shattering into fragments with the impact: insults and slammed doors, silences that lasted weeks, hands meant to care and caress turned into weapons, every sickening moment of what their so-called marriage had become burning a hole through her soul so wide and ragged and raw that she wondered if it would ever truly heal.

Kirsty took another breath. And another. She forced herself to stand up straight—no, not just straight but *tall*—to close her eyes for a moment, and to just focus on the small things: the wind in her hair, tussling it and playing with it and tying it in knots; the faint scent of dampness from the moorland beneath her feet; her heartbeat gradually slowing after the adrenaline surge from the flashbacks; the warmth of her goose down jacket, the sweet bright taste of Kendal Mint Cake still lingering in her mouth, the welcome ache in her muscles after a full day of walking.

Opening her eyes, Kirsty took another deep breath, then stared out at the view in front of her. And what a view it was, she thought, briefly wondering why it had taken her so long to get to where she was right now, gazing out across the hauntingly beautiful landscape of Swaledale. What a place! But that didn't matter, not right now. What did, was the fact that she had finally made the break, kicking Daryl out on his arse a week ago to the day, and this moment, this tiny celebration of what she'd done, was, for the first time in years, her time alone, and she was going to make sure that she enjoyed every sweet-tasting and wonderful second of it.

FOR KIRSTY, Swaledale had been a refuge since childhood holidays had left her forever haunted by its embrace: the sweeping valleys and hills laced together by the thin, ancient threads of drystone walls; houses huddled together in cosy clusters against the elements as though squeezed shoulder-to-shoulder to share heat; the ghosts she half-imagined still worked the tumbledown mines which rose from the heather and bracken like the broken dwellings of a civilisation lost to time.

Fifteen minutes later Kirsty had managed to erect her tent, thin pegs pinning it safely to the ground, the flysheet tied back to give her a small porch area in which to cook up her supper. Behind her, rolled out and looking very cosy and welcoming indeed, her four-season down sleeping bag lay on top of a surprisingly comfortable camping mattress, and next to it a novel she'd purchased a couple of days ago from the little independent bookshop back home.

Kirsty giggled then, and she almost jumped at the sound of it, because laughter and happiness were things which had become so alien and distant to her that they were little more than the ghosts of memories haunting her mind. But she wasn't so scared of them now, not anymore, and as she unpacked her brand-new stove—well, everything was brand new, but that only served to make it all so much more exciting!—ready to cook up the food she had brought with her for the evening ahead, she was filled with the sense that this was a new beginning and that from here on in, life was only going to get better.

Despite knowing Swaledale since childhood, the actual final destination for Kirsty's trip in the dale had come about thanks to a Facebook group about wild camping she'd stumbled on during one of her numerous tedious hours at work. Being a partner in an accountancy firm was an achievement, of that Kirsty had no doubt, and was also something which her parents reminded her about at every opportunity, and the money was quite the reward, for sure. But the monotony of it —the people, the dreary day-to-day of advising companies on their budgets, producing numerous spreadsheets, and really trying her best to always be so very excited indeed about pivot tables—well, there was only so much of it that she could take. And having her own office gave Kirsty sufficient privacy to occasionally just drift among the flotsam and jetsam of the internet.

Kirsty had never really thought about going camping, not now that she was an adult. Her idea of roughing it was a king-sized bed in a Premier Inn. Cooking outdoors, well, that was a pizza oven in a gastro-pub garden. As for exercise, one of the perks of the company was that it had its very own gym, and she had admired it each and every day when she passed it by on her way towards the lift while carrying fresh coffee and a warm bagel from the fancy little shop on the corner. And yet, despite all of this, she'd been drawn to search for activities which promised adventure and escape.

The daily postings on the group page had hooked her in quicker than she had expected. Members posted photos of their solo wild camps and Kirsty found herself scrolling through them in wonder, fascinated by the idea of just buggering off into the hills on her own. Then, one evening, as she'd been heading home and dreading what awaited her beyond her own front door, she had taken a small detour and ended up wandering around a superstore dedicated to all things outdoors. An hour later, she had walked out carrying a bag of things which, only a few weeks before, she hadn't even known existed.

That had been the beginning, the first snip at the wire

fence which had hemmed her in and imprisoned her for so long.

Over the next few weeks, Kirsty had taken further trips into the same store, slowly building up enough gear and equipment to venture out on her own and become a solo wild camper, all while following the advice of the others in the wild camping Facebook group. The idea of it was complete insanity, she knew that for a fact, but as her secret pile of purchases grew steadily larger, so did her excitement, which was made all the more acute by the fact that Daryl Didn't Know.

Truth be told, Kirsty hadn't planned to combine her first-ever solo camping trip with doing to her marriage what a blast from a shotgun does to a melon. It was just the way things had turned out. Originally, her plan had been to wait until Daryl was away on one of his numerous business trips, and then sneak off and bathe in a stolen moment of freedom. Instead, what had actually happened was she'd come home from work to find Daryl waiting for her at the dining room table, in front of him a long list of her apparent misdemeanours from the previous month, and by his side, a bottle of whisky already opened and poured into a very expensive glass.

With the early evening sun bathing the earth in a deep golden hue, Kirsty stirred the boil-in-the-bag beef stroganoff, which she'd heated up in water boiled on her stove, and the memories of that evening dancing around her a little too gleefully, she thought. But the food wasn't just hot, it was surprisingly delicious, and the cheeky bottle of rather expensive red wine she'd brought with her only added to her enjoyment. There was nothing that her past could do to her now that would make her regret what she had done.

That fateful evening, back home from work and sitting down at the table directly opposite Daryl, Kirsty had stared at her husband and known immediately that she'd had enough. When he'd opened his mouth to start at the top of his list, she'd got in there first.

'I want a divorce.'

'What?'

'A divorce, Daryl. Begins with *dee* and ends with fuck you! I want one. I'm not doing this anymore. Not any of it. I want you to pack whatever you need and get out. Now.'

Daryl had stared at her, hadn't he? Those cold grey eyes narrowing to thin slits of meanness, his face wrestling with the mixed emotions of rage and confusion and arrogant disbelief.

'You can't tell me what to do.'

'I can and I have. Get out.'

Then he'd been up on his feet, the list clasped in one hand, the other waving around in the air as he spat a vitriolic salvo of rancorous bile her way, his words barbed with poisoned spite and a mean cruelty he had honed over the years of their marriage.

'How dare you! How bloody well dare you! I'm your husband! You belong to me! You don't get to tell me what to do, you hear? You just don't! And to think of all the years, all the time and effort I've put in to protecting you and looking after you! After all I've done! You absolute shit! You are mine! You made a vow! And you will not break it! I won't let you! I won't!'

With the memory of those words fading in her mind, Kirsty poured her wine into a plastic cup and drank deep, the rich ruby liquid gliding across her tongue, filling her senses with tastes of chocolate and berries and the faintest hint of leather. God, it was good, and all the more so for where she was having it. But that memory still had more to give and its numerous tiny hooks caught her and pulled her back in.

'I've already contacted my solicitor, Daryl.'

It had been a lie, but right then it hadn't mattered, because she absolutely would be doing so the following day, and did.

'You have no grounds for divorce. None! I won't allow it. I'll delay it. I'll do everything within my power to destroy you before—'

'Destroy me?'

It was those two words which had made up her mind in the end and Daryl, unused to being interrupted, had stared back at her in shock. So Kirsty had continued, her voice measured and calm, and yet burning with an anger so hot she was sure her skin had tingled from it.

'It's all you have ever done, Daryl, you know that don't you? You made it your life's work to break me down, to scoop out every last bit of who and what I am, to turn me into a shell, just an empty thing chained to you like a slave!'

'But—'

'No, Daryl! No! There is no but, there is no excuse! None! What did you think? That I'd take it forever, happy to be the creation of a sick artist? Because that's really what you are, isn't it? An artist with a twisted mind, desperate to make me into something I'm not. Well, it's over! I'm done! It's finished!'

'An artist? You're not making any sense!'

Daryl had had a point, Kirsty knew that, but she had been on one, and the years of torment had been her fuel and right there and then she simply hadn't cared.

'This is the most sense I've made in years! So just get out! Get out of this house and get the hell out of my life!'

Daryl had thrown the whisky bottle then, hurling it at her with the roar of a god cast into hell by the people it thought were its believers. Kirsty had ducked, just in time, and she could still remember the faint gust of wind that caressed her as it flew past only millimetres away from her face. That she hadn't responded in kind had been her shining moment because she knew that was what Daryl had wanted. Her retaliation was what he had needed, an excuse to really go for it then, to come down on her with everything he had, and in his own twisted mind, all for her own good.

Instead, she had stood up, walked from the dining room into the kitchen, picked up the phone, and decided that right there and then, he could have the bloody house, the bastard. For now, anyway. She'd get half of it as part of the divorce, so why worry now? And with that, she left the dining room, grabbed her keys, and walked out of the house. If she needed anything, well, she'd just buy it. At that moment, with her soon-to-be ex-husband's face growing redder and redder, with the vile torrent of abuse pouring out of his spit-lashed mouth, all that had mattered was that she'd broken the one thing keeping them together. Now it was time to set a course for a new horizon, even if that particular horizon was a Travelodge hotel on the edge of town. It didn't matter. It was over. She was free. And that was the last time that she'd seen her husband.

Plastic cup empty, Kirsty poured another, then pulled from a pocket some photographs she'd brought with her for just this moment. She lit her stove once more then touched the corners of the photographs with the vivid blue gas flame in front of her. The photographs quickly set alight, their edges curling inwards as though welcoming the flame, and Kirsty dropped them into the empty metal pan she'd used to boil up the water for her dinner. For the next few moments, she stared at the frozen memories in front of her, watching them turn to ash.

Darkness was drawing itself across the world now, though the evening was still yet to turn gloomy. But the horizon was now the edge of a thick duvet promising cosy slumber, and with a toast to the brightest moon she had ever seen, Kirsty edged back into her tent, zipped the approaching night away, and slid into her sleeping bag. By torchlight, she managed to read a few pages of her new novel, but the wine did its work quicker than she expected and so, with eyes barely able to stay open, she fell asleep.

CHAPTER THREE

HARRY GRIMM STARED AT MIKE THE MECHANIC, HIS IED-damaged face looking uglier by the second as he tried to take in what the man had just told him.

'But it was fine yesterday,' he said, nodding to his car, an old Fiesta the colour of a football field after a school sports day in the rain. 'You're sure there's nothing you can do?'

Mike shook his head. 'Nowt at all,' he said. 'You see, it's got an unfortunate flaw.'

Harry leaned in, ready for Mike to lay out the technical reasons as to why his car was a goner. 'And what's that, then?'

'It's a bit buggered, like, isn't it?'

'Ah,' Harry said. 'I see.' Even though he didn't. Not really. Because mechanical stuff just didn't interest him.

The Fiesta had died on him earlier that afternoon. He'd been out to meet with a farmer after the theft of a couple of dozen sheep and, chat over, had headed off back towards the office at the Hawes Community Centre. But a few miles into the journey something under the bonnet had made a horrible clank, then something else had joined in with a worrying crunch, and the car had rolled itself to a stop immediately after. Thankfully, Jim Metcalf, one of the local PCSOs, had been able to come out and tow him back to town. But that had taken the rest of the day and now it was early evening, he was tired, the weekend was only a few hours away, and Harry was looking forward to not doing much with it other than falling asleep on the sofa.

'Like I said, nowt I can do,' Mike continued. 'It's not worth the money it would cost to fix it. It's scrap value now, really, if I'm honest.'

'Which is what?'

Mike looked thoughtful, rubbed his chin. 'About fifty quid, give or take a quid.'

'Bollocks!'

'I'm serious!' Mike said, and Harry heard the note of hurt in the man's voice, as though Harry was questioning his proudly held professional opinion and expertise on all things car-related.

'No,' said Harry. 'I mean bollocks as in what the hell am I supposed to do now without a car?'

'Ah, right, yes, I see your point,' Mike said, stuffing his hands into the pockets of his overalls. He looked out of the large entrance of his garage and Harry followed his line of sight to a small collection of vehicles huddled together outside like teenagers around a shared cigarette.

'And you're sure it can't be fixed?' Harry asked, sending another glance at his Fiesta.

'The timing belt snapped,' Mike explained as though everyone in the world should know what that actually meant.

'But that's just a belt,' Harry said, with absolutely no idea what he was talking about. 'Surely that's not exactly expensive, is it? How much?'

'It isn't,' Mike replied. 'The belt, that is. But it's the damage the belt caused by snapping that's the problem. Bent valves, knackered cylinder head, twisted camshaft, not to mention possible piston and cylinder wall damage. It'll be a right mess in there, I promise you.'

'I was with you up to *that's the problem.*' Harry sighed.

Mike walked out of the garage towards the vehicles. Harry followed and was pretty sure he could already hear his credit card sobbing in anticipation of what was coming next.

'I've not got much in at the moment,' Mike said, 'but have a look and see if anything takes your fancy. I can offer credit as well if you need it.'

Harry stood next to Mike and stared at what was on offer. Not wanting to come across as completely disinterested, he moved away from the man and walked over to the vehicles to get a closer look. It didn't help, and neither did leaning in to glance through windows or crouching down to see what was what underneath.

'Anything you like the look of?' Mike asked.

Harry stood back up and walked round to the back of a small red hatchback. For some reason he decided kicking one of the rear tyres was a good idea, the kind of thing someone who knew all about cars would do.

'If you don't like it, there's no need to kick it,' Mike said.

Harry looked over at the man, rather embarrassed, only to see the faintest hint of a smile creasing the mechanic's face. 'Look,' he said, moving away from the red hatchback, 'it's just that, well, I'm not really a car person, you see.'

'Thought as much,' Mike said. 'So why don't you try that one on the left there. Good runner. Solid. Will go for years. Engine is bombproof.'

Harry walked over to the vehicle Mike was referring to.

It was a four-by-four, but smaller than most of the ones he'd seen on the dales' roads over the past three months. As to its colour, Harry wasn't so sure. It had the look of brown to it, but he wouldn't have liked to put money on that having been the colour it had come off the factory floor with.

'Toyota RAV4,' Mike said. 'It's old, but it's in good nick, like. Low mileage, one owner, even has its complete service history, all of it done by me. Permanent four-wheel drive as well, and you'll be thankful for that, I can tell you, once summer's over and winter is on its way. Not exactly economical, but it's the best here, that's for sure.'

'How much?' Harry asked.

'You don't want to take it for a test drive?'

'Why, is there something wrong with it?'

The shock at the mere suggestion was almost too much for Mike to bear. 'No, of course, there isn't!' he spluttered. 'I've got my reputation to think about, you know! I can't go flogging stuff that's knackered now, can I?'

'So how much is it?' Harry asked again.

'Seven hundred,' Mike said. 'Full service and M.O.T. as well.'

'I'll take it,' Harry said.

'What, just like that?'

'Yes, just like that,' Harry said, then turned from the vehicle and strolled back inside the garage to settle up.

ALTHOUGH HARRY'S new home was not even a mile away, back up in the centre of Hawes, he decided that having just bought the vehicle, it would probably make sense to go for a little run in it, if only to make sure that he wouldn't go leaving the lights on and running the battery down or something equally stupid.

The evening was bright and clear and the sun was rolling towards the horizon, dragging ribbons of shadow with it which would eventually knit together to become night. Not wanting to go too far, or to get lost, Harry set off out of Hawes towards Hardraw, then took a right to head up over the fells and on towards Thwaite, over the famous Buttertubs Pass. He had done the road a number of times before and had quickly understood why it was a favourite of drivers and bikers alike, promising not just an exciting drive but views to feed your soul.

The road was clear and wide, occasionally pinching in at points, and lined by drystone walls on each side. Then, after a couple of miles, the walls stopped and open moorland welcomed him and Harry sped on, windows down, enjoying the rich, cool air now blasting in at him, his right arm leaning out of the window.

The three months that he'd been in the dales had flown by and Harry was beginning to come to the startling conclusion that he was as happy now as he had ever been. Back when he'd been sent up north by his boss, Detective Superintendent Alice Firbank, he had hoped that the placement would only be for a couple of weeks, a month at best. He'd been sure that he would miss Bristol, a city that danced to its own beat, where vintage shops rubbed shoulders with high-end designer outlets, where an evening out could involve a Michelin-starred restaurant, a microbrewery pub, and a funky new nightclub, and a place he had called home for more years than he cared to remember. Now though, and although it was absolutely something he wouldn't mention to anyone, not even in the strictest confidence, he was beginning to think that if it never came to an end, well, he wouldn't exactly be complaining.

Wensleydale, Harry had come to realise, had somehow got under his skin. Yes, the dale itself was a beautiful and rugged thing, which looked very good on postcards and biscuit tins, but there was so much more to it than what the eye could see and what the tourist board could squeeze into a little brochure. It was a living, breathing place, where the lives of the people who lived there were a part of the soil, with families farming the same land for generations. He had made friends, good ones, too, and much to his surprise, had even bought a pair of Wellington boots. The only thing he had yet to make peace with was the whole Wensleydale cheese-with-cake thing so loved it seemed by everyone he'd met, but that wasn't exactly a deal-breaker. If people wanted to ruin good cake with some stinking pats of off milk, then that was their business; he would just continue to forgo the white, crumbly horror, and stick to eating cake on its own, not counting the copious mugs of required tea, obviously.

Harry spied a layby ahead and pulled in, swinging his newly purchased vehicle around to face back down the way he'd come. So far so good, he thought, as the RAV4 purred quietly and he accelerated homeward. The vehicle was certainly a lot comfier than his old Fiesta, Harry thought, and in considerably better condition, too, but then he hadn't exactly looked after it, and the passenger footwell had served as much as a rubbish bin as anything else. It was pretty basic, but that was something he liked. Harry wasn't one for fancy built-in cameras, in-car entertainment systems which could turn your heating at home on and off, leather interiors, or cruise controls. The car had air conditioning and a CD player and that was about as far as it went in terms of luxury.

It also had, quite to Harry's bemusement, a little instrument perched on the dashboard just in front of the steering wheel, which not only showed the level of incline and lean of whatever slope the vehicle happened to be on, but also a compass to show direction. Useful, Harry thought, though for what exactly, he hadn't the faintest idea.

Back in Hawes, Harry parked up then walked on towards the flat which had been his home for the past couple of months. He had some food in for the evening ahead and as he opened the door he was very much looking forward to eating just enough to send himself to sleep on the sofa. He'd managed to lose a bit of weight over the past few weeks, thanks to regular runs, which were no faster but a little less painful, so booze was off the menu.

Wandering through to the kitchen, Harry dropped his keys on the table and was about to make his way over to the fridge when his phone rang.

'Grimm,' Harry said, his gruff voice sounding tired even to him.

No answer came, but Harry heard breathing.

'Hello?' Harry said. 'Who is this?'

Still nothing, just breathing.

'Look,' Harry said, not in the mood for either a prank call or some poor bastard working cold calls to pay the rent, 'it's a Friday night, I'm tired and I'm hungry, so if this is important, speak. If it isn't, then—'

'Hello, Harry.'

Harry's world slammed into an invisible wall and he reached out to steady himself against the kitchen door. He recognised the voice, but it couldn't be . . . No, it was impossible, surely! There was just no way . . .

'Harry, it's your dad.'

And there it was, the voice of the devil introducing himself.

'I know who it is, you murderous bastard,' Harry growled, his voice the deep, guttural snarl of a wolf ready to kill.

Two decades crumbled to nothing and Harry was reliving moment after godawful moment, every single second he'd spent with the man clattering into him like rounds spat from a machine gun. Dad, the man may have been, but he was certainly no father.

'Don't hang up.'

'What do you want? How'd you get this number?'

'That doesn't matter right now.'

'Oh, I think it does,' Harry said, his voice a whisper, his blood boiling now, the heat of it setting fire to his veins. 'It matters a great deal. And unless you're calling me to finally give up and hand yourself in for what you did, then we have nothing to say to each other.'

'This isn't about me.'

'Oh, it bloody well is,' Harry said. 'It's always been about you.'

'You need to listen, Harry.'

Harry fell quiet, not because he was listening, but because the rage inside him was unbearable and he knew of no words in existence that he could conjure up to adequately express what he needed to say right then in that moment.

'You're in danger.'

Harry choked on a laugh. 'I'm sorry, what? Danger? Me? You're the one who threatened Ben! You're the one who killed Mum!' Harry was shouting now, his words spitting out like bolts of fire. 'You want to know who's in danger? Because I don't care how long it takes, I'm going to find you, and when I do, I'll be making absolutely bloody sure you—'

'What do you mean, threatened Ben?'

Harry couldn't believe what he was hearing. 'I'm not having this conversation,' he said. 'So why don't you do us both a favour and stop talking shite?'

'I'm not,' Harry's dad replied. 'I honestly don't know what you're talking about.'

It was all Harry could do to not throw his phone at the wall and watch it splinter into a thousand pieces of shattered glass and twisted metal. 'You sent a message to him in prison,' Harry said. 'Scared him half to death. Your own son, you bastard!'

'It wasn't me. It was them.'

'I'm sorry what?'

'It wasn't me, Harry! It wasn't! I don't even know where the hell Ben is!'

'And yet you were able to somehow find my number?'

For a moment neither man spoke.

'I'm not calling you to ask for forgiveness,' Harry's dad said. 'Neither am I about to give myself up for what I did. But I have changed, Harry.'

'I'm sorry,' Harry said, 'but I don't understand a word you're saying, because you seem to be talking bollocks.'

Harry heard a slow, deep breath down the line.

'They're going to try to get to me by coming for you,' Harry's dad said.

'They? Who's *they*?'

'That doesn't matter! You just need to be careful, okay? I've done more than enough in this lifetime to accept what's coming for me, but I can't have it touch you or Ben.'

'What are we, your get out of jail free card when you get

to the gates of Hell?' Harry roared. 'Because we both know it's not going to be enough! Not enough by half, you hear?'

'I have to go,' Harry's dad said, and Harry heard panic in the man's voice. 'I'll contact you again when I can.'

'No, you bloody well won't,' Harry said. 'Not unless you're calling me to come put you behind bars for the rest of your pathetic life!'

No reply came, just the thin whine of a broken call.

Harry roared then and punched the kitchen door hard enough to splinter a panel and bloody his knuckles.

CHAPTER FOUR

KIRSTY WOKE WITH A START, HER HEART BEATING HARD enough for her to see the rhythm counted out on the outer surface of her sleeping bag. At first disorientated, she quickly remembered where she was, reached for her torch, and switched it on. As to what had actually woken her, she wasn't entirely sure, and for a moment the only sound she could hear was that of her blood thumping through the veins in her head. Around her, the tent seemed like a cocoon, a strange almost alien thing into which she'd been stowed, as though in some form of stasis, safe and secure not only from the outside world but from the life she'd lived up until just a few days ago. She remembered then, the sound of something hitting the outside of the tent, a sharp tap, like a solitary raindrop falling from the sky. At least that's what she thought she remembered, but whether or not such a thing had happened, she had no idea at all, her mind sluggish from sleep and a polished off bottle of wine, the fading remnants of dreams already twisting into forgotten wisps of the imaginary.

As she lay there thinking about the mysterious sound

that she may or may not have heard, a yawn pushed itself out and Kirsty stretched as best she could, her hands pressing against the material of the tent, her toes doing the same as her heart rate started to slow. The ache in her muscles from the walk the day before had eased a little, but she was stiff now, and she rolled onto her front in an attempt to loosen up the tightness she felt through her whole body. Unfortunately, all that did was put weight on her bladder and Kirsty knew immediately that she would now have to venture out into the night to nip to the loo. Sitting up, Kirsty yawned once again, then unzipped her sleeping bag and the inner tent, and twisted round to ready herself to slip out into the outside world.

Boots on, Kirsty slipped her head torch on, reached forward, and with a sudden awareness of the chill creasing the edges of the night air, unzipped the flysheet to stare out onto a dark and foreboding moor. She shuffled out quickly, her gaze drawn upwards almost immediately by the vastness of the black bespeckled heavens above. She checked the time, amazed to see that it wasn't even gone ten yet. But it seemed so late and it felt as though she had been asleep for hours. The moment reminded her of being a child, of waking in the night to a silent house, the world so still she was sure it was listening in.

Kirsty paused then, desperate to relieve herself, but at the same time equally as keen to not let this moment pass. She had seen dark nights before, yes, but none so bright and clear as this, the thick blanket of stars working together to make the blackness beyond them even more deep and endless. It was a wonder to behold and she was here to witness it because she had decided to take control of her life at last. In some ways it felt like a reward, Kirsty thought, as though the universe was rubber-stamping her actions by showing her just a little of what she had to look forward to now that she was free of Daryl.

A shiver raked its nails down Kirsty's back, and she pulled herself away from stargazing to deal with the fact that her bladder was about to burst. Served her right for drinking all the wine, she thought, but it had absolutely been worth it, if only to let her steal a private moment with the stars.

A quick scan of the surrounding area with the torch gave Kirsty plenty of choice for things to duck behind, from old drystone walls to a few bushes and a gnarly, windswept old tree. But the wall won out and Kirsty raced over, hiding behind it from what exactly she had no idea, but right then she didn't care. It was cold, dark, and more than a little bit spooky, so the sooner she was back in the cosy false security of her sleeping bag and tent, the better.

Crouching down in the darkness, Kirsty heard something behind her, a sort of faint, soft rustling, as though a curtain was being pulled back. She froze, her senses suddenly heightened to the world around her. The darkness seemed to rise around her then and fall inwards, a great and impossible wall to suffocate her. Her breath caught in her throat and the silence, right then, seemed to be overwhelming, deafening almost.

Kirsty was up on her feet in a heartbeat, pulling her trousers back up as she hobbled forwards across the tufty grass back to her tent. She had no doubt that what she'd heard was a fox or a badger, perhaps even a deer, but it had still spooked her, and she sped up, the beam from her torch swinging back and forth, casting white light in front of her like spilled milk on the grass.

Another sound this time, only it sounded like a growl. Or was it a laugh?

Kirsty stopped, couldn't move, afraid that if she did, then whatever it was that was out there in the darkness beyond would hear, and equally afraid that if she didn't, if she stayed exactly where she was, then it would get her anyway. But what would get her? she thought. It couldn't have been a growl, not up here on the moors. Yes, there were urban myths of big cats released by their rich owners to fend for themselves, but such legends were of other places, not here, not Swaledale! It was her mind playing tricks, an overactive imagination putting the willies up her, as her father would say. It wasn't the best of phrases to use, and it had always made her laugh how completely incapable he was of seeing why it sounded so inappropriate, and yet here, right now, it seemed to fit better than anything else she could think of.

Back to the tent, Kirsty . . . Back to the tent and get yourself back to sleep . . .

Kirsty moved, her feet dancing out a flurry of fairy footsteps as she swept through the grass to dive headfirst into her tent, the cold air snatching at her as she fell forwards. Then, she was inside, the fabric cave enclosing her with a sense of security she knew to be misguided yet to which she grabbed on tightly anyway.

Turning quickly around to face back out through the door, Kirsty stabbed at the darkness beyond her tent with the torchlight, using its beam to take scythe-like cuts at it, turning the gloom into ripped sheets of black. And out of it something shot forth, too quick for her to see, but powerful enough to smack into her left cheek and cause her to squeal out, not just in pain, but shock and fright.

Kirsty rubbed her face where whatever it was had hit her

and she turned around in the tent, expecting to find an unconscious wasp or bee.

A sharp stab lanced its way up Kirsty's back as something else smacked into her, the sting of it lighting her up with enough pain to elicit a flurry of swearing.

Kirsty snapped around to stare out of her still open tent when once again pain coursed through her, this time from something bouncing off her forehead. The only difference was that this time she saw it land.

Resting by her right hand, on the surface of her sleeping bag, small and innocuous, was a white ball no bigger than a few millimetres in diameter. Yet the fact that it was there at all gave it such weight that for a moment Kirsty felt as though she was being drawn down towards it, sucked in by an impossible gravity.

Kirsty reached out towards the ball with her left hand. When she touched it, the ball jumped away, rolling to a stop further down her sleeping bag. She reached out again, pinched it between finger and thumb, then brought it up close to her face.

The tiny, white sphere was plastic, Kirsty noticed, staring at it, as baffled by its presence as she was disturbed by it. It was the kind of ball she had seen in the toy guns one of her friends had bought for her two sons, except those had been bright red.

A sharp tap of something landing against the inside of the tent had Kirsty staring at another of the balls. And at that point a thought, cold and sharp, pierced her mind: someone was out there in the dark, shooting at her. And she had a pretty good idea who it was.

'Daryl!' Kirsty yelled, thrusting her head outside of the

tent, her torch beam sent out to cut the night in two. 'Daryl, you pathetic bastard! Where are you?'

The night hung above her, a breathless thing, expectant and full of threat.

'Daryl? Daryl! Come on then and show yourself, or are you too pathetic to even do that, hiding in the shadows? Call yourself a man? You disgust me!'

Pain lit Kirsty's face as another of the small white balls pinged off her cheek. When Kirsty spoke again, her voice was years of anger and frustration and fear, and it clawed out of her throat, hacking its way out to scream at the night.

'What the hell is wrong with you? Shooting at me with a toy gun? Is that what you've come to? Is it, Daryl? Really? You're that pathetic that you'd follow me out here just to scare me? Oh, you're such a man, aren't you? Such a powerful, strong man! Well, guess what? You're not! You're pathetic! You're a weak, pathetic man with about as much backbone as a mollusc! Now sod off home, will you, and I'll make sure my solicitor calls to say hello in the morning!'

As the last word left Kirsty's mouth something grabbed her hair and dragged her from her tent, and she was sure her scalp was being torn off. She twisted left and right and reached up to find a gloved hand hooked into her. Clawing at it did no good as she was dragged out into the open air then hurled forwards onto her face.

Kirsty, the wind knocked from her, gave in to the pure, white-hot fury which consumed her, and twisted over onto her back ready to attack Daryl, torch in hand and shining out, as a weight slammed into her, crushing her to the ground, and then a sharp, impossible pain to her throat stole away her voice.

Kirsty tried to speak, tried to move, but could do neither.

In front of her face, the night seemed to have formed itself into a human shape, sketched out in the flickering beam from her torch. But all she could see of the thing's face were eyes and a mouth, both glistening in the weak torchlight.

She was afraid now, terrified, because something was wrong with her body, her everything. She was cold suddenly, as though the heat was draining from her, and all Kirsty wanted to do was to curl up inside her sleeping bag, to fall asleep, and to wake to a new morning. Yes, that was what she wanted, wasn't it? Because this was a nightmare, a mix of tiredness, over excitement, too much wine, and her imagination taking a fast train to crazy.

Then grey light slipped into her mind and Kirsty faded into it, folding into its deep, endless embrace, her eyes closing to the face before her, her last breath, still sweet from the booze, drifting out to be tasted by her attacker's tongue.

Laying the body down, the killer stood up, then set to work with the killing knife on one final task, every sweet moment recorded for his fans.

CHAPTER FIVE

HARRY SAT UP SO QUICKLY HIS HEAD SPUN, THE VIOLENT trill of his phone ripping him from his dreamless sleep so violently that for the briefest moment he was pretty sure that someone had come into his bedroom to attack him with a dentist's drill. Rubbing his eyes and mumbling a few profanities, he reached out and grabbed it, fully expecting to recognise the number from the call he'd received just a few hours before from his father. Only it wasn't, which was a relief of sorts, except that he knew full well that a call at this hour was never ever good. No one ever rang someone in the early hours to say, 'Hey, guess what! I'm going to give you a thousand quid!' or, 'Have a promotion and six months extended leave!' No. It was always and without fail bad news.

'Grimm,' Harry answered, weariness in his voice, but the reply came in before he'd even finished saying his own name.

'Boss, it's Dinsdale. Did I wake you?'

'Yes, of course, you bloody well woke me!' Harry snarled back at the voice of Detective Sergeant Matthew Dinsdale, glancing at the time. 'It's half two in the sodding morning!

What did you think I was doing? Watching the late-night shopping channels to try and grab a bargain?'

Harry had given up trying to stop his team from calling him boss. At first, he hadn't wanted the title because he'd been adamant that he wasn't going to be around long enough to warrant it. Now, though, he didn't really mind, and it was certainly a lot better than a good number of other things they could call him, and probably did when he wasn't around.

'We've found a body.'

That news was enough to have Harry not just awake but alert and quickly out of bed. 'Who has? Where?'

'Swaledale Mountain Rescue,' Matt explained. 'Had a call out just before midnight. We're up above Gunnerside.'

Harry remembered Matt telling him about his role as a member of the local rescue team. But it wasn't just people lost on the moors they dealt with, but folk who had somehow gotten themselves into trouble in one of the numerous caves and potholes in the area. Harry still couldn't get his head around why anyone would use the word 'fun' to describe an activity which involved crawling on your belly in mud and water through tunnels deep underground.

'So why are you calling me?' Harry asked. 'Death from exposure or falling off a cliff in the middle of the night isn't really police business. You're a DS. You can handle it.'

'It's a bloody mess, boss, that's why,' Matt said, and Harry heard the dead tone in his voice, one that told him his night of sleep was over. 'Jim's on his way to pick you up. I need you here ASAP.'

Harry yawned, his body forcing out an involuntary stretch at the same time. 'A mess in what way? How do you mean? What's actually happened? What have you found?'

'I think it's best you see for yourself,' Matt suggested.

'I've secured the crime scene and no bugger's going near it, that's for sure. Not until you get here, anyway. I can't make the call on what happens next, but I think we need to throw everything at this.'

Harry sensed a headache coming on but forced it back down. And although he didn't want to admit this to Matt, he was impressed with his professionalism for calling him in the first place. 'You can give me more detail than that. What are we dealing with?'

There was a pause down the line and Harry sensed that Matt was working out the best way to deliver the most information in the shortest amount of time.

'Female backpacker, looks like a stab wound to the throat.'

That was a new one on Harry. A murdered backpacker? He had a fleeting memory of the film *American Werewolf in London*, but quickly quashed it. 'Anything about the victim's identity?' he asked. 'Any ID?'

'We reckon, well we think, I mean, well, it looks like she's called Stacy,' Matt said stumbling over his words.

Harry was confused. 'It looks like? What the hell does that mean, *it looks like?*'

'Just that,' Matt replied. 'We think that her name's Stacy.'

'And why's that?'

The pause from the other end of the line was thick and heavy.

'Well?' Harry pressed, already dreading where this phone call was leading.

'Because,' Matt said, his voice suddenly quieter, even more grave, 'it's been carved into her forehead and written on her tent in blood, which is probably hers, I'm thinking.'

A cold so violent came over Harry that it was as though

he'd been suddenly caught in the path of an avalanche. 'Bloody hell.'

'Yeah, exactly.' Matt sighed.

'Best you call Swift then,' he advised. 'If it's as bad as it sounds then there's no point delaying the rest of the team.'

'You sure?'

'Absolutely,' Harry said. 'And make it seriously bloody clear to everyone there right now that they tell no one. No friends, no family, not someone they've never actually met on whatever social media they're on. I don't want to wake up tomorrow morning to a pile of bollocks in the press sparked by a careless message or some other horseshit nonsense on Faceshite, you hear?'

'Yeah, I hear you, boss,' Matt said. 'See you in a bit.'

No sooner had Matt hung up than there came a knock at Harry's door.

'Alright, just a minute!' he shouted. 'I'm not even bloody dressed yet!'

'It's Jim!' a voice called in through the letterbox.

'I know it's Jim!' Harry snapped back, now wrestling to get stiff legs into his trousers which, by some dark and mischievous magic, had in the night somehow managed to twist themselves into impossible knots. 'Who the bloody hell else would it be?'

'I'll wait outside, then,' Jim called in, as Harry tripped and crashed down onto the floor.

'Bastard trousers!'

'Sorry, what was that, boss? You okay?'

'Nothing,' Harry hissed through gritted teeth. 'Just give me five, alright? I'll be out in a jiffy.'

Back up on his feet, Harry couldn't remember the last

time he'd used the word 'jiffy', but use it he had, though he had no real idea how long one actually was.

Dressed, at last, Harry went to the front door and opened it to find Jim standing outside as though on protective duty. He liked that about Jim; he was keen. He may have been only a PCSO in the eyes of most people, so not a real copper, but that seemed to have no bearing at all on how he worked. And Harry had grown to respect him as much as any of the others on the team.

'Just need to put my shoes on,' Harry said.

'You'll need your boots, not shoes,' Jim said. 'We'll be out on the hills, like. Up by the old lead mines above Gunnerside. It's not exactly muddy, but chances are you'll snap your ankle if you go up in those.'

Harry agreed, heaved himself into them, pulled on a jacket, then left the flat and followed Jim over to his Land Rover. 'I'm assuming you or Matt have been in touch with the rest of the team, yes?'

'Liz is away to a funeral,' Jim said. 'Gordy's on leave for the week now, up in Scotland somewhere, visiting family I think.'

'What about Jenny and Jadyn?'

'Jenny and Jadyn will be in Hawes first thing,' Jim said.

Opening the passenger door, Harry was greeted by a small flash of white and black, which leapt at him and attacked his face with a wet tongue and oversized paws.

'What the bloody hell . . .?'

'Oh, right, yes, about that,' Jim said, climbing into the driver's seat. 'This is Fly, my new Collie pup.'

Harry grabbed the dog with both hands and slipped himself onto the passenger seat, slamming the door behind him. 'And it's with us why?'

'He's ten weeks old,' Jim said, 'so I'm getting him used to being out and about with me, like. He needs to spend as much time with me as possible so that he sees me as boss.'

Harry stared at the small, overly friendly ball of fur, which was now sitting on the storage box between him and Jim. Its tail was wagging so hard that its backside kept sweeping round and sending it to tumble off and onto his lap.

'And how's that going for you?' Harry asked, as Jim sparked the engine to life.

'Not too bad,' Jim replied, rolling the Land Rover forward to head down through the marketplace and on to their destination. 'He's a good lad. Keen. Bright. But a right soppy bastard as well.'

As if on cue, Fly leapt at Harry's face with his massive paws. Harry caught him before impact only to have his hands licked with frantic enthusiasm.

'Sorry,' Jim said. 'I should've asked first if you're okay with dogs.'

'Oh, I'm okay with them,' Harry said, 'but I don't think it's general police practice to turn up at a crime scene with a puppy. Sniffer dogs, yes. Puppies, probably not.'

'I'll be leaving him in here,' Jim explained. 'He'll just go to sleep in the footwell.'

It was pretty clear to Harry that sleep was the last thing on Fly's mind, as the dog swiped at him with his left paw, so he grabbed the pup and shoved him down to sit at his feet. Much to his surprise, the dog sat down quite calmly and didn't even try to get back up. Instead, it chewed the toes of his boots.

'They're bright dogs,' Jim explained. 'Too bright, to be honest. He'll be easy to train.'

Harry reached down and ruffled the hair on Fly's head.

The dog leaned into it, clearly very happy, before trying to nibble his hand.

'So, have you got any more to tell me other than what Matt just filled me in on?' Harry asked as Hawes gave way to rolling countryside the colour of ink beneath a clear night sky lit by stars.

'Female, mid-thirties,' Jim said. 'Found near a tent. Matt reckons she was walking the old Corpse Road from Keld to Grinton. It's a popular path.'

'The what road?' Harry asked, fairly sure he must have misheard what Jim had said.

'Corpse Road,' Jim said again.

'And just what in God's name is that?'

Jim dropped a gear to accelerate up a hill. 'Back when folk used to have to take their own dead to church to bury them, and before the church in Muker was built, the nearest church was in Grinton, so that's where the path finished,' he explained. 'It's a nice walk. About sixteen miles, I think. An easy one to do over a couple of days.'

'So when was this, then? It's not still done is it?'

'No, it was centuries ago,' Jim said, a laugh curling the edges of his reply.

Harry wasn't one for giving much truck to the notion of bad omens, but the fact that a body had been found on a place called Corpse Road struck him as more than a little ominous.

'How long till we get there?'

'About another twenty minutes,' Jim said. 'Then we've a bit of a trek at the other end, up the beck along Gunnerside Gill. It's pretty special. My dad used to sing a song about the place.'

'How do you mean?'

'Likes a bit of folk music,' Jim explained. 'There's a local group, called Fourum or something. Still around I think. He used to go see them play in the local pubs.'

They were over the other side of the hills now and coming down into Swaledale. The night was still dark and Harry wasn't exactly looking forward to walking along a footpath before the sun was up to show them the way.

'Don't suppose you've got a torch?' Harry asked.

'Don't worry, I bought a couple,' Jim said. 'There's always one in here anyway, and I grabbed another on the way out. That's something else you should probably think about getting for yourself. The roads around here are pretty dark come evening and in winter it's full dark. Pretty unnerving if you're not used to it.'

A few minutes later and they were zipping along the bottom of the valley, the road a thin grey line stitching together fields and hamlets.

'I'll have to bring you out here during the day,' Jim said, as they wound their way at last into the small village of Gunnerside. 'The King's Head pub is fantastic.'

Jim pulled the Land Rover to a halt on the left in front of a large house which Harry could see in the headlights had a small red post box set in the wall.

'We just head over the bridge,' Jim said, gesturing with his thumb behind them. 'The path follows the beck. Right, you climb out and I'll keep a hold of Fly.'

Harry handed the dog to Jim and climbed out of the vehicle and spotted just a little way off the smallest village green he had ever seen in his life. On it sat three wooden benches facing inwards. It was dotted with flowers and he was sure that in the bright light of day it was actually rather pretty.

'Come on, then,' Jim called out, walking round to meet Harry at the back of the Land Rover and handing him a torch. 'It's a bit of a trek, so the sooner we get cracking the better.'

Harry followed Jim and soon they were heading down a path which, as Jim had said earlier, followed the beck up into the moors. To their left, the beck chuckled and giggled its way through the rocks. It was dark and gloomy, overhung with trees on the bank, but after a while, the path wandered away from the busy chatter of the water to make its way through low fields and stone stiles.

Neither man spoke as they walked, and Harry did his best to rid his mind of thoughts of his father, and what the man had said on the phone, wanting to have a clear head to deal with whatever was waiting for them at the end of their journey.

Further on, Harry spotted what he assumed were the ruins of the mines Jim had mentioned. The land here was scarred still, the wounds of long ago carved deep into the ground, gashes and grazes of gravel and grit riding silent rifts down to the beck below.

Rounding a corner on the path, Harry spotted lights ahead. 'That'll be where we're heading then,' he said.

'That'll be it,' Jim replied. 'Come on, we'll be there in ten I reckon.'

As they drew closer, Harry saw that not only were there a number of people milling around waiting for them, but also a vehicle, which was yet another Land Rover, however, this one was kitted out with rescue gear, including, Harry guessed, a stretcher, plenty of first aid, and whatever else the team had decided was needed for this particular call out.

A figure strode over to meet them.

'Now then, Boss.'

'Detective Sergeant,' Harry replied, as DS Matt Dinsdale came to stand before him, handing him some PPE for what was to come. He nodded towards the vehicle. 'I see you took the easy way up.'

'Not me,' Matt replied. 'Only enough space in it for a few of us, the rest had to walk. Not a bad little stroll though, is it? Though, there are better reasons to go for one.'

Harry caught the sombre tone in Matt's voice and glanced over his shoulder, spotting some cordon tape glinting in the torchlight. 'So, what have we got, then?'

'Best you follow me,' Matt instructed.

Stepping in behind the DS, Harry and Jim walked past the rest of the mountain rescue team and on towards the reason they'd been called out in the first place. Ducking under the tape, with gloves now on and a face mask hooked behind his ears, Harry was soon staring down at the kind of scene usually reserved for horror movies.

'Bloody hell . . .'

'Yeah,' Matt said. 'Not much I can add to that, if I'm honest.'

CHAPTER SIX

BLOOD WAS THE FIRST OBSERVATION TO THRUST ITS hideous way to the front of Harry's mind because, as they slipped quietly through the rough grass, he just couldn't take his eyes off it.

'Jim?' Harry's voice was low, gruff, and sombre, the awfulness of what was in front of them reaching inside him and twisting his gut.

The PCSO, who was still behind the cordon tape, glanced up at Harry.

'I need you to be Scene Guard,' Harry said. 'I'll take it from here with Matt.' Then he added, 'And I'm not asking because I don't think you can handle this, okay? The opposite is true. In fact, I'm pretty sure that you can handle it as well as any of us, but I need someone back there to keep an eye on things. Okay?'

'No problem,' Jim said, and Harry could see the steely look in Jim's eyes telling him he wasn't just fine with it but understood the responsibility and the seriousness of what they were dealing with.

As Jim turned to leave, Harry said, 'And make sure no one comes through that cordon tape without your say-so, you hear? You're in charge and don't let anyone tell you any different. You're my gatekeeper and I want this by the numbers. Divisional surgeon first, then the photographer, then everyone's favourite pathologist and the rest of the scene of crime team, okay?'

Jim gave a quick, casual salute, then turned away and headed off back towards the rescue team.

'Right, then, so who was first on the scene?' Harry asked, turning his attention to Matt, if only to add a pause to the proceedings, and to give him a moment to compose himself. He wasn't exactly in a hurry to get any closer to the carnage in front of them and could already see more than enough of it, even though they were still a few metres away.

'Actually, I was,' Matt said. 'I'm a fast walker, you see, not that you'd know it from looking at me, right?'

Harry, a little surprised at this minor revelation, saw Matt tap his belly. It wasn't huge by any stretch of the imagination, but he had a point. He was a man who looked built more for a stroll than a march. But looks were often deceiving, and that was something Harry knew about better than most, he thought, scratching at the scars on his face as though suddenly bothered by the pain from the wounds, which had faded long ago.

'You?'

'Well, yes and no,' Matt said. 'I mean, I was first in an official police capacity, but the actual first on the scene was Adam Bright.'

'So, you weren't actually the first on the scene at all, then.'

'Second,' Matt said. 'That's a silver medal in the Olympics.'

'This isn't the Olympics.'

'Yes, but if it was, I'd be up there on the podium, getting my medal, and you'd be cheering, all proud, like.'

Harry liked Matt, but there were times when he had an unshakable urge to slap him. This was very much one of those times.

'Right now, the only thing you're close to getting is a boot up the arse,' Harry growled. 'So, how's about we get on with the job in hand, eh?'

'Sounds like a plan,' said Matt.

'It's not a plan, it's procedure,' Harry said, keen to get on, the chill of the night starting to bite into him. 'Right, now then, so this is how you found the scene, yes? Nothing's been moved or disturbed?'

Matt shook his head. 'I cordoned the whole site off immediately. Didn't want to risk having any of the rescue team wander where they shouldn't.'

'What about this Adam Bright bloke you mentioned?'

'He didn't touch a thing.'

'You're sure?'

'You can ask him yourself, but yes, I'm sure.'

Matt gestured back at the rest of the rescue team, who were currently all standing around the rescue vehicle warming themselves with quiet conversation and mugs of tea poured from large, metal flasks. Harry saw that Jim was with them and not just talking but taking notes. That lad is certainly keen, he thought.

'He waited for me because he knew this was a police thing,' Matt explained. 'Not just a rescue.'

'So what about the initial call, then?' Harry asked. 'Who was it?'

'Adam's younger brother,' Matt said. 'He was heading back from the pub I think, saw lights up on the hill and spoke with his brother. Adam lives near Gunnerside so he ran up here to check, seeing as he was close while calling it in.'

'Lights?' Harry said. 'I just assumed this was a nine-nine-nine.'

Matt shook his head.

'No phone call,' Matt said. 'Just a flashing light.'

'And that was enough?'

'Considering what's in front of us, it really wasn't,' Matt said. 'Sadly, it was too little too late.'

Harry wondered how much time passed between the flashing light and the scene in front of them.

'I'll want a chat with this Adam then as soon as we're done here.'

'I've already told him that,' Matt said. 'He's expecting a chat.'

Harry moved closer towards the tableaux of horror, aware now of the growing scent of death. It always surprised him how quickly the stink of it would infect the air. It was worse when a body had suffered trauma severe enough to sever limbs, crush skulls, rip open a person's torso. And here, as far as he could tell, the body was intact, but the blood, that was enough. The metallic tang of it was slipping around them now and growing ever stronger the closer they got to the victim.

'Jim tells me this is an old Corpse Road,' Harry muttered, his voice quiet and sombre.

'That it is,' Matt replied. 'You think this was done here because of that?'

Harry didn't answer immediately, his mind still trying to take it all in. 'Whether it is or not, I don't know, but it certainly makes it all the more sinister, doesn't it?'

'Yeah, it does.' Matt sighed.

'So, why didn't she use her mobile phone?' Harry asked. 'A woman out here on her own would have one with her, surely, right?'

'Not always,' Matt said. 'Not that we know yet, so we'll just have to wait to see if the CSI bods find one, but a lot of folk head out into the hills without their phones because that's the very reason they're going out into the hills in the first place. You know, to leave all that bollocks behind for a while. I do it myself now and again, just to have some bloody peace! And the last thing you want if you're trying to get away from it all is to be constantly checking social media or your emails or getting phone calls.'

'I feel like that just sitting down to grab some lunch,' Harry said. 'If it's there, you're always checking the damned thing.'

'Exactly,' Matt agreed. 'Daft really, isn't it? I mean, you don't sit at home and get up every five minutes to go and check if someone's at your door, do you? So why do we feel the constant need to keep checking our phones?'

Harry took a few more steps, pulling himself to a stop when he was just a metre or so away from the body. Close enough, he thought, to see what was what, but not so close that the pathologist, Rebecca Sowerby, would have reason to complain.

'And you're absolutely sure she didn't call the police?'

'No one's told any of us otherwise. Poor lass must've been in a right state, and to end up like this? Whoever did it, they're a bloody animal.'

Harry was listening to Matt's voice, but his attention was now fully on the scene before him. He was also forcing all thoughts about the call from his supposed father from his mind; he would deal with that at the right moment, and that wasn't now.

For Harry, these initial observations, these first minutes at a crime scene before anyone had disturbed the site, they were always useful. He had, over the years, come to feel as though what he was doing in such early moments at a murder scene was very much akin to stepping into an art gallery before the public was allowed in, albeit the kind no sane person would ever want to visit. This was a private viewing of someone's handiwork, and it was his chance to view it and assess it without his thoughts being contaminated by the words and suggestions and ideas of others.

The woman, Harry noted, was laid on her back, her dead eyes open and staring at the night sky, her legs and arms outstretched. She was fully clothed, which suggested that she hadn't been raped, but that was never a certainty, not until the autopsy had been done. She was barefoot and the wound to the front of her neck, just above the collar bone, was clearly visible. Harry could see that something had been thrust into it, just above the collar bone and blood covered her torso. What exactly, he couldn't say, again something which would become clearer at the autopsy. Regardless, Harry knew enough about violence to know that she had not died well, if such a thing could ever be said of dying at the hands of another. It would not have been quick, her lungs filling up with blood, suffocating her.

Harry forced himself to keep on with the observations and to not dwell too much on the nightmare that had been endured by the victim. He spotted a torch near the woman's left hand, no doubt the one she had used to signal for help. He glanced then over at the tent and saw that it, like everything else inside it, looked brand new, hardly used at all. There was an empty wine bottle just inside the door, a stove, a pan—the remnants of her last meal no doubt.

'You think she drank that all by herself?' Harry asked.

Matt looked to where Harry was pointing.

'Looks like there's only enough kit for one,' Matt said.

'One sleeping bag, one rucksack, so I guess so.'

'Unless there was someone else and they cleared off after?'

Matt offered nothing, neither agreeing nor disagreeing with Harry's thoughts.

Harry's focus was back on the body, his left hand raised to point not at the wound to the neck, but what had been carved into the woman's forehead. He remembered then, Matt telling him about it on the phone. The warning hadn't made it any easier in the viewing.

Matt asked, 'You ever seen anything like it before?'

'No,' Harry replied. 'And I'd be happy to never see anything like it ever again.'

At first, the wounds to the woman's forehead had looked like nothing but cuts scratched into the skin, with no obvious shape or form. But then, on closer investigation, it had become clear that the marks were indeed letters cut into the flesh and the letters spelled a name.

'Stacy,' Matt said, saying out loud the name formed of deep gashes in seeping flesh. 'Like I said earlier. So, do you think that's her name?'

'I guess,' Harry said, though he had caught the sound of uncertainty in Matt's voice.

'But why carve it into her forehead?' Matt asked. 'What

kind of sick person does that? Does any of this?'

'The kind of sick person it's our job to find,' Harry said. 'And quickly.'

CHAPTER SEVEN

As Harry dipped back under the cordon tape and away from the crime scene, bright lights flooded the area in front of him, bringing into stark relief the team of volunteers who had all been called out to rescue someone who now lay dead just a short walk away. The grumble of engines accompanied the lights and Harry saw a trio of four-by-fours in convoy pull up behind the rescue vehicle. The darkness of the night was receding now, with dawn working its slow, relentless way towards them, but the night was still clinging on, the darkness now the grubby grey of rainwater racing down a roadside.

Harry called Jim over and nodded at the new arrivals, all of them now out of the vehicles and busily getting themselves into the white paper suits required for what was to follow.

'Remember what I said, okay? You're the Scene Guard, so you run this. No one gets past without your say-so. Record their details, entry and exit times, everything,'

'I'll make sure of it,' Jim said.

'Oh, and one more thing,' Harry said, 'is there a reason why we walked up here when all these buggers just drove?'

'It's a roundabout route with a vehicle,' Jim explained. 'And off-roading at night isn't that sensible unless you know what you're doing.'

'You saying you don't?'

Jim shook his head. 'Oh, I do, but like I said, driving up here isn't as direct as you'd think. Plus, I didn't want to risk us getting into trouble and then having to call someone away from the crime scene to come and help us.'

'Ah, I see,' Harry said.

'The walk takes about the same amount of time,' Jim added. 'And to be honest, I thought it might be sensible to walk in anyway just in case we spotted anything or whatever. I mean, the route we took here is the quickest way down, so if this turns out to be a murder, then it could be the way whoever did it left the scene.'

A cough interrupted Harry and Jim's conversation and Harry looked up to see a man laden down with a heavy bag and a large camera.

'Hi,' the man said. 'Am I okay to go in?'

'It's all yours,' Harry said, then nodded at the bag the man was carrying. 'You want to leave that with us?'

'This? Yes, that would good, if you don't mind.'

Harry took the bag, which weighed considerably more than he'd expected. 'What the hell have you got in here?'

'Drone,' the man said. 'When the light's up a bit, I'll send that up as well, film the site from the sky. Might catch something interesting, might not. Have to see.'

Harry had nothing to say to that so stood back and let the photographer carry on with his duties, Jim having made a note of his attending the scene.

Looking back to the newly arrived vehicles Harry spotted two faces he recognised, the divisional surgeon, Margaret Shaw, and her daughter, Rebecca Sowerby, the pathologist. Having caught their eye, Harry sent a lacklustre wave in their direction.

'I'll go and see how the rescue team are doing,' Matt said, as the two women made their way over towards him and Harry. 'And I'll have a word with Adam, make sure he doesn't go till you've spoken to him.'

'You mean you're running away,' Harry said.

'Yes, absolutely,' Matt said, and was gone.

'Chief Inspector!'

The divisional surgeon's voice was the kind any army sergeant would be proud of, Harry thought, as the woman approached. It was clear, loud, and demanded attention. It was the kind of voice which could, he was sure, command people to do pretty much whatever it wanted.

'Morning,' Harry replied, as Margaret came to stand in front of him. 'Sorry to have to drag you out so early on a Saturday morning.'

'What have we got?' Margaret asked, ignoring Harry's concern, and striding over to the cordon tape.

'Female, mid-thirties at a guess, stab wound to the neck,' Harry said. 'Shouldn't think the photographer will be all that much longer.'

As if in answer to Harry's words, the photographer dipped under the tape and walked over to collect his bag.

'Thanks,' he said, taking it from Harry. 'Don't think the drone's going to be much use, to be honest. It's too dark to pick anything out that I won't have done from the shots I've just taken.'

'So that's you then, is it?'

'Yes. And I'll get these to you as soon as I get back and have everything loaded up and checked.'

'Good,' Harry said.

The photographer made to leave, but paused. 'Who does something like that, do you think? I mean, why? It doesn't make sense.'

'No, it doesn't,' Harry said. 'Not to us, anyway. But to whoever did it, then it's probably all very easy to justify. Which is as scary as it sounds, because the irrational act has become rational to them.'

Shaking his head, the photographer walked off, only to be replaced by Margaret Shaw, who was under the tape and to the body in a few strides. A few minutes later she was back with Harry and Rebecca.

'Sorry you had to see that,' Harry said.

'All part of the job,' replied Margaret. 'Poor lass. What a mess.'

'So, you're happy to confirm death?'

'My boy, not even our good Lord and Saviour could bring her back.' She turned her attention from Harry to Rebecca. 'You sure you're going to be okay with this one? I mean, you know—'

'Yes, I'll be fine,' Rebecca said, her voice snapping the divisional surgeon's voice in two. 'I can handle it. Now, if you'll both excuse me, I'll get on with my job.'

Harry watched Rebecca give a wave to the rest of her team, and then they were off, a parade of white phantoms marching towards a grizzly puzzle they were now all tasked with trying to solve.

'What was that about?' Harry asked.

'You mean you don't know?'

'Know what?'

Margaret looked serious for a moment and Harry could see that she was wrestling with something, her brow furrowed deep. Then she grabbed hold of his arm and led him away just enough to give them some privacy.

'She was eighteen when it happened,' Margaret said. 'And it's why she decided to become a pathologist in the first place. Changed her degree to do it, moved universities. It's why she's so on edge all the time. It's not personal, she's just, well, focused, shall we say.'

Harry had no idea what the surgeon was getting at. 'When what happened?'

'She was walking home from a club with a friend,' Margaret explained, her voice surprisingly soft and quiet. 'They were attacked. Rebecca retaliated but was punched and kicked unconscious. When she came to, her friend was gone. She blamed herself for not being able to do enough.'

A sliver of ice slipped down Harry's spine as he guessed exactly where the rest of this story was leading. The crime scene was busy now, a tent being erected over the body, evidence being collected.

'Her friend was found two days later,' Margaret said. 'She'd been raped then strangled to death.'

'Jesus Christ . . .'

'Indeed,' Margaret said. 'He was caught soon after. Rebecca ID'd him and the forensics evidence ensured that he went away for a very long time.'

Harry scanned the crime scene, watching Rebecca and the rest of the CSI team go about their business.

'Cases like this are the worst,' Margaret continued. 'Stir up old memories. And I'm just a concerned mother, that's all.'

'Well, thanks for telling me,' Harry said.

'Perhaps best you don't tell her that I did,' Margaret whispered. 'But I thought it sensible that you know, particularly considering the circumstances of what's happened here.'

'No, right, yes, thanks,' Harry said, stumbling over his words.

Without another word said, Margaret turned and headed off back to the vehicles.

'That looked serious.'

It was Jim and Harry turned to face him.

'Most conversations are at a crime scene.'

Jim folded his arms, his eyes now on the CSI team. 'What exactly is it that they're looking for?' he asked. 'I mean, I know they're looking for evidence, I'm not a complete idiot, but what specifically? I'm not making any sense, am I?'

'You are,' Harry said, 'because you're asking questions, and that's the only way any of us can learn.'

'That's a relief.'

'Basically,' Harry explained, 'they're looking for two things, one being anything missing that we'd expect to find.'

'Like what?'

'A phone, for example,' Harry said. 'We'd expect to find that here, wouldn't we? So if it isn't here, then we start asking questions, like where is it, why isn't it here, did she leave it somewhere, did someone take it and if so who and why? That kind of thing. You see, something missing automatically forces us down lines of enquiry.'

'Makes sense,' Jim said. 'What's the other thing?'

'Basically, the opposite of that,' Harry said. 'Anything that doesn't belong. That could be anything from something that clearly doesn't belong to or has nothing immediately obvious to do with the victim, to blood or body fluids, anything with possible DNA traces on it, like cigarettes or whatever, anything that could have fingerprints on it, physical marks like footprints and tyre prints.'

Jim was quiet for a moment. 'So we're looking for things that are there which shouldn't be, and things which should be, but aren't.'

'Exactly that. Couldn't have said it better myself. You ever considered moving up from PCSO?'

Jim shook his head. 'I'm good with what I'm doing at the moment,' he said. 'Anyway, can't see why I'd be needed. With everything you've just said going on, makes you wonder how anyone gets away with anything really, doesn't it?'

'That it does,' Harry replied. 'Anyway, I need to go and have a chat with this Adam bloke.'

'Brighty?' Jim said, then pointed at a man chatting with Matt. 'You can't miss him, what with hair as curly as his. He says it isn't permed. No one believes him.'

Harry spotted who Jim was talking about. His hair was definitely on the curly side, he could see that from where they were standing, but not in an 80s glam metal kind of way, which was what Jim's short description had painted in his mind. Instead, it was cut short and was so black that Harry was reminded of the hair his *Action Man* toys had back when he was a kid.

'See you in a bit then,' Harry said, then added, 'And when that lot is done, you can head off back to that dog of yours before it chews its way through your seats out of boredom. I'll grab a lift with Dinsdale.'

CHAPTER EIGHT

To Harry's mind, Adam Bright was every bit the postcard image of what he imagined most people thought of when it came to someone who rescued people from the wilds —rugged, worn, and fit. In many ways, he was the very opposite of Matt, Harry thought. Adam was tall, with the build of someone who could clearly walk mountains for days and never quit. He wasn't skinny, like a fell runner, but built with a size that told the story of a man who was strong and lean. He was dressed, as were the others in the rescue team, in all the appropriate outdoor gear. As Harry approached him, a smile reached across his weathered face like a deep crack in a worn cliff. He was wearing a black beanie hat and Harry could see the ends of a curly fringe sprouting from beneath it.

'Hi,' Harry said, reaching his hand out to the man. 'I'm DCI Grimm.'

Adam took Harry's hand and shook it warmly. 'Sorry about this,' he said. 'Early morning call out isn't what anyone wants, is it?'

'Hardly your fault,' Harry said. 'Can you spare a few minutes? Just want to go through what you found.'

'Yeah, no problem,' Adam replied, and Harry led them away from the group to get a bit more privacy.

'Firstly,' Harry said, 'I just need to take your details down. Name, age, address, telephone number, if that's okay.'

'Yeah, no worries,' Adam said, then gave Harry the details he'd asked for.

'Thirty,' Harry said, shaking his head. 'I remember that like it was a long time ago.'

'You're not exactly old,' Adam said.

'On the outside, no,' Harry agreed, 'but inside? It's another story, let me tell you.'

Harry paused for a second or two, glanced once again over to the crime scene, then was back to Adam. 'I need to ask how you're doing, with all this?' he said. 'I ask because this isn't the kind of thing anyone's really prepared for. I am, because I've seen plenty of awful things in my time on the force, but this is probably a bit different from what you usually get sent out for.'

'I've seen dead bodies before,' Adam replied.

'We both know that this is no normal dead body,' Harry said. 'There's a huge difference between finding someone dead of exposure to someone dead through violence enacted upon them by someone else.'

'I'm okay, though,' Adam said. 'Really, I am. But thanks for asking. I appreciate that.'

Accepting what Adam had said, Harry said, 'DS Dinsdale tells me you're the one who called it in.'

'Yes and no,' Adam said, correcting Harry. 'My brother, Gary, saw the lights on the hill so I went to check.'

'Ah, yes,' Harry said. 'And that was enough to have you calling in the rescue team?'

'It was enough for me to go out and check, seeing as I live the closest. Out of the rest of the team, I mean. And it's just a short walk really, and an even shorter run.'

Harry had no doubt that Adam would have flown up the path he'd just walked himself with Jim.

'We, all of us, every member of the team I mean, have a grab bag at the door, you know, another in the car. Emergency kit. We're all a bit kit obsessed, really. And I had enough with me to deal with an emergency while waiting for the others to turn up. Can't say I was expecting this, though.'

Harry pondered on how Adam had described the walk he had just done himself to the crime scene as a short run. It wasn't far, for sure, probably just under three kilometres, but running it, in rescue kit, carrying a bag of emergency equipment was another thing entirely. Which also reminded Harry he needed to go for a run himself later on, if only to stop Jen from badgering him about it and quizzing him on his fitness goals.

'And you were at home?'

Adam shook his head. 'On my way back from work.'

'Pulling a late one?'

'All part of the job,' Adam said.

'How did your brother describe the lights, then?' Harry asked, dragging his mind back into the now. 'What was it about them that caught his attention?'

'He said it looked like someone was signalling,' Adam said.

'You mean like morse code?'

'Well, if it was, Gary wouldn't have known,' Adam said, laughing. 'No, he just said that there was a flashing light up on the hills and that it didn't look quite right, all sort of erratic, so I thought it was worth heading out to check just in case. Which is what I did.'

'I'd like to talk to your brother,' Harry said.

'He'll be at home,' said Adam.

'He lives with you?'

'For the moment, yes,' Adam said. 'He's saving up having just finished university and applying for jobs.'

'So he's what, twenty-one, twenty-two?'

'Twenty-two,' Adam said. 'Web design is his thing. Definitely not mine, though.'

'And what about yourself?'

'Me? Outdoor education,' Adam said. 'I have to work outside or I'd go mad. I'm deputy head at Marrick Priory, just down the valley, the other side of Reeth. Lovely little place.'

Harry wasn't at all surprised and could easily see how the role suited Adam. He had a naturally confident air to him and Harry had no doubt that he was well-liked by the kids he threw off cliffs and down rivers.

'So you were there yesterday evening?'

Adam shrugged a 'Yes', then said, 'We were doing what we call a Night Owl exercise. Send the kids out when it's starting to get dark and have them do an easy orienteering course. The staff patrol it to make sure they don't get lost. It's a lot of fun and makes sure they're knackered enough to actually go to sleep.'

'Sounds fun,' Harry said.

'It is. I love my job. I'm very lucky. I basically spent the whole evening out on the hills, just observing the other staff, making sure they're all on it, if you know what I mean. It's best to step back, you know? Give them space, observe from afar. Otherwise, they're always looking over their shoulder, and that's not good.'

Harry asked, 'When's the best time to catch Gary, then? And can I have his number?'

'Sure,' Adam said, pulling out his phone and flicking through his contacts. 'And any time is fine at the moment. Like I said, he's applying for jobs, but it's not easy. And he's doing a bit of work from home when he can get it. Freelance stuff. To be honest, I've not a clue about any of it. His room looks like something you see in the movies, all screens and keyboards and little red lights going on and off.'

Harry wrote down Gary's number. 'So, do you want to tell me what you found when you arrived? What you saw?'

Harry noticed Adam shuffle a little on his feet, clearly uncomfortable with the memories his questioning had stirred.

'It was quiet,' Adam said, his voice dropping a notch, as though talking about death automatically required the kind of volume generally reserved for funerals. 'I mean, it's always quiet up here, up on the moors, but it seemed quieter, though I'm probably reading too much into that.'

'Not necessarily,' Harry said. 'I've experienced the same, when you walk into a crime scene and the horror of it just seems to have sucked out the usual atmosphere of a place, turned it sombre or something, like the volume on the world has been turned down.'

'Yes, it was like that,' Adam nodded. 'It was the tent I saw first. Nice one, too, actually. Decent bit of kit. Some folk go out with stuff that I wouldn't even use in a back garden on a sunny day. But this one wasn't bad at all. Looked new, too, I reckon.'

'And was there anything odd about what you saw?' Harry asked.

'Like what?'

'Was there anything you noticed around the tent, any sign of disturbance? Anything that didn't look right, was out of place? Something that shouldn't be there that was?'

'Just the blood,' Adam said. 'And I only saw that when I got close. At first, I just thought it was damp, like there'd been a quick shower up here and it was still drying out. Weather can change like that, you know? I've been in my garden and seen rain lashing down at the other end of it while I'm sitting just a few metres away in the dry.'

'What did you do when you realised it was blood?' Harry asked.

'Not much,' Adam said. 'I'd already called it in with the team, so I knew Matt was on his way, so police involvement was sorted.'

'Then what?'

'I stayed pretty well clear of the site while I looked for whoever had been signalling with the torch,' Adam said. 'I didn't want to disturb anything. I saw that the tent was empty and I called out to see if there was anyone around, if they were injured nearby or something. Then I saw the body.'

'Did you notice anything else?'

'What like?'

'Anything at all,' Harry said. 'Anything out of the ordinary or strange or not quite right.'

'Just the body and the blood,' Adam said. 'It was pretty hard to see anything beyond that, if I'm honest.'

'Well, if you think of anything, let us know, right?'

'No worries,' Adam said. 'Just let me know if I can be of any more help.'

'I'll just need to talk to your brother for now,' Harry said, 'but if I do need to have another chat, I'll let you know.'

And with that, Harry let Adam return to the rest of the rescue team, before wandering over to the cordon tape to wait as patiently as he could for some kind of update from the pathologist and the rest of the SOC team.

CHAPTER NINE

MORNING CREPT OVER THE HORIZON, BURNING WITH the red-orange glow of a stoked furnace. The dew-wet grass at Harry's feet glistened and shone in the new-born light, the faintest of mists hanging low in the valley, like the wayward remnants of clouds caught in fields and trapped between houses. The air was cool and rich with the sweet earthy notes of peat and bracken and Harry breathed it in deep, filling his lungs with it as though necking a draft of the finest ale. The still, almost watercolour artwork of the view before him seemed all the starker because of what lay all but a few metres away from where he stood, his legs stiff, his back aching, his feet numb. He wondered how many other dark tales the valley of Swaledale held beneath its heavenly bed of grass and wall, river and tree, how haunted the beauty of the place truly was by a past no one now remembered.

'Here,' Matt said, coming up alongside Harry with another mug of hot, sweet tea. 'Get this down you.'

'Where exactly are you getting all of this from?' Harry

asked, taking the drink and a sip. 'Is that rescue vehicle little more than one massive tea urn?'

'Everyone brings a hot drink,' Matt explained. 'Tea, coffee, hot chocolate, we've got it all. Does wonders for folk if they've been out and things have got a bit sketchy for them.'

Harry knew very well from his days in the Paras just how important a good hot drink was. It was something some of the US lads he'd fought alongside had always said about British soldiers, how even in the middle of hell, they'd stop to get a brew on.

'Any reason you lot are still hanging around?' Harry asked.

'Most have headed back,' Matt said. 'A few have stayed on, just to see if there's any help needed. It's the weekend, so being up here is no chore really, not with a view like that, right?'

Matt swept a hand out across the valley below them.

'Yeah, it's pretty lovely, all in all,' Harry agreed.

'If these hills could talk,' Matt muttered.

'Well, that would make our job a lot easier, wouldn't it?' Harry replied.

'Anything from that lot yet?' Matt asked, with a nod at the SOC team.

Harry said, 'Can't be long now. They've been at it a good while.' He checked his watch. 'Bloody hell, it's nearly six!'

'Time flies when you're having fun, right?' Matt said.

Harry yawned. 'We've a busy day ahead. There's going to be a hell of a lot to do, that's for sure.' He pulled his phone out and brought up the number for Adam's brother, Gary. 'You mind giving him a call, just to let him know we'll need to speak to him at some point today?'

'What, now?'

'Yeah, you're right, it's a bit early. I just want to know what he actually saw, which I'm sure is sod all, but something might crop up.'

Matt said, 'I'll give him a call now, leave a message, then call again at eight if he's not returned it.'

'Good plan,' Harry said, as a movement caught his attention and he turned to see Doctor Rebecca Sowerby strolling towards him. The paper suit and face mask gave her the air of an apocalyptic messenger, as though she was returning from some bleak land blasted by a plague.

As Matt headed back to the rescue team, Harry reached out and lifted the cordon tape for her and she walked through with a short nod of thanks.

'So, how are you doing?' Harry asked.

'And what's that supposed to mean?' Rebecca snapped back.

'Just asking,' Harry replied, stepping back just a little. 'I mean, it's a pretty rough crime scene as things go.'

Rebecca pulled her facemask up to snap back onto her head. 'Yes, it is,' she said. 'Bloody awful, frankly.'

Silence slipped its cunning way between them then as Harry tried to work out the best way to continue the conversation. After what he'd been told by Margaret Shaw, Rebecca's mum, he was looking to avoid any and all confrontation with the pathologist. He simply wanted to know what they'd found. Obviously, there would be more to come, following the autopsy, but right now he needed something to go on so that he could set the team to finding whoever was responsible.

'I've got a few things you can take away with you now,' Rebecca said. 'You don't want to be hoofing it over to the property store in Richmond every time you need to look at something, so just use the temporary one in Hawes.'

'Will do,' Harry replied, wondering who would be best to be put in charge of it.

'Right, so her name's Kirsty Emily Jackson,' Rebecca said, her voice buckled with the weariness she was clearly feeling, not just from a night of no sleep, but one disturbed by the unthinkable horror they were all dealing with. 'She's thirty-seven. Lives over near Darlington in Stapleton on Tees. I don't need to do an autopsy to tell you that she was killed just a few hours ago. That much is clear just by looking at the site.'

This information from the pathologist had Harry immediately confused. 'Kirsty? That's her name? You sure?'

Harry hadn't meant it to come across as a questioning of the pathologist's skills and ability, but it was clear from the expression on her face that this was exactly how it had been heard.

'No, I made it up!' Rebecca said. 'In fact, I've spent the last couple of hours looking over a dead woman and her belongings chuckling to myself about how funny it would be to tell you a completely made-up name!'

'That's not what I meant.'

'Well, of course, it's her bloody name!' Rebecca said. 'She had a purse with her. So, you know, driving licence, credit cards, a few photos, that kind of thing. And, though perhaps this will also come as a massive surprise to you, I can actually bloody read! And—oh look!—here it is! The purse!'

Rebecca revealed an evidence bag containing the purse in question and handed it over to Harry. It was larger than he expected and seemed to have been stitched together from very expensive carpet. Perhaps that was the fashion now, he thought.

Harry took the purse and decided the best course of action was to nod and stay very, very quiet as Rebecca worked to calm herself back down with a few slow, deep breaths.

'Moving on,' she said, 'there doesn't seem to be a phone, which is strange.'

'Apparently, it's not,' Harry said, remembering what Matt had told him and sharing the information with Rebecca. Then he decided to try asking about the name again, but more sensitively this time. 'About her name . . .'

'You look confused.'

'I am,' Harry said.

'The name cut into her forehead and painted on the tent then, yes?'

'Yes,' Harry said. 'That. Stacy. I just assumed that was what she was called.'

'Well, it isn't,' Rebecca said. 'Don't ask me why.'

'Could be a nickname?' Harry suggested. 'You said there were photos?'

'Yes, here, have a look.'

Rebecca handed an evidence bag to Harry. He glanced at the contents. Three photos: one of Kirsty with a couple of friends; one of an older couple, perhaps her parents, Harry thought, and a photo of Kirsty, looking somewhat younger, on her wedding day, cheek-to-cheek with her new husband.

'We also found the burned remains of some other photos,' Rebecca said, handing over another bag. 'In a metal pan inside her tent, next to the empty wine bottle. These are a little bit more interesting I think, though perhaps the word is incriminating.'

Harry stared at the remains then glanced back to the photos from Kirsty's purse. He remembered spotting the metal pan earlier.

'Looks like the same bloke, right?' Rebecca said.

'Very much so,' Harry agreed. 'Which makes me think two things immediately. One, that perhaps Kirsty was saying goodbye to a marriage. I mean, why else would she burn the photos of the man she's just got married to in that other picture? And two—'

'That her husband wasn't too happy about it, followed her out here, killed her, carved Stacy into her skull for some reason, and has done a runner?' Rebecca said, snatching Harry's thoughts from his head.

'Love and hate—two sides of the same coin.'

'And very bloody easy to flip,' added Rebecca, then handed Harry a set of keys. 'She drove, by the way. One of those is definitely a car key, the clue being that the fob says Porsche. The others could be house keys.'

'Anything else?' Harry asked, dropping the keys into a pocket, glancing back over at the crime scene, hoping that what had happened to Kirsty was nothing more than the work of a very, very angry husband and nothing worse. That there could be worse, well, that was something Harry knew for sure.

'Only that she works for an accountancy firm, which would explain the expensive ride. There's a pass in her purse for the office the company works from. And a gym membership card, too, and a few receipts. Usual purse stuff.'

Harry shuffled through the evidence bags, at the same time sifting through his thoughts. In his hands now he had pretty much everything he needed to really get going on investigating a prime suspect, that being the husband, whoever he was. But something still bothered him, because it just didn't fit. Not yet, anyway.

'I just don't get why the name cut into her isn't actually hers,' Harry muttered, as much of himself as the pathologist. 'And it being a nickname just doesn't seem right, does it?'

'That's for you to figure out,' Rebecca said. 'Some couples play games, if you know what I mean. Roleplay. Could be that.'

Harry pondered that thought for all of two seconds.

'Everything else you're pretty much aware of, I should think,' Rebecca said. 'The stab wound to the neck, signs of a scuffle around the body, though it doesn't look like she actually fought back.'

'Really?' Harry said, thinking most people would fight back if someone attacked them.

'Probably didn't have much of a chance,' Rebecca said. 'An injury like that, if it came at her by surprise, she'd have been dead pretty soon after. There are no defensive wounds on her hands or arms, nothing like that at all. Whoever did this stuck her with the knife before she even realised what was happening.'

'What about the . . .' Harry then gestured to his forehead, signifying the name carved into the victim's skin.

'Probably done with the same weapon that killed her. A very sharp knife is my best guess. The lines aren't hacked, just carved, nice and clean.'

'So she was killed first, then?'

Rebecca nodded. 'There's no way she was alive when it was done. She'd have to be unconscious or seriously restrained, and even then, the cuts are just too clean. If she shook her head at all, even if it was being held, then the wounds would show that, and they don't.'

Harry mulled this over. They had a name now, so that was good, but they also had a place of work, keys to a car, and potentially a house, the address of which was on Kirsty's driving licence. And they had evidence of something going very wrong in a relationship courtesy of the burned photos. 'Any sign of where the attacker came from?' Harry asked. 'It's a pretty weird place for something like this to happen.'

'Hard to say,' Rebecca said. 'There are too many footprints around the area to tell, what with it being a popular route for walkers.'

'But why attack here?' Harry asked, almost as though the question was directed at the moors which lay silent around them. 'That's the bit I can't get my head around.'

'Well, she was definitely here alone,' Rebecca said. 'The tent is for solo camping. No way could you fit two people in it. All of her kit is for one person. No additional food. No footprints from another tent either. It was her, out here on her own, and then someone came in and, well, you know the rest.'

'Looks pretty new, as well,' Harry said, remembering what Adam had said.

'Every bit of it does,' Rebecca agreed. 'It's like she went out and bought the lot in one go then headed up here with no experience in the slightest. Why do that?'

'If her marriage has gone tits up, then perhaps she just decided to escape,' Harry suggested. 'Spur of the moment thing, perhaps?'

'Oh, one other thing,' Rebecca said. 'We found these as well.' She then revealed an evidence bag at the bottom of which sat a collection of tiny white balls each about five millimetres in diameter.

Harry stared at the bag. 'What are they, then?'

'I haven't the faintest idea,' Rebecca said. 'Quite a few were found in the tent, a small number just outside. Any ideas?'

'None,' Harry said with a shake of his head. 'That it?'

'We think the blood on the tent is the victim's,' Rebecca said, 'but I'll confirm that later. Other than that, what we know for sure right now is that a woman called Kirsty drove here from up near Darlington, for an unknown reason, to end up dead on the moors.'

Harry could see now that the scene of crime team was bagging up everything from the site, the tent now being broken down. It would all be heading back to the lab for tests in the faint hope that somewhere there was a fingerprint or a hair, just something that would give them a strong lead to whoever was responsible.

'Right then,' Harry said, deciding that there was now little else to be said, 'I expect I'll be hearing from you later today then, right?'

Harry saw the pathologist's eyes narrow.

'Expect?' said Rebecca. 'You'll hear from me when I'm done and no sooner.'

'That's not what I meant,' Harry said, but it was too late, his words bouncing harmlessly off the retreating back of the pathologist.

With little left to do, and no expectation on his part to be getting any further information from the scene of crime team until later in the day, Harry figured now was as good a time as any to head off. The path back down into Gunnerside was clear to see from where he was and seeing it in the early morning light would probably do him a lot of good.

Harry strolled over to Matt and told him that he was going to take a walk back down to Gunnerside and to pick him up from there. Then, after a quick word with the remaining members of the rescue team, and a repeated thank you to them and to Adam, he headed off back down the gill.

As he wandering away from the scene, the sound of the beck dancing ahead of him and beckoning him on, a call pulled him up sharp.

'Excuse me!' the voice said. 'Sir?'

Harry turned around to see one of the rescue team chasing down towards him, a woman with ice white hair in a ponytail and an energy in her step which he found almost terrifying.

'Yes?' Harry said. 'Something up?'

The woman held out her hand. 'I found this,' she said. 'Don't know if it's important or not, but thought I'd get it to you anyway. You never know, right?'

Harry glanced down to see another white plastic ball in her palm, the same as the ones found by Rebecca and the rest of the SOC team.

'What is it?' the woman asked, staring at the ball then back up at Harry.

Harry picked it up then slipped it into an evidence bag pulled from his pocket. 'I've no idea,' he answered. 'You?'

The woman shook her head. 'It caught my eye just away over in the bracken,' she said, pointing away from the actual crime scene. 'I'd picked it up before I'd even thought about what I was doing. I hope I've not done anything wrong.'

Harry shook his head, staring at the thing in his palm. 'You ever seen one before?'

'Can't say that I have,' the woman said. 'Like I said, it's probably nothing. Looks like a bearing, but for what I wouldn't have the faintest idea. And bearings are usually metal, right? That's just a small, hard plastic ball.'

Harry tucked the evidence bag back in his pocket. 'Thanks,' he said. 'If you can just give your name and contact details to Detective Sergeant Dinsdale, that would be great.'

'No bother at all,' the woman replied, then turned on her heel and jogged back to join the rescue team.

Harry watched on for a moment or two more, his head now a confused mix of determination and drive to get on with the case and get justice for the victim, and a deep sadness at what had happened to her only a few hours ago.

And so, with the ruins of the old lead mines around him, and the beck skipping its way ever onwards in front, Harry turned away and walked back down towards Gunnerside, every step feeling as though he was heading further and further back in time.

CHAPTER TEN

Harry, with Matt strolling in close behind, strode into the office used by the team at the community centre in Hawes, to be met by a full-on assault to the senses. The first thing he noticed was the rich, salty smell of bacon, which immediately set his stomach to rumbling. Next was the aroma of coffee. Good coffee, too, he noted rather happily. The usual drink of choice for the team was tea it seemed, but coffee turned up occasionally, and for that, on a day like today, after a night like he'd had, he was very grateful.

Harry saw that the briefing board was already in the process of being filled out on what had happened over on the moors in Swaledale, with a few notes from Jim giving brief descriptions of the scene, the victim, and the names of people already spoken to, such as Adam, and ones they hadn't, such as Gary. Harry had some additional details of his own now, thanks to the chat with Sowerby, and some additional details handed to him as he was heading down the trail to Gunnerside, and he would be sharing those soon enough. There was a lot of chatter around the board as well, with Jen and Jadyn being updated by Jim on what had happened. Then finally there was Fly, who, on seeing Harry at the door, threw himself across the room like a furry missile, leaping up at him, only to be whistled and shouted at by Jim.

'Fly! Down!'

The dog, Harry could see, didn't exactly give much heed to the command and simply continued to bounce up and down, the bounce eventually becoming so violent that it sent the dog onto his back, belly up. Now on the floor, the daft animal kept wagging his tail, which only served to have him slowly cartwheel around in a clockwise direction, his enthusiasm for Harry's arrival not diminishing in the slightest.

'Sorry, boss,' Jim said, jogging over to grab the overly exuberant Fly and take him away. 'I guess he just likes you.'

'I guess he just likes everyone,' Harry replied as Jen headed over and ruffled the fur on the dog's head, the dog trying to lick her hand.

'He's such a cute little bugger, don't you think?' she asked. 'You should get one for yourself, boss.'

'Not bloody likely,' Harry said. 'I've managed to get to my age without having children, so why would I ruin that run of luck by getting myself a dog?'

'Now don't be like that,' Jen said, and Harry saw the grin creasing the corners of her eyes as much as her mouth. 'I can just see you with a little furry friend following you about.'

'You lot do that enough as it is,' Harry muttered. 'So, if I can smell coffee and bacon, am I right to assume there's some left for me? Or have you all wolfed the lot?'

Jadyn strode over carrying a large, steaming takeaway cup, and a paper bag which was transparent in places from the greasy goodness inside. 'Here you go,' he said. 'I couldn't remember if you wanted ketchup or not, so it hasn't got any.'

Harry relieved the young officer of his offering and made his way over to a chair and sat down.

'And what about me?' Matt asked, now that Harry was no longer blocking his path.

'What about you?' Jim said.

'You're not being serious, surely,' Matt replied. 'Where's mine?'

Jim handed Matt a coffee, which the detective sergeant took gratefully.

'And the bacon butty?'

'Yeah, about that,' Jim said, then glanced over to Fly who was sitting in a small dog cage in the corner of the room.

'You have got to be kidding me! That furry little sod ate my breakfast?'

Fly stared over at Matt, tail wagging.

'Don't you go thinking the *I'm really cute* thing is going to allow you to get away with this,' Matt said, staring at the hound. 'Rude, that's what it is. Unbelievable!'

A beat later, Jadyn handed another paper bag over to Matt. 'Here you go, I popped out and got you another,' he said. 'Seemed only fair.'

Harry saw the look of abject disappointment on Matt's face get swept away by a sudden wave of happiness.

'You keep this up, you'll go a long way in the force,' Matt said, patting Jadyn on the shoulder then opening the bag to remove the butty.

'You mean by bribing senior officers with food?' Harry said.

'Don't give me that look, boss,' Matt said. 'You know as

well as I do that bacon is the currency everyone understands, so my view is, the more you spend the better!'

Matt bit into the butty then sat down by Harry. 'So, what now, then?'

'Simple,' Harry said. 'We catch the bastard.'

Harry hadn't meant his words to come out so aggressively, but he was tired, and sometimes, well, that was just what happened. And it was clear that their effect had been to have everyone suddenly fall quiet and stare at him expectantly. He turned to Matt.

'Brief everyone on what happened,' he instructed. 'I know Jim will have covered it, but this is the first time we've all been together, so there's nothing wrong with running through this properly.'

Matt stood up, swallowed his last mouthful, then quickly ran through what they knew so far, from the reporting of the light on the hill through to what he was aware of from the SOC team, which he read from his personal notebook.

'So, she's not called Stacy?' Jim said once Matt was done.

'No,' Harry said, 'she's not. So, let's start getting this stuff written down, everything we know so far, and everything we're about to do. I'm assuming we've got an Action Book to hand?'

Jen went over to some drawers in one of the desks and pulled out a book, waving it in the air.

'Good,' Harry said, then he turned his attention to Matt. 'You're good on details, right, Detective Sergeant?'

'Absolutely,' Matt replied. 'Do my best to not miss anything. Eagle-eyed Matt they call me.'

'No, they don't,' Harry said, 'but regardless of that, I'm appointing you as office manager.'

'But am I not more use out and about?'

'Gordy's not here,' Harry said, 'and until she is, I need you and your experience and skills to run things and to keep an eye on whatever we have to lock away in the temporary evidence storeroom here. You also know your way around HOLMES, so you'll be able to keep it up to date.'

'It's not very sexy though, is it?' Matt complained.

'Well, if you were looking for sexy, perhaps joining the police in the first place wasn't your best plan. This is hardly the Chippendales, you know.'

Harry noticed that everyone, bar Matt, was staring blankly at him. 'Chippendales?' he said. 'Famous strip show? You know, buff lads, all pecks and penises, strutting around on stage in their leather budgie smugglers while knickers rain down on them from the audience?'

Jim shrugged, shook his head. 'Nope, no idea, boss.'

'Good job, too, by the sound of it,' Jadyn added.

'Hey, I could give those lads a run for their money,' Matt said. 'I've got the moves!'

'Yes, and we've all seen them,' Jen said. 'The bacon butty strut, the doughnut twist. God, the idea of you doing a striptease!'

Matt turned a hurt eye towards Harry. 'They're bullying me, boss,' he said. 'You're not going to just let it go, surely?'

'Oh, I think I will,' Harry said. 'You're a big boy. You can look after yourself. Now if we can get back to what we were talking about, I'm not expecting you to lock yourself away in here, Detective Sergeant. I just need you to take responsibility for it. And seeing as you've got that nice, new shiny detective qualification, I think we should be making full use of it, don't you?'

Matt took the Action Book from Jen.

'Right then,' Harry said, 'back to where we were.'

'Which was where, exactly?' Matt asked, pen poised. 'I mean, I remember, but I'm just keeping you all on your toes.'

It was clear to Harry that no one believed Detective Sergeant Dinsdale at all.

'Stacy,' Jim said, 'and the fact that it's not the victim's name. So what has it got to do with what happened?'

Jen was up at the board again. 'Could be a friend. Maybe Stacy is the killer's name and it's a betrayal thing?'

'Be a bloody fool to tag the scene with their own name,' Harry said. 'But it obviously means something and is key to the whole thing, so we need to find out everything we can about Kirsty. Pathologist thought it might be something to do with roleplay?'

'Could be,' Jen agreed. 'Everyone likes to add a bit of spice to their love life.'

'Do they, now?' Matt asked, raising an eyebrow.

'Well, perhaps not everybody,' Jen explained further. 'But maybe Kirsty and her husband were into it? You know, pet names for each other, scenarios and whatnot. Some people pretend they're Han Solo and Princess Leia.

'Stacy, though?' Jim said. 'I can understand the *Star Wars* thing, but what kind of roleplay would involve being called Stacy?'

Jen shrugged. 'Each to their own, right?'

Moving the conversation along, Harry said, 'And we've got a few things to go on from the SOC team.' He looked over to Jen to check that she was ready. Then he pulled out the evidence bags from the pathologist and the set of keys.

'So what've we got?' Jim asked.

Harry went through the bags, one by one. 'Purse,' he explained, 'containing driving license, photos, access card for where she works, gym membership card, receipts. Next, we've got burned photographs found at the scene in a pan, looks like they were set fire to by Kirsty. They didn't burn completely and the person in the photographs corresponds to one of the photos in her purse, namely her husband. There are the keys, obviously, and also this bag of weird little plastic balls.'

Jen picked up the bag of burned photographs. 'So, a bonfire of the ex, then,' she said.

'Exactly that,' Harry agreed.

'Motive, right there, then,' Jadyn added.

'Indeed,' Harry nodded. 'No escaping that. But we can't just roll on over to wherever he is and arrest him. There's no evidence that we know of yet linking him to what happened.'

'And those keys could be house keys, right?'

Harry gave a nod. 'Which means we have a pretty solid lead, that being the husband. And I, for one, hope that it is him, because if it isn't then who knows what the hell we're dealing with.'

'It has to be,' Matt said. 'We just need to find him, ask him where he was last night, and have him confess.'

'If only it were so easy.' Harry sighed.

'What else?' Jen asked, jotting notes on the board.

'The gym's worth checking out,' offered Jadyn again. Doing his best to impress, Harry thought. 'They'll have an emergency contact number so that could give us the husband's number, parents maybe. I can give them a call.'

'The receipts are from an outdoor shop,' Harry said and read out the name of the shop. 'And there's a discount card.'

'Someone might remember her,' Jim said. 'Worth a look.'

'What about Gary?' Matt asked. 'Still want me to head over for a chat?'

'Has he replied to your message?'

Matt shook his head.

'Then yes, get over there when we're done here.'

'I'll head over to Keld,' Jen said. 'The Corpse Road starts there, and there's a hotel there, so I'm guessing that's where she left her car. And I reckon a Porsche is going to be pretty easy to find.'

'Sounds good,' Harry said. 'Why don't you both just head over together then?'

'So long as I get to drive, that's fine,' Jen said.

Matt laughed.

'Jadyn,' Harry said, turning to the young officer, 'how are you with HOLMES, seeing as Matt is going to be out now?'

The computerised system used by the Home Office to record information gathered in investigations across the country was something which Harry could accept as a vital and very clever resource, but it was something he generally left for other people to fathom. But then he was still having trouble with the remote control for his television back at the flat. Computers just weren't his forte.

'He's better at it than any of us,' Matt said. 'I mean, I know how to use it, but Jadyn's all over it like a rash. Not only does he bring food, but he also understands technology! Reckon we should definitely keep him.'

'As a replacement for you, you mean?' Jim said with a laugh.

'What about photographs, report from the scene of crime team, the pathologist?' Matt asked wisely changing the subject. 'Any idea when we'll hear something on all that?'

'Later today I hope,' Harry said, then tapped a finger on the bag containing the plastic balls. 'But while we're waiting, we've enough to be getting on with, including whatever the hell these little buggers are.'

Jim picked up the bag and peered closely at its contents.

'Turns out, there were a lot of these at the crime scene,' Harry said. 'Sowerby found a fair few in the tent, and some outside of it, too. And one of the rescue team found another one further away, although I'm not exactly sure where.'

'That was Helen,' Matt said. 'Told me she'd had a word with you about something.'

'I can give them a call, if you want?' Jadyn offered.

'You do that,' Harry said. 'Matt will give you their numbers. Then I want you to head back out to Swaledale. Do a wider search of the crime scene. See if you can find anything to suggest that someone else was out there.'

'Like what?' Jadyn asked.

'More of these might be a start,' Harry said, shaking the bag in his hand. 'This wasn't a random event. This was planned. You don't just take a walk up onto the moors in the hope that you'll find someone in a tent who you can murder. No. Whoever did this, whether it was the husband or someone else, they either made their way up there to kill Kirsty or were waiting for her. Both of those possibilities take planning. And there might be some signs of that.'

'The rest of you know what you're on with?'

Harry saw nods all around.

'What about me?' Jim asked.

'You're with me,' Harry said. 'Otherwise, I'll get bored on the journey.'

'Journey? To where? And what about Fly?'

'Fly can come,' Harry said. 'We're heading over to Kirsty's house, see what we can find. By which I mean, her husband.'

'And if he is, we arrest him?' Jim asked.

Harry shook his head. 'Like I said, there's nowt here,

other than some burned photos, that even comes close to suggesting that he was responsible. All we've done is put two and two together and come up with five. So, right now, all we can do is tell him about Kirsty and ask him some questions. We need a hell of a lot more than what we have right now to justify bringing him in.'

Harry stared at the team around him once again, a lighthouse casting a blinding light of warning. He wasn't going to suggest that if the house was empty then he'd be using the keys to enter without permission, but it was an option, albeit not one exactly by the book. 'If you find anything, any of you, you call me, understood? No bollocks about thinking it's not important or whatever. We need to all be on this, sharing data, and finding the bastard. We clear?'

More nods, during which Jim reached over for the evidence bag containing the white balls and took it from Harry.

'You think you know what that is?' Harry asked.

'No, I don't,' Jim said. 'It's just that it looks like . . .' He paused for a moment, then handed the bag back to Harry. 'No, it can't be. Ignore me.'

Harry didn't ignore anything when it came to investigating a murder. 'What is it, Jim? What do you think it is?'

'I don't know what it is,' Jim said. 'It just looks like the kind of thing I used to shoot out of toy guns as a kid.'

'You're right, it does,' Jadyn added. 'I had one, but the little balls just sort of fell out of the barrel when you fired it. I had one with disks as well, which was way better. Went for miles!'

'Can't see why anyone would be out on the moors with a toy gun,' Harry said, shaking his head.

Outside, with the rest of the team cracking on with their

tasks, and with Matt making sure that his rank counted for something, Harry made his way back down through the marketplace to his new vehicle, Jim and Fly trotting along behind. He was glad Jim was coming along, and that he had the stupid puppy with him, because not only was it a long journey ahead, there was every chance that the end of it was going to be deeply unpleasant.

As they approached the car, Jim called over to Harry and said, 'You also need to watch yourself a bit, by the way. You're starting to turn, if you know what I mean. You stay here much longer, you'll go fully native.'

Harry was confused. 'Why? What are you on about?'

'Earlier? You said *nowt* instead of *nothing*. It's a slippery slope, boss. A very slippery slope. Dangerous, too, if you're not careful.'

'Good God.' Harry sighed. 'What an awful thought.'

Jim laughed. 'Before you know it, you'll be just like the rest of us, and you know what that means, don't you?'

Harry stopped and turned to face the PCSO. 'No, what?' he asked.

'Cheese and cake, Boss.' Jim grinned. 'Cheese and cake.'

CHAPTER ELEVEN

Sitting in the passenger seat of the Vauxhall Astra Incident Response Vehicle, Matt was doing his best to not give Jen the impression that he was absolutely bloody terrified. But that was a little difficult to do, with the car skipping along the Cliff Gate Road and through the Buttertubs Pass, like a happy bouncy mountain goat, and being driven by someone who, as far as Matt could tell, obviously had ambitions to be a getaway driver.

'You okay, there?' Jen asked, dropping a gear for a corner just ahead before taking it with ease.

And she was whistling, Matt noticed, which didn't help, either. It wasn't that she was driving like a complete idiot, just that she was driving fast and with exceptional skill, and it was rather unnerving. He realised then that he had somehow managed to brace himself tightly into his seat, his knees jammed against the glovebox, hands gripping anything they could find. 'Oh, I'm fine, yes,' he said, attempting to relax. 'So, where did you learn to drive like this, exactly? The Dakar Rally?'

'I did the advanced driver response course a while back,' Jen said. 'Remember?'

Matt certainly did remember, but he'd not been in a car with her since then, and the difference in the way she handled the vehicle was as dramatic as it was traumatic.

'So, you enjoyed it then?'

'Yeah, it was great fun,' Jen said. 'You should have a go yourself.'

'No, I'm fine, thanks,' Matt said, as another corner came and went as though it wasn't really there.

Outside the car, the weather was on the turn, Matt noticed. It hadn't quite started raining, but the sky was certainly grey with depressing promise. The clouds were low, erasing the fell tops from view. The bright greens of the fields and moors had fallen to a darker shade, and he could see wind dancing through the long grass and the tall ferns of bracken which cloaked the fells. God, it's a beautiful place, he thought, somewhere he knew he could never leave. It was also somewhere he would always do his best to serve, and to somehow try and preserve that beauty in whatever way he could. Because the beauty wasn't just in the place, the physicality of the ancient, glacial landscape that they were now speeding along, but the people, the history. And that made it all the more important to do what he could to get to the bottom of what had happened the night before.

'So, how long have you been with the rescue team?' Jen asked.

They were at the bottom of the road now, and she took a left, turning onto the road which led through the small village of Thwaite, its grey stone, slate-roofed houses sitting low and quiet under the watchful gaze of Kisdon Hill.

'Can't say that I know, to be honest,' Matt said. 'Years.'

'So why did you join?'

'Because I made a tit of myself when I was young and stupid,' Matt said. 'You know, before I became all old and wise.'

Jen raised an eyebrow. 'How so?'

'Got lost down an old tin mine.' Matt sighed, the memory of it all as fresh as the day it had happened. 'It was my nineteenth birthday. Got pissed the night before with a couple of mates, on Thunderbird, would you believe? The next day, off we went, thinking we were invincible.'

'Seriously?'

'Oh yes, very seriously,' Matt said. 'Lost down a tin mine. Not fun at all.'

'No, I mean you got pissed on Thunderbird?' Jen's voice cracked with laughter. 'I mean, who drinks that?'

'We did,' Matt shrugged. 'It was all about bang for your buck back then.'

'So what happened?'

'Well,' Matt began, sifting through the memories to make sure he had them in the right order, 'you see, one thing you always take with you, whether you're above ground or below, is a map, right? I thought my mate Dave had it. He thought I had it. And the other lad, can't remember his name, well he thought I had it as well. But none of us thought to check who actually had it until we'd been underground for over an hour.'

'Ah,' said Jenny.

'Yes, ah, indeed. Blame the Thunderbird! And tin mines, they're pretty wet as well, like. So, there we are, lost in this mine, and we come across this cavern. A flooded cavern. We've no idea where we are, which route to go back, and we have no choice but to swim across the bloody thing to this huge rock in the middle, which had clearly fallen from the roof at some point, which didn't exactly make us feel any better. It was an experience, I can tell you.'

'All sounds very *Raiders of the Lost Ark*,' Jen said. 'So, what happened? You clearly didn't drown.'

'No, but our lights died, didn't they? Thankfully, we'd had the good sense to leave details with another mate just in case we didn't get back when we said we would. Which we didn't.'

'So, the rescue team was sent out?'

'Yep. He called them out and they found us a few hours later, cold and pretty scared to be honest. We'd kept ourselves occupied by scoffing the food we'd taken with us in an old army ammo box, you know, Mars bars, Kendal Mint Cake, and a flask of hot chocolate. Marzipan, too.'

'Wait, what? Marzipan?' Jen exclaimed.

'Don't knock it,' Matt said, waggling a knowing finger. 'What you do, right, is get it out of its packet, flatten it out with a rolling pin, wrap it in cling film, then stuff it up inside your caving helmet. Genius!'

'Yes, but marzipan?' Jen said again, her expression one of abject horror. 'That stuff is disgusting!'

'Anyway,' Matt said, 'we were rescued. We weren't in any real danger, but we were starting to suffer from the cold. I've never been so happy to see anyone in my whole life as I was when the rescue team turned up in that mine. So, I decided afterwards to give back by joining them. I also married one of them a few years later.'

Ahead, Matt saw the road fork and just beyond it, on the left, stood Keld Lodge.

'Just pull up in front,' Matt said, and Jen eased the car off the road, up against a drystone wall.

'You don't mention Joan much,' Jen said, unbuckling her seat belt. 'How is she? Haven't seen her for a while.'

'Not the best,' Matt said. 'Misses the hills, you know? Bloody arthritis, and she's only a couple of years older than me. Not that it stops her hammering about on that wheelchair of hers. Calls it her chariot. She's more dangerous than you are in this!'

Outside the car, Matt pushed away thoughts of his wife, which wasn't exactly easy when they were with him every hour of every day. Not that he resented it, just that he wished he could do more for her, the same he knew she would do for him.

'Never been here,' Jen said, as they climbed out. 'Bit posh for me. Driven past a fair few times though.'

'On your way up to the Tan Hill pub, I should imagine?'

'Love it there,' Jen said. 'Bleak and beautiful. One of those places where the worse the weather gets the better the pub is.'

Across the road, Matt led the way through the front door. Inside, the air was rich with the smell of the breakfast which had been served a couple of hours ago, all sausages and black pudding and fried bread, and Matt's stomach rumbled. A man and a woman walked past him, fully kitted out with walking gear, chatting away, faces full of smiles. He tried not to think about how Kirsty had been the day before, setting off into the hills, excitement in every footstep, but doom waiting for her on the moors. They reminded him of himself and Joan, back when they'd been able to head out onto the hills together. Good times, long ago now.

In the bar he found one of the staff to talk to, a young woman, dressed smart, with a smile that could have given the sun a run for its money when it came to brightness.

Matt introduced himself and was greeted with even more smile and a friendly New Zealand accent.

'How can I help?' she asked.

'Just need to ask a few questions about someone we think might have popped in here yesterday,' Matt said. 'Do you know who was on duty?'

'I was,' the woman said. 'Fire away.'

Jen came over to stand with Matt.

'Can we take your name and phone number first, if that's okay?' Matt asked. 'Just in case we need to follow anything up?'

'Sure,' the woman said, giving her name as Ellie Matthews, then her mobile number. 'So, what do you need to know?'

Jen pulled out the car keys. 'First off, do you have a Porsche in the car park?'

'Not sure, but you can go check,' Ellie said. 'Just out the back, through those doors over there.'

Jen nodded thanks and made her way out through the doors, following some quick additional directions from Ellie. A couple of minutes later, Jen popped her head around the door. 'Yep, the car's out there. I'll just call it in then go out for a closer look.'

Jen gone again, Matt turned to Ellie. 'The photo I'm going to show you is a few years old now, but if you saw the owner of the car yesterday, you'll recognise her from it I'm sure.' He then pulled out the photo of Kirsty on her wedding day which Harry had shown them all earlier.

Ellie glanced at the photo. 'Yes, I remember her. Is she okay? Has something happened?'

Matt ignored the question. 'Can you tell us anything

more about her? If she said anything about why she was here or what she was doing?'

Ellie looked thoughtful for a moment. 'She was very chatty and excited, like she'd never been camping before. Said she used to come up to Swaledale as a kid and that was why she'd come back, sort of a homecoming kind of thing I think.'

Matt jotted notes as Ellie spoke. 'Anything else? Did she mention if she was meeting anyone, for example?'

Ellie shook her head. 'No, not that I can remember. She was on her own, asked if she could leave her car here, and that was it, really. We don't usually allow people to do that, because the car park is for those who are staying overnight, but she has a room booked for this evening anyway, so it wasn't a problem.'

'So, she was due to stay here tonight, then?' Matt asked. 'Did she leave anything with you to look after while she was away?'

'Yes,' Ellie said. 'There's a suitcase up in her room. Oh, and she said that the trip was a little treat for herself, that she was getting away for a bit of "me time," I think.'

'And you're sure she didn't mention anyone else?'

'As sure as I can be,' Ellie replied.

Jen appeared once again through the doors and walked back over to Matt and Ellie. 'Ellie, has anyone else been in asking for her at all?'

Ellie shook her head. 'Not me, anyway. Perhaps one of the other staff. I can ask.'

'No, that's fine,' Jen said.

Matt thanked Ellie for her time then followed Jen back outside. 'You think someone followed her?'

'No,' Jen said, 'I know someone followed her. Look . . .'

Matt looked down to see that Jen was holding an evidence bag, inside which was a short note written on a piece of plain paper.

'Shit,' Matt said.

'Exactly,' Jen replied.

CHAPTER TWELVE

THE POST HAD GONE LIVE AN HOUR AGO AND THE messages were still pouring in. The ones who got it, the ones who understood, who shared his pain, his rejection, they were loving his work. Loving it!

The adrenaline had been such a rush that he was sure that even now, over twelve hours later, he was still riding high from it. And it felt good.

The look on her face! Ha! Served her right. Served them *all* right, didn't it? Because she was just the first of so many more, and they were all going to get what was coming for them. And it was a storm, that's what it was, a righteous storm against every Stacy and every Chad. They had it coming, every single one of them, and a surge of adrenaline rushed through him at the thought of it.

A storm . . . Yes, that was absolutely the right word. This was a storm and he was the wind that started it. And soon others would join in, would follow him, and together they would wreak such havoc that the world would have no choice but to sit up, to take notice, and to listen.

And this was why he'd picked her first, the ungrateful bitch. Everything she had, her nice house, her posh car, her husband, and she still wasn't happy, wasn't satisfied? Yeah, she'd had it coming and she'd deserved it. She'd been made an example.

So, who was next? He'd been planning the first for a few weeks and hadn't given much thought to the next stage— where he would go from here. But there had to be another one if this was going to have the impact he wanted it to, if he was going to have any chance of making this storm really happen. One just wasn't going to be enough. Yes, one was a start, but another, well that meant things were continuing, didn't it? And then there would be another, and another . . .

He checked his post again, the messages still increasing in number, filling his screen with praise and adoration.

You're our soldier!

Dude, you're our hero!

Who's next? Who's gonna get it?

Can't wait to see the next Stacy get what's coming!

All hail the new Ultimate Gentlemen!

These messages were for him! People he'd never met in his life, from all over the world, sending messages just to him, saluting him, praising him, worshipping him!

He liked that some of them were calling him their soldier. Because that's exactly what he was, right? He had all the gear, had read up on everything he needed to, spent too many hours to ever count watching YouTube videos to make sure that what he did was as good as it could ever be. And he'd practised and practised until he was unstoppable.

He leaned back in his chair, resting his head in his hands, and stared at the ceiling. This first operation had been such a success, he giggled at the thought of it and what he was going to do next. He was excited, that was for sure, and felt more alive now than he ever had done in his entire life. But now, he needed to think. To put his mind to where to take his crusade next because really, that's exactly what it was.

And then an idea struck him. Of course! Yes! Why hadn't he considered it before? It was so obvious, wasn't it? And no one would expect it, would they? It would be the most wonderful surprise!

The simplicity of this idea made him giggle, and as he opened a new window on his screen to see a tiny flashing dot against a map, the giggle soon became a laugh, and one which was as cold as the steel blade he'd used the night before.

CHAPTER THIRTEEN

Harry pulled his car into the drive of a detached house with a large, double-door garage to its right, and enough lawn out front to play a good game of croquet.

'You ever played croquet?' Harry asked, his thoughts deciding to give themselves an airing.

'Can't say that I have,' Jim said with Fly on his lap, licking his chin. 'Why?'

'You're not missing much,' Harry said. He hadn't a clue as to why anyone would want to play such a stupid game. He'd never seen the point. But then, he felt like that about most games and sports. He just couldn't get excited about winning, or losing, a game. It was fun to have a game of cards down the pub, throw some darts, but the winning, well, that had just never grabbed him. He'd tried a few times to show interest, particularly during his years in the Paras, because loads of the lads had been into football or whatever. Since then, though, he was pretty sure he'd not watched a single game.

'You don't see it on television, do you?' Jim said.

'What?'

'Croquet,' Jim said. 'There's darts, isn't there? Snooker. Croquet's kind of the same.'

'Is it?'

Jim gave a convincing nod. 'They're not sports, are they, they're games? So why isn't croquet on TV?'

'Bowls is,' Harry said.

'Exactly!' Jim exclaimed.

'I think you're onto something here,' Harry said. 'A new Saturday afternoon show, perhaps.'

'There's other things you could show as well,' Jim said, Fly now on his back across Jim's lap, enjoying a tummy tickle. 'Quoits, for example.'

'Good one.'

'Skittles.'

'Now you're talking.'

'Welly wanging.'

At this, Harry frowned.

'Welly wanging?'

'Did you not go to the Hawes Gala?' Jim asked.

Harry had indeed ventured into it for a whole afternoon, thanks to much haranguing by Liz and Matt. And it had certainly been an experience. Not least, because he was pretty sure that, from the moment he'd stepped across the bunting-strewn entrance and onto the field it was held in, he'd actually travelled back in time.

'So, you'd have seen the welly wanging!' Jim said.

Harry was none the wiser, but he could very much remember his day at the Gala. Not just because the fancy dress parade, which had trundled through the marketplace before ending up in the field, had been a joy to behold, so long as your definition of joy was to witness the true horror that people can achieve when given too much time, an awful lot of crepe paper and paper mâché. But also because of the stalls that had surrounded the edge of the field, with everything from the coconut shy booth and wooden boat swings, to the local Methodist minister being locked in the stocks, a pet show, and even a very popular activity which involved sliding along a horizontal pole to crack an opponent across the face with a hefty pillow and send them into the mud below.

'You'll have to show me, sometime,' Harry said and switched off the engine. Then he stared up at the house, wondering what it was that had caused Kirsty to leave it and head off to Swaledale.

'I see there's a car in the drive,' Jim said. 'So, I guess someone's home.'

The other car in the drive was a black BMW, and Harry did his best to force himself to not automatically assume that the owner, who he figured must be Kirsty's husband, was a tosser. But the odds weren't exactly in his favour, not least because Harry had spotted the M3 emblem at the back.

Harry undid his seatbelt and turned to face Jim. Only it wasn't just Jim staring back, but Fly, too, his long tongue flopping out of his mouth which, Harry was pretty damned sure, was fixed in a permanent doggy grin. 'So, Jim, do you remember the last time we had to do this? Tell someone a relative has been killed?'

Jim said, 'I do. George Hodgson, when we found his wife at Semerwater.'

It had been Harry's first week in the dales. And what a week that had been, he thought. And here he was, just over four months on, doing the same thing.

'Well, that's good,' Harry said. 'We'll just see how it goes, okay? You can never tell how someone's going to react.'

Climbing out of the RAV4, Harry was about to make his way over to the house, when his phone rang. The number flashing up did not make him happy. He looked over to Jim, who was pointing a sharp finger at Fly, who was sitting on the passenger seat and staring at him through the passenger door window. 'Just need to take this,' he said. Then, with the phone up against his ear, he said, 'Good morning, sir. To what do I owe the pleasure?'

At the other end of the call, Detective Superintendent Swift emitted a very clear huff of annoyance, which wasn't a good sign, particularly as the conversation hadn't really even started yet.

'I understand our run of quiet months is over,' the DSup said. 'How long were you going to wait before informing me?'

'I was going to call you later today,' Harry lied. 'You know, when we had a bit more information through from the SOC team. Didn't want to bother you otherwise, knowing how busy you are with, er, whatever it is you do that keeps you busy.'

'It's my job to be bothered!' the DSup snapped back. 'I get paid to be the one you and everyone else bothers. It is what I am for, bothering. Just so long as you only do it when something is important. And this, I believe, is important, agreed?'

'Well, now that I know that, sir, I'll make sure that I bother you as much as I can.'

The line fell silent for a moment.

'So, what do we have, then?' the DSup asked. 'And what exactly are you all doing about it?'

Harry gave a quick run-through of what had happened,

where Kirsty's body had been found, and what the rest of the team were up to right then.

'And you're two officers down as well,' the DSup said. 'Which means I'll have to cancel my weekend and come down to keep an eye on things.'

'There's no need for that, sir, I'm sure,' Harry said. 'Honestly, everything is in hand.'

'Yes, but they're your hands, Grimm, are they not?'

Harry sucked in a slow, deep breath. The DSup had taken a dislike to him from the moment they'd first met. Harry hadn't exactly worked to discourage him from it either. 'Detective Inspector Haig and PCSO Airey will be back next week,' he said. 'In fact, I think Liz is back Sunday evening. So I'm sure we'll be fine until then.'

'Regardless, I'll be on my way as soon as I've sorted a few things. Where are you right now, Grimm?'

'The victim's house,' Harry said. 'With PCSO Metcalf.'

'And where is that exactly? The house?'

'Somewhere up near Darlington,' Harry said

'Well, then, I shall no doubt see you later today at the community centre. And I shall expect a full and complete update.'

'Yes, of course,' Harry said, willing the conversation to end with just the power of his mind.

'Anything else?'

'No, not at all,' Harry said, wondering how his superior had managed to make it now sound as though it was he who had initiated the call and not the other way around.

'Good,' the DSup said and hung up.

Harry stuffed his phone back into the depths of his pocket. He'd always been of the opinion that the mobile phone was responsible for an awful lot of time being wasted in people's lives, not just because of things like social media, but also because it gave everyone far too much access to everyone else. How many phone calls happened when they just didn't need to? he thought. Well, that had been one, hadn't it? And how many times were people called about something that just wasn't important or didn't need to be said? And the impatience which had come with the mobile phone, hand in hand almost, well that was something else, wasn't it? The absolute expectation that if you called someone, then they simply had to answer, and if they didn't, well then the only conclusion to be had was that they were either rude or in dire straits. And with Harry, it was generally because he was rude. If he didn't want to answer, then he just didn't. It was as simple as that. It was someone else's decision to call him and his if he answered or not. Usually not.

Walking over to the front door, with Jim alongside him, Harry briefly rested his hand on the hood of the car.

'Warm,' he said.

'So, someone's in then,' Jim said.

'Looks that way,' Harry said. And that someone, he was pretty sure, had to be the husband. Which meant that this visit wasn't going to be just a simple chat, was it? No. It was going to be a little more awkward than that. Giving the news of someone's death to their nearest and dearest was something that no training on earth ever made easy. Yes, it ensured that you were able to do it correctly, but that was about it. Harry knew that having Jim with him for support, not just for the person who was about to get the news, but himself, too, was a very good thing indeed.

Harry was at the front door. He caught his reflection in one of the glass panels and saw staring back at him a face that looked like its only purpose was to deliver the worst news imaginable, which this pretty much was. He was half tempted to stand Jim in front of him, have him be the first face seen by the husband, but instead, he stretched out a hand to press the doorbell.

The door flew open, at exactly the same moment as the bell rang out, and Harry was assaulted by a filthy cackle riding on a cloud of perfume, aftershave, alcohol, and the background scent of musky sweat and garlic.

'Ah, sorry,' Harry said, stepping back from the door and into Jim, who tripped and fell backwards onto the lawn, as a woman stumbled out backwards and into him. She was wearing just enough to hide what was necessary, and what there was of it was leaving nothing to the imagination.

Harry glanced round to Jim, who was quickly pushing himself back up onto his feet. 'You okay, Jim? Sorry about that.'

Jim said nothing and instead stared at the woman in front of them, who turned around to face Harry and then fell into him just a little bit further.

The woman's breath folded over Harry with the rich scent of wine and whatever else she had eaten and drunk the night before. It was thick, Harry thought, almost chewy.

'No, my fault,' the woman said, pushing herself away to reveal a man standing behind her in the doorway, to whom she threw a carefree wave then blew a kiss. 'Thanks for a lovely evening! Surprising, too, you naughty thing! Call me and we'll do it again!'

The man at the door stared at Harry, at Jim, his eyes hard, then turned his attention to the woman. 'Yes, absolutely.'

He was tall and broad, Harry noticed, his black dressing

gown doing little to disguise the gym-built body beneath. His face was all chiselled angles. But his expression was one that reminded Harry of how politicians stared at the public—a mix of disdain and superiority.

The sound of a car's engine caught Harry's attention and he turned to see a taxi pull into the drive behind his vehicle. The woman half-walked, half-stumbled towards it and climbed in, offering a flirty wave out of the window as the taxi reversed back out then sped off into the rest of the day. In his car, Harry spotted the small black nose of Fly peeking up above the lip of the passenger door window, steam blasting across the glass.

Harry turned his attention back to the man in the doorway. 'Mr Jackson? I'm Detective Chief Inspector Harry Grimm,' he said, showing his ID. 'And this is PCSO James Metcalf. Can I, I mean we, come in, please?'

The man rubbed his eyes and shook his head. 'Look, whatever this is about, and I've honestly got no idea how or why that mad bitch has sent you here, but I'm tired, I need to shower, and really it would be much better if you came back later. Actually, no, it wouldn't. So, thank you, and goodbye.'

Mr Jackson went to close the door, but Harry's hand was on it and stopped it dead.

To make doubly sure the door wasn't about to move without his say-so, Harry slipped his fingers around its edge, clamping it tightly in his grip. 'I worded it as a polite request,' he said, 'but it wasn't. Can we come in?'

Up until the moment the door had opened, Harry had been preparing himself mentally to deal with a man who he assumed was dealing with a failed marriage the reasons behind it being none of Harry's business, though from what they'd found at the crime scene it was key to Kirsty heading off into the wilds—and would then on top of that, be sat down and told that his wife had been murdered. Impending divorce or no, that was still going to be horrendous news to receive. Now though, however, Harry realised that he was dealing with an entirely different animal. He didn't quite want to jump to conclusions, but the evidence before him was presenting him with the kind of person he just didn't like. Okay, so he wasn't in a position to judge, and that wasn't his job either, and people dealt with marriages going wrong in numerous different ways, but right there and then, Harry wasn't getting much in the way of regret or remorse. Plenty of *mind your own sodding business*, but that was about it.

Mr Jackson didn't move.

Harry ever so slowly and ever so surely pushed against the door. Mr Jackson tried to resist, but it was no good, and Harry could see the look of mild surprise in the man's eyes.

'You'd better come in, then,' Mr Jackson said, annoyance in his voice.

Harry stepped through the door and into the house, Jim behind him, but not so close as to come a cropper again. 'Is there somewhere we can talk?' he asked.

'Will this take long?'

'I think it would be best if we sat down,' Harry said, then nodded towards a door to their left. 'Is the lounge through there?'

He didn't wait for an answer and made his way over to the door and pushed it open. On the other side was a room containing yet more evidence of the night before. Three empty bottles of wine were on a glass-topped coffee table, along with a small board containing the remnants of cheese and crackers. The sofa had been stripped of its cushions, which were on the floor in front of a gas fire. Scattered around them were various items of clothing clearly torn off in the throes of drunken passion. A packet of condoms, ripped open, the contents scattered, discarded. Harry stared for a moment at the scene before him, not so much shocked by it as intrigued as to how the woman he'd just seen leaving the house still had enough clothing left to put on, what with so much of it left behind.

'We can talk in the kitchen,' Mr Jackson said, and Harry and Jim turned from the room and followed him across the hall into the kind of kitchen he had only ever seen on television.

'Coffee?' Mr Jackson asked.

'Your car,' Harry said, ignoring the question as he made his way over to a stool perched around a central workstation with a granite top.

'Yes, what about it?'

'Just wondering if you've been anywhere this morning?' Harry asked.

'I went to the shop to get some things for breakfast,' Mr Jackson said.

'In your dressing gown?' Harry asked.

'Of course, not,' Mr Jackson replied.

'And you think you were safe to drive?'

'You mean the wine, I assume? I had one glass twelve hours ago. I rarely drink. It messes with my training.'

'One glass?' Harry asked. 'Are you sure about that?'

'I'm very sure about that indeed,' Mr Jackson snapped back. 'I will be at the gym later and alcohol doesn't exactly mix well with the routines I do. Now, what is this about? Why has Kirsty sent you? What I do now is my own business and has nothing at all to do with her!'

'Please,' Harry said, 'could you just sit down? I do think it's for the best.'

Shaking his head, Mr Jackson headed over to sit opposite Harry. Jim, however, stayed on his feet.

Harry didn't respond, deciding instead to just get on with the information every police officer dreaded having to deliver. 'Mr Jackson, I have some very bad news I must tell you,' he said, the words in his mouth as welcome as gristle, their inherent wrongness so clear, their intent so obvious, that Harry wished to God he was anywhere but where he was right then. 'Your wife, Kirsty, was involved in an incident in Swaledale last night. I'm sorry to tell you that she was killed.'

CHAPTER FOURTEEN

'Bollocks!' Mr Jackson exclaimed, jumping to his feet. 'I don't have to listen to this! Who the hell do you think you are, anyway? Did she put you up to this, is that it? Try and mess with my head? That's absolutely bloody typical of her! Unbelievable! And if she thinks she's even getting a tenth of what this house is worth then she's got another thing coming!'

'Please, Mr Jackson,' Harry said, keeping his voice flat and calm, which wasn't easy when deep down he had an undeniable urge to give the man a massive, meaty slap. 'I need you to sit back down. I know this will come as a shock, but—'

'A shock? A shock? I'll tell you what will come as shock, my foot up your arse as I kick you out of my house, that's what!'

Mr Jackson was around and into Harry's face in a beat. Then Jim stepped in and ever so gently and yet with more than enough force, eased the man back and away from his superior.

'Mr Jackson, please,' Jim began, his hands now up in some attempt to calm down the clearly enraged man, but Mr Jackson was having none of it and was leaning into him now, words spitting out of his mouth with rage, and Jim did his best to lean away from the verbal attack.

'He's not taking it all that well, is he?' Jim said, turning around to Harry.

'He's not really taking it at all,' Harry replied.

Mr Jackson started to shout again. 'What, she thinks she can just kill a marriage and then start having people join in with her insane stories to somehow get back at me, does she? Is that it?

'We are the police,' Harry said, his voice emotionless, although this was quickly becoming difficult to maintain. 'Please, Mr Jackson, sit down.'

'And for what? That's what I want to know!' Mr Jackson continued, not listening. 'How much did she pay you to do this? Not much, judging by the look of you. But I'll pay you three times as much to just get the hell out of my house, how's that sound?'

Harry ignored the unnecessary dig at his attire and tried once again to calm the man down, but it didn't work.

'So, you're just going to sit there, are you? Well, we'll soon see about that, won't we!'

With a roar, Mr Jackson heaved himself past Jim, knocking him across the floor and onto his knees, then lunged at Harry, grabbed him by the lapels of his jacket and threw all of his weight into one enormous heave to have Harry up and onto his feet.

Except, it didn't work.

Harry sat on his stool, staring up at the mad man in front

of him, an immovable object that no amount of swearing and heaving was going to shift.

Jim was back on his feet. 'Can I arrest him, Boss?'

'Mr Jackson,' Harry said, fully aware that his complete lack of being affected by Mr Jackson's protestations and physical attack was only serving to make the man even angrier. 'I can understand the shock and upset that you must be feeling, but you need to calm down. I really don't want to have to arrest you, not at a time like this, but you need to sit down, to calm down, and listen to me, okay?'

For a moment, it seemed as though Mr Jackson wasn't going to do anything of the sort. Then he let go and stepped away.

'Do you understand, Mr Jackson?' Harry asked, pushing the point. 'Please, sit down.'

When Mr Jackson spoke next, his voice was barely an echo of the shouting which had come before. 'I . . . I need to have a shower,' he said, and before Harry could say anything more, the man turned and walked calmly out of the kitchen and into the hallway, the sound of his footsteps disappearing up into the house.

Harry followed him. 'Mr Jackson? Please, you need to listen to what we've just told you. Do you have any family we can call? Someone who can be with you, now, at a time like this? Also, I need details for Kirsty's parents, if you have them.'

The only response Harry received was the sound of a shower being switched on.

Jim came to stand with Harry. 'Well, that went well,' he said.

'Hmph,' was about all Harry could manage, so he added

a, 'Buggered that right up,' just in case Jim wasn't quite clear on how annoyed he now was.

Harry and Jim spent a minute or two at the bottom of the stairs trying to work out what they were dealing with, while from upstairs the sound of the shower was drowned out by electronic dance music. The kind Harry had always assumed was for late-night dance floors in warehouses, or illegal raves, not Saturday mornings after a one-night stand.

'This ever happened to you before?' Jim asked.

'Can't say that it has,' Harry said.

'Well, that's something.' Jim wandered into the kitchen then came back out again to join Harry. 'Quite a place, isn't it? Must both earn a fair whack to afford it.'

'You've seen his car,' Harry said. 'And it looks like Kirsty was driving a Porsche.'

'Not for me though,' said Jim. 'I need the hills.'

'Is your dog alright?' Harry asked. 'Won't have pissed on my car seat, will it?'

'I'll go let him out,' Jim said.

With Jim gone for a moment or two, Harry continued to wait at the bottom of the stairs, as though on some odd vigil. Mr Jackson was unlike anyone he'd ever met, and he'd only been in the presence of the man for about fifteen minutes at the most. Who the hell goes and has a shower after hearing that their wife is dead? And as for that comment about what he was wearing, well, that was just unnecessary, wasn't it?

Make yourself a coffee, Harry decided, so that's what he did.

When Mr Jackson presented himself about fifteen minutes later, he was dressed in jeans, a polo shirt, and was wearing a jumper slung over his shoulders. Jim had already come back inside and, to Harry's relief, shared the news that

Fly hadn't done anything untoward in the car. In fact, he'd been curled up on the driver's seat, fast asleep.

'Made ourselves some coffee,' Harry said, stating the obvious.

Mr Jackson said nothing in reply, poured himself a glass of water, then sat down. 'I'm . . . I'm sorry,' he said. 'It's just that, well, I'm not very good with bad news. And it's all rather a terrible shock, isn't it?' He sipped from the glass, his hands shaking. 'She's dead? You're sure about that? You're sure that it's her? Kirsty, I mean. It's not someone else?'

Bad news? Harry thought. At what point is the murder of your wife only bad news?

'I'd like to ask you a few questions if I may?' Harry said, pulling out his little notebook and a chewed Biro, keen to push on now that Mr Jackson had calmed down. He was also smelling faintly of mint, which although pleasant, didn't exactly add anything to the proceedings. 'And do you have someone you can call who can come over at this difficult time?'

Mr Jackson shook his head, then handed over a slip of paper with a telephone number written on it. 'You said you wanted Kirsty's parents' details,' he said. 'They'll be home I'm sure. They live over near Catterick. Unless you want me to tell them? You don't, though, do you? I mean, I can, but I . . . well, I'm not sure I—'

Harry took the paper. 'I'll have someone sent out to visit them,' he said, handing the note to Jim. 'We could do with Gordy here for this,' he said. 'Can you give Matt a call?'

Jim left the kitchen and headed outside to make the call.

There was no response from Mr Jackson. Instead, he just sat there, staring into the middle distance.

'So, Mr Jackson,' Harry said.

'Daryl,' Mr Jackson replied. 'Please, call me Daryl.'

'Okay, thank you, Daryl. Now, I do have to ask you this, I'm afraid, but can you tell me where you were last night?'

Horrified shock twisted the man's face. 'What, you don't think I did it, do you? I mean, you can't! Why would I? You're insane!'

'We need to ask the question,' Harry explained, as carefully and calmly as he could. 'It's important, I'm sure you can understand that.'

'Yes, but I'm not a suspect, surely! I'm her husband!'

'Can you answer the question, please?'

'I was here, wasn't I?' Daryl said, raising his hands in a sweep around him. 'I mean, you saw who I was with, didn't you?'

Yes, I did, Harry thought, but still . . .

'Would you be able to give me her details?'

'Oh, so you don't believe me! Good God, what is wrong with you police nowadays?'

'It's all procedure,' Harry said. 'If I can corroborate your whereabouts then that's better for everyone I think, as I'm sure you can understand.'

'Well, I'll have to see if I can find them,' Daryl said. 'We didn't exactly spend our time exchanging personal details and information.'

'But you must have her phone number,' Harry said. 'Know where she lives?'

Daryl shrugged. 'Can't say that I do. We met in a bar, you see. One thing led to another. She came back here.'

Harry waited, expecting Daryl to say more, but he didn't.

Jim came back into the kitchen.

'Sorted?' Harry asked.

Jim nodded, although there was something hidden

behind it that Harry wasn't quite sure about. 'Everything okay?'

'Yes, totally,' Jim said. 'All good.'

And that was enough to tell Harry that, once they were over here, he would be pressing Jim on exactly what it was that he wasn't telling him. For now, though, he wanted to deal with Daryl. 'That taxi, earlier, Jim,' he asked. 'Did you catch the name of the company?'

Jim frowned, then said, 'Sandy's Taxis, I think.'

'Good. Give them a call, see if you can find out any details about the woman we saw here earlier.'

'What's her name?'

Harry looked over at Daryl, eyebrow raised.

'Claire, I think,' Daryl said.

'You think?' Harry said, with the emphasis clearly on *you have to be kidding me.* 'Surname?'

'No idea.'

Jim said, 'I'll see what I can find out,' and turned once again to head back outside to make a call.

Harry focused once again on Daryl. 'Can you tell me the last time you saw your wife?'

'About two weeks ago,' Daryl explained. 'She told me she wanted a divorce and she told me to leave. I refused, so she left instead. No idea where she's been. Friends I suppose, or a hotel. I called her parents but they said they hadn't seen her.'

'Did you know she was going walking and camping?'

Daryl let out a laugh, only it sounded like the short, sharp bark of a small, annoying dog. 'Camping? Kirsty? Are you kidding? So that's what she was doing?'

'So, you didn't know?'

'Know what?'

'Where she was going, what she was doing?' Harry said.

Daryl shook his head. 'No. And why should I? I've heard nothing from her since she left. Well, unless you class a letter from her solicitor that is. Camping, though? Really?'

Harry asked, 'Can you think of any reason as to why someone would want to harm her at all? Anyone she's had an argument with, someone at work perhaps?'

'She's an accountant,' Daryl said. 'Unless someone got very angry with her about some spreadsheets or tax or profit and loss, then I doubt it.'

Harry noticed that the man was still talking about his wife as though she was alive. 'You don't know then, for sure?'

'We didn't talk much about work,' Daryl said.

'Just out of interest,' Harry asked, 'what is it that you do yourself?'

Daryl seemed to puff out his chest a little then.

'I'm a stockbroker. Work for myself. Do rather well out of it, too, as I'm sure you've noticed.'

Harry watched as Daryl rolled his eyes around the kitchen as though inviting Harry to gasp in wonder at the clearly very expensive cabinets and worktops. He didn't.

'So you had no idea that your wife was going away?'

'No,' Daryl said. 'As I've explained, I've not seen her since she walked out two weeks ago. And I can't say that I care.'

Harry was having a problem dealing with someone showing so little remorse for his dead wife and was glad when Jim walked back in. 'Any luck?'

Jim shook his head. 'No name. Paid in cash.'

'What about where she was dropped off?'

'Middle of town,' Jim said.

'Yes, that's where she'll have left her car, I should think,' Daryl offered.

Harry checked over his scant notes then rose to his feet. 'Mr Jackson, we really are very sorry for your loss. And I can assure you that we will do everything in our power to find who was responsible.' He was about to conclude the little chat when he remembered the strange little white balls found at the scene. He pulled out the bag. 'Do you have any idea what these are?'

Daryl leaned in close and stared at the bag. 'Little white balls,' he said.

'Do you have any idea what they could be from, or used for?'

Daryl shook his head. 'Haven't the foggiest,' he said.

Harry slipped the bag back into his pocket. 'Our family liaison officer is currently on leave, but we'll have someone contact you later today.'

Daryl stood up and led Harry and Jim out into the hallway. 'Yes, well, it is terrible news. Awful. But I'll be fine, I'm sure.'

'Regardless,' Harry said, 'someone will contact you and a follow-up visit will be arranged, and further support provided.'

'There really is no need.'

'You may think that now,' Harry said, 'but trust me on this, okay? You'll need the support, so take it.'

Daryl said nothing more, just smiled an emotionless smile, led Harry and Jim to the front door, then waited for them to leave.

At that moment, Harry had quite a lot he wanted to say to Mr Daryl Jackson. His callous attitude, his bizarre behaviour, all of it had served only to rankle and rattle Harry to the point where, right now, what he really wanted to do was grab the man by the scruff of the neck and yell at him. But as he stared at him, standing there in his preppy clothes, smelling of mint, his chiselled face showing about as much emotion as a barrel of dead fish, his too-obvious toned pecs, he found his anger turn to pity. This was a man who was already running around bars seeking solace between the legs of other women, someone who was quite astonishingly keen to have his kitchen noticed, a man who viewed the death of his supposed life partner as nothing more than bad news. It really did take all sorts to make up the world, Harry thought. But why the hell that had to include men like Daryl, he hadn't the faintest idea.

Outside the house, Harry remembered something and turned back to Daryl as he was closing the door. 'One more thing . . .'

'What?'

'Does the name Stacy mean anything to you?'

'Stacy?' Daryl said, repeating the word and chewing on it like gristle. 'Not in the slightest. Why?'

'Nothing to worry about,' Harry said. 'Thanks for you t—'

The sound of the door being slammed cut Harry off. He breathed deep the midday air. 'Well, that was interesting,' he said, as he made to follow Jim over to the RAV4.

'Do you think he understood what we were telling him?' Jim asked.

'Haven't the faintest idea,' Harry said, opening the car door to be assaulted by Fly's enormously oversized paws and very slobbery tongue.

Inside the car, Jim now sitting next to him, Harry remembered the PCSO's strangeness earlier. 'So Matt's heading out to see the parents, is he?' Harry asked.

As he was clipping in his seatbelt, Jim paused just long enough to confirm for Harry that something was amiss.

'What is it?' Harry asked. 'What aren't you telling me?'

'I didn't speak to Matt,' Jim said.

'No? Then who?'

'It was Swift,' Jim said. 'He's gone to see the parents.'

It was the best news Harry had heard all day, and as he reversed out of Mr Jackson's drive, he was very aware of the smile on his face at the thought of Swift having to do something other than complain.

CHAPTER FIFTEEN

A CALL CAME THROUGH ON JIM'S PHONE AND HE answered it on speakerphone.

'How you doing, Matt?' Jim asked. 'Found anything?'

'You could say that, yes,' Matt replied. 'Where are you?'

Jim checked his watch. 'Left the house about fifteen minutes ago. Bit of an odd one too, the husband.'

'So you're not there now, then?'

'No,' Jim said. 'Why?'

'Well, I think you need to turn around sharpish and get back there.'

Harry shoved himself into the conversation. 'What's up? Why do we need to go back?'

'We found the car,' Matt explained. 'Kirsty's Porsche. It's parked behind the Lodge, up in Keld.'

'Where the Corpse Road starts,' Jim said.

'Exactly,' Matt replied. 'Kirsty was here yesterday. Left it overnight. Had a room booked for this evening as well.'

'What are you getting at?' Harry asked, pressing for Matt to get to the point.

'Jen found a note on the car window,' Matt said. 'Jammed under the windscreen wiper.'

'A note?' Jim said. 'What about?'

'It's not just what it's about,' Matt said. 'It's about who we think it's from.' There was the briefest of pauses, and then he asked, 'Did he say where he was last night?'

'Didn't really need to,' Jim said. 'We turned up as his hot date from the night before was leaving.'

Harry eased off the accelerator, instinct telling him what was coming and what he was going to have to do.

'He was there,' Matt said. 'Her husband. He knew where she was.'

Harry glanced ahead, saw a road on the left to turn around in, and swung the RAV around, wishing he was at the very least in a patrol car with flashing lights. And that was something he would absolutely be bringing up with Detective Superintendent Swift when he saw him next.

'You sure it was him?' Harry asked, checking both ways, before pulling out and heading back the way they had just come.

'I'll read you the note,' Matt said. 'And I apologise in advance for my language.'

The briefest of pauses, Harry accelerating hard through third and up into fourth.

'*I'm watching you, bitch. I'll never let you leave me. Ever.*'

'Bloody hell.' Jim sighed, rubbing his forehead in frustration. 'That lying—'

His voice dropped off.

'Bastard?' Harry finished for him. 'It's okay to swear in front of me, you know that, right? Matt?'

'Yes, Boss.'

'What time was he there?'

'Trying to find that out now,' Matt replied. 'Just having a spin through some security camera footage. But that's not all, I'm afraid. We've found something else.'

Harry's mind was racing ahead now, readying himself for whatever Daryl Sodding Jackson and his posh kitchen were going to throw at them next to explain exactly why he'd lied to them so easily and freely. 'What's not all?' he asked. 'You've got something else? What is it? What have you found?'

'I had a quick look around the car,' Matt said. 'We've called forensics, obviously, and they're on their way to collect it, and yes we've left it the hell alone, but I spotted something underneath, just under where the passenger sits. Sending you a photo through now.'

A ping sounded from Jim's phone a couple of seconds later and he opened the file to show to Harry. On the screen, Harry could see a small, black box, about the size of a cigarette packet, stuck to the underside of Kirsty's car.

'Shitting hell!' Harry exclaimed, teeth clenched, the words hissing out as angry as a kicked viper.

'What is it?' Jim asked, looking at the photo himself.

'I think it's a tracking device,' Matt said.

'No way!' Jim gasped. 'But that's like spy shit, isn't it?'

'No, it isn't,' Harry said. 'You can pick them up online for bugger all.'

'Why?'

'People use them as a security device, to keep a track of the kids, anything really. I think some insurance firms even give lower premiums if you have one. Spy more, pay less, that kind of thing.'

'Yeah, well, I'm guessing Kirsty had no idea it was there,'

Matt said. 'You'd have to be looking for it to find it, if you know what I mean.'

They were less than a mile away now from Daryl. But that mile just couldn't zip by quick enough.

'We're nearly back at the house,' Harry said. 'What about you and Jen?'

'We were just about to head over to speak with Adam's brother,' Matt said. 'Just to check up on what he saw up on the moors, the lights and whatnot. Just wanted to get this development to you first.'

'Right,' Harry said. 'Good job. Well, you crack on with that, see what Gary has to say. But get a message through to Jadyn to contact Swift and tell him what we're up to.'

'Will do, Boss.'

Harry told Jim to hang up. 'We're nearly there,' he said, dropping speed now as they passed into a residential zone. 'We've no idea how he's going to react when he sees us again. And we've no idea either as to why he lied to us about not knowing where Kirsty was. But we're going to find out.'

'Are we arresting him?' Jim asked.

Harry shook his head. 'We've nothing like enough to be doing that, no. But we need to have him come with us for questioning. He's lied, and that's cause for serious concern. We can scare him with the suggestion that we have every right to charge him with wasting police time.'

'Or perverting the course of justice,' Jim added.

'Exactly. And that should hopefully be more than enough to have him comply and to come along quietly. But if he doesn't, well, we'll just have to deal with that if it happens,'

'Got you,' Jim said. 'The house is just ahead.'

Harry swung into the drive and swore loudly and expressively, hammering a clenched fist against the steering wheel.

'Car's gone,' Jim said.

'Too bloody right it's gone,' Harry snarled. 'I'm guessing he buggered off as soon as we left.'

'Where to, though?' Jim asked. 'And why? I mean, if he's not guilty, then this isn't exactly helping, is it?'

'No, it's not,' Harry said. 'Us turning up to question him has set him running. If he's not guilty, then he's panicking because he thinks we reckon him to be our prime suspect. Fair enough really, all things considered.'

'And if he is guilty?'

'Then he probably wasn't expecting to be dealing with the police so soon after the fact. So he's legged it.'

Jim unclipped his seatbelt. Fly sprang off his lap and over to Harry's, then licked the DCI's chin.

'He likes you!' Jim said, opening his door as Fly's tail wagged faster and faster and he pushed himself up on his front legs to get to the rest of Harry's face.

Harry grabbed Fly, plopped him in the passenger footwell, then climbed out of the car.

'Here,' he called over to Jim, then threw the PCSO the keys that the SOC team had found on Kirsty. 'Go see if one of those fits the front door.'

'What if the house is alarmed?'

'I'm going to put a fiver on our friend Daryl leaving in too much of a rush to worry about anyone stopping by to nick his silver candlesticks and oil paintings,' Harry said.

At the front door, Jim tried the keys and was first-time lucky. Pushing it open, they both waited for the alarm, but none came.

'See? Told you so,' Harry said. 'Wisdom of the old, right there.'

'You're not old,' Jim said.

'I don't half bloody well feel like it sometimes, though,' Harry said. 'Hanging around with you isn't helping either. Now get in and see what you can find.'

Harry followed Jim into the house. It was quiet, oddly so, he thought, but only in the way he'd noticed numerous times before. It was as though a house knew if its occupiers had left its embrace for good or ill. The air was too still, almost as though the very walls themselves had been caught off guard and didn't quite know what to do with themselves.

'Check upstairs,' Harry instructed. 'And be careful. For all we know he's still here and someone else took the car.'

'Really?'

'I doubt it,' Harry said, 'but regardless, stay sharp.'

As Jim dashed upstairs, Harry did a sweep of the ground floor, starting with the lounge. It was the same as before, a tableau of the previous night's drunk and debauched evening of alcohol-fuelled fun and frolics. So, Daryl hadn't even bothered to tidy, which said a lot.

Further down the hall, Harry checked an office-cum-gym room, which had French windows staring out of a large, well maintained, and somewhat overly designed garden, which was all angles and gravel and unnecessarily strange-looking bushes. The gym equipment looked expensive, as did the flatscreen television on the wall. Outside in the garden, he spotted a water feature front and centre, which to Harry looked like an enormous, melted chocolate bar, still in its foil wrapping. Water dripped down it a little pathetically. He had no doubt that it cost a small fortune. Much like everything else in Daryl and Kirsty's life, he thought, pondering the fact that he'd lost count of the number of times he'd seen houses like this, dedicated to money buying happiness, only to be proved terribly, horribly wrong.

After the office, Harry found himself in a smaller reading room, the walls lined with bookshelves and art on the walls, then a utility room, with a door leading off to the side of the house by the garage. Finally, he made his way back into the kitchen and dropped down on the same stool he'd occupied barely an hour earlier, to listen to Jim scootch around upstairs.

'Anything?' he asked when Jim finally appeared.

Jim shrugged. 'To be honest, I wasn't really sure what I was looking for, but whatever it was, I didn't find it.'

'The daft sod's definitely done a runner, then,' Harry said. 'May as well just tattoo GUILTY onto his forehead at the same time, whether he is or not!'

'I've got the number plate,' Jim said. 'Jotted it down when we arrived.'

Inside, Harry beamed. Jim really was bloody good at his job. 'Right, call that in and see if we can't get him found. Guilty or not, we need him back at the station to answer a few more questions.'

Jim laughed. 'Back at the station! Not sure our couple of rooms in Hawes can ever be described as that.'

'Force of habit,' Harry said. 'Though I can't think what else to call it. And I'm not going to be blurting out, *Right, let's get him back to the rooms at the Hawes Community Centre* every time we need to take someone in for a chat, that's for sure!'

Once outside, Harry saw that Fly was sitting on the driver's side of the RAV4 again, staring at him, tail thumping.

'You're a silly sod, you know that?' he said, staring at the dog.
Fly's tail simply thumped harder and faster.

'Right, they're on it,' Jim said, joining Harry at the vehicle. 'Now what?'

Harry checked his watch. The afternoon was leaving them behind and rushing towards evening. 'Let's get back,' Harry said. 'Gather the team together and see where we are.'

Jim, Harry noticed, was staring back at the house.

'You alright?' he asked.

Jim shrugged and turned back to face Harry. 'You think he did it?' he asked. 'The husband, I mean.'

'Majority of murder victims are killed by someone they know, someone close to them, a friend or a family member,' Harry said, his voice flat and devoid of emotion.

'So, that's a yes, then?'

'No, it's a statement of fact,' Harry said. 'Research shows that's just the way it is for most murders like this. But there's always those that buck the trend. Always.'

'Still, it's looking pretty obvious right now, isn't it, what with him scarpering and all?'

'There's a world of difference between what looks obvious and what the truth actually is,' Harry said. 'But yes, it is starting to look a bit obvious.'

Jim frowned. 'You're speaking in riddles.'

'I'm just saying that there'll be no jumping to conclusions,' Harry said. 'Some of what we have fits, some of it doesn't. And it's the some-of-it-doesn't that's bothering me.'

CHAPTER SIXTEEN

'Doesn't exactly look like anyone's in, does it?' Jen said, standing beside Matt outside a small, terrace cottage of grey stone. Then she noticed the car parked out front, a small, white hatchback with alloy wheels. It had clearly been polished to within an inch of its life. 'Wow!'

'Wow?' Matt said, staring at the car, somewhat baffled. 'What's wow about that? It's at least thirty years old!'

Jen raised an eyebrow, staring at him from the other side of the car's bonnet. 'You do know what this is, right?'

'A car,' Matt said. 'Do I get a prize?'

'What, a coconut?'

Matt laughed, remembering one of their DCI's more bizarre phrases.

Jen was walking around the car now, a huge smile on her face. 'This is a Peugeot 205 GTi! And it's in mint condition! Look at it!'

Matt was looking at it. He was staring hard at it wondering what all the fuss was about. Then he turned his attention to the beautiful scenery surrounding them. Behind the cottage, in the distance, he saw how the fells rose gently, ancient beasts slumbering under a blanket of green. Above them floated a clear sky home to candy floss clouds, and on the air came the faint sound of sheep calling to each other in the fields at their feet.

Matt pulled himself back to Jen and her bubbling excitement then knocked again at the door before leaning the side of his head against it to listen for any sound from the other side. 'Looks like we'll have to come back tomorrow,' he said.

As Matt turned away from the cottage to walk back to the patrol car, the sound of a door opening behind him had him stop and turn around.

'Er, hello?'

Standing in the doorway was a young man. He was naked from the waist up, sweat pouring from his brow, a small towel in his hand. He was slim, built like a climber, with dark hair, which only looked more so against his pale skin. It flopped over his eyes and he attempted to tuck it behind his ears.

'Police,' Matt said, stating the blatantly obvious, what with Jen being in uniform. He realised this probably sounded a little abrupt, so smiled far too broadly, then added, 'Just wondered if we could have a little chat?'

'Why, what's happened?' the young man asked, stepping out of the cottage and into the light of the day. 'Is it Adam? Is he okay?'

'Yes. I mean, no, it's not about Adam,' Matt said. 'Though, I'm sure he's fine. It's about last night? The lights that you saw?'

'You are Gary, yes?' Jen said, stepping forward, moving away from the Peugeot. 'Gary Bright?'

The young man nodded, then wiped his face with the

towel, a smile creasing his face as he looked over at Jen. Pushing his fringe out of his eyes again he said, 'Sorry, just been working out.'

'You mind if we come in?' Jen asked, gesturing to the open door behind him.

'Yeah, no problem,' Gary replied. 'Just give me five while I shower and change.'

Before either Jen or Matt could say anything, Gary turned and disappeared back into the cottage.

Following him in, Jen and Matt stood in the small lounge waiting for Gary to return. Matt wandered around the lounge, not looking at anything in particular. The room was cosy, with an open fire, comfy-looking sofa and armchair, and shelves heaving under the weight of books and DVDs. Matt cast an eye over the shelves. He'd been right about Gary looking like a climber, he thought, spotting classics such as The Games Climbers Play and numerous climbing guides, standing alongside books by Andy McNab and Lee Child. He pulled out one of the DVDs. 'Bloody hell, I've not seen this in years.'

'What is it?' Jen asked, walking over to join him.

'*Stone Monkey*,' Matt said. 'Absolutely amazing stuff. Gritstone climbing. Johnny Dawes.'

'You mean you used to climb?'

Matt saw the look of disbelief written across Jen's face. 'I used to look like that once, you know,' he said. 'Back in the day.'

Jen laughed. 'You, a six-pack?'

'Well, perhaps not that, no.' Matt sighed, slipping the DVD back on the shelf. 'But I was really into my training. I think I've even still got my weights somewhere. Maybe I should get them out again.'

'And then again, maybe you shouldn't,' Jen said.

'What are you saying?' Matt said, doing his best to look hurt.

'I'm saying that you shouldn't go looking at someone half your age and use that as the motivation to get fit. If you do, you'll do yourself a mischief.'

'Easy for you to say,' Matt said. 'All that running you do, up and down mountains all the time.'

'You need to ease yourself into it,' Jen said. 'Like Harry is with his running.'

'He's still doing it, then?'

Jen nodded. 'He's kept at it. Does three five-kilometre runs a week now.'

'How absolutely bloody terrifying!' Matt said. 'Can you imagine seeing that massive angry bastard charging down the road towards you, sweat pouring off that face of his, the air thick with him swearing in that weird West Country accent of his?'

He then did what he assumed was a good impression of Harry running, waving his arms around, and huffing and puffing and swearing.

'Best you don't do that in front of him,' Jen said. 'If you want to live to see the next day, that is.'

'Ah, get away with you,' Matt said. 'He's just a big cuddly bear under all that gruff and grump.'

'You sure about that?'

'No,' Matt said. 'Not in the slightest.'

Gary entered the lounge fully dressed now, though just as red in the face courtesy of the shower. He looked straight over at Jen. 'Can I get you a drink?'

'No, we're good,' Jen said.

Gary took a seat. Matt and Jen did the same.

'So,' Matt began, 'can you tell us what happened last night?'

'Not much,' Gary said, leaning back. 'Saw some lights on the fells, that was it really.'

'What made you think something was wrong?' Jen asked.

'Not sure,' Gary replied. 'Just looked strange, I guess. It was a clear, dark night, I saw the lights, mentioned them to Adam, and he thought it was worth heading up to check out.'

'He called it in though,' Jen said. 'He must have thought it was serious enough for that.'

'I suppose so, yes,' Gary agreed.

'And where were you when you saw this?' Matt asked.

'On my way back from the King's Head,' Gary said, then flicked a look over to Jen. 'It's the pub in Gunnerside.' He brushed the hair back from his face. 'You ever been?'

'Can't say that I have,' Jen said.

'You should,' Gary replied, smiling. 'It's really friendly. If you ever want to go, you know, for a pint or whatever, just let me know.'

There was a pause in the conversation as Jen glanced over to Matt who was staring at her now, an eyebrow raised and the faintest hint of a smile on his face.

'So, you were at the pub for the evening, then?' Jen said, kick-starting the conversation again.

'Nipped in for last orders, like I usually do on Fridays,' Gary explained. 'I was walking back after closing time and that's when I saw it, the lights, I mean.'

So what were you doing for the rest of the evening?'

Gary smiled. 'I was round next door with Mr Harker. He's on his own and in his eighties so I go round and keep him company now and again. He plays a mean game of draughts and pours a generous measure of whisky.'

Matt wrote the details down, making a note to check in with Mr Harker, and took his phone number down as well.

'He's not got a mobile and has no idea what the internet is,' Gary said.

'What is it you do yourself?' Jen asked.

'Web design,' Gary answered. 'Looking for a full-time job after university, you know, so I'm filling my time with odd jobs here and there when I can get them.'

'Where were you at university?' Matt asked.

'Lancaster,' Gary said. 'Nice place. Good times.'

'Is there anything else you noticed last night?' Jen asked.

'Like what?'

'Anything unusual,' Jen suggested.

Gary looked thoughtful for a second or two then said, 'There was this bloke who turned up at the pub,' he said. 'He sort of just walked in, looked around, then left again.'

'Can you remember what he looked like?'

'Tallish, thinnish,' Gary said.

Matt reached into his pocket and pulled out the photo that he'd shown Ellie back at the Lodge in Keld. He showed it to Gary.

'Yeah, that was him,' Gary said. 'Older though.'

'What time was this?'

'No idea. Late evening anyway.'

Matt stuffed the photo back into his pocket. 'I think that'll do for now,' he said, rising to his feet. 'Thanks for your time, Gary. Very much appreciated. And well done on spotting the lights on the fell. Most folk wouldn't have thought to do anything about it.'

'No problem,' Gary replied. 'You sure there's nothing else I can help you with?'

Matt noticed Gary's eyes stray over to Jen again. 'No, we'll be heading off now, leave you be.'

Outside the cottage, Jen saw the Peugeot and turned back to Gary. 'This yours?'

'Yep,' Gary replied. 'I've had it for years. Renovated it myself. You like it?'

'I love it!' Jen said.

'Well, perhaps I can take you for a ride in it some time, let you have a spin?'

'Perhaps,' Jen replied with a smile.

Gary closed his front door and Matt went to climb into the passenger seat when he remembered something. 'Just a mo' . . .'

Jogging over to the house next door to Gary's, he gave the front door a knock. There was no answer, so he tried again, harder this time.

'Away, then,' Jen called from inside the patrol car. 'We've got his number. We'll give him a call later.'

Matt turned away from the house, climbed into the car, and turned to Jen as she clipped herself in and started the engine. 'Think you've an admirer there.'

'Not my type,' Jen said, with a laugh. 'The car though? That's definitely my type! Back to Hawes?'

'As quick as you can,' Matt said. 'This is urgent.'

Jen keyed the engine into life. 'I know. He saw Kirsty's husband.'

'Well, yes, that, obviously,' Matt said. 'But there's something else, too.'

'What?' Jen asked, snapping round to face Matt.

'Cake, Jen,' Matt said, deadpan. 'Cake. And it won't get eaten all by itself, now, will it?'

CHAPTER SEVENTEEN

HARRY LET HIS HEAD FALL BACK A LITTLE JUST SO THAT he could stare up at the ceiling. He then rubbed his eyes hard enough to see sparks, before rolling his head forward again in the hope that things had changed.

They hadn't.

Having arrived back at the community centre about half an hour ago, with Jim and Fly in tow, he was as tired as everyone else looked. It was gone five in the afternoon, it had been a long day, the kind which had decided to stretch out its greedy hands across the night before, and everyone didn't just want to go home, they needed to. The trouble was, that wasn't about to happen anytime soon. Not because he had ordered them to stay. Quite the opposite, actually. Once everyone had reported back on anything they'd found, or not, he'd told them all to bugger off home and get a good night's sleep, because they needed it. Harry was pleased with what Jen and Matt had found, not just over at the Lodge in Keld, but from the chat with Gary, Adam's brother. And he and Jim shared what had happened with the husband, his very obvious late-night escapades, his behaviour, and then him doing a runner. Then, Detective Superintendent Swift had arrived and, well, that had been the end of that, hadn't it?

'Grimm?'

Harry rested his glare on the pale, pallid face of his superior, his hands clasping the enormous pint mug Matt had bought him a few months ago. It was still half-full with tea and Harry spotted a few crumbs from the cake he'd had with it a few minutes ago. He'd managed, once again, to avoid the horror of adding crumbly Wensleydale cheese to it, averting his eyes as he'd watched Matt cut a slab of the creamy white stuff, then lay it on top of a slice of cake from Cockett's and shove it into his mouth with unbridled glee.

Swift's complexion, Harry thought, was akin to that of a resident of a morgue, caught as it was in the insipid glow from the filament bulb lighting the room directly above his head. He had the look about him of a cadaverous letch, a thing refusing to die because there were so many other mean, hideous, and cruel things left to do. And one of those things was to get right up in Harry's face about the last twenty-four hours.

'I asked you a question.'

Harry realised that he'd drifted off from whatever it was Swift had been talking about and said, 'I was trying to think of an answer.' As he also tried to remember what the question was.

'Trying?' Swift said. 'Trying? You mean you don't have one?'

'Oh, I have one,' Harry growled quietly to himself, remembering the question, then said somewhat louder, 'but I don't think it's one you'll want to hear.'

'I'll be the judge of that.'

Harry pulled himself up in his chair, then drained his mug of the rest of the tea, before sitting it underneath his chair. 'I think we need to wait for him to show himself,' Harry said, remembering at the last minute that the DSup had been pushing for more to be done about bringing in the husband. 'He won't have gone far. He's probably holed up in some hotel or Airbnb somewhere, hoping everything will die down soon.'

'Really? That's your answer?'

'I did say that you wouldn't want to hear it.'

'So, you're suggesting that we simply wait for the chief suspect to just show himself?'

Harry nodded.

'And until then we just sit around, do we? Waiting?'

'No, we've plenty to be getting on with,' Harry said. 'Forensics will be in tomorrow. We've photos to look through, lots of evidence to examine, I want to go and have a walk around the crime scene tomorrow—'

'Yeah, sorry about that,' interrupted Jadyn, his eyes flicking from Harry to Swift and back again. He made to continue speaking, but Harry shook his head. He could tell the lad felt awkward, having been pulled away by Swift from what Harry had asked him to do.

'Don't worry, you had other things to do.'

'You don't think this is a bit more urgent, then?' Swift asked. 'A murderer at large?'

Harry gave himself just a moment to his own thoughts, his head cocked just a little to one side, his eyes staring up and away from Swift. 'If it was the husband,' Harry began, 'and I do mean *if,* then this all looks like it begins and ends with Kirsty up on the moors. Whether he planned to do it, whether it was heat-of-the-moment, it's done. He'll turn up, sooner or later, probably stinking a bit and sleep-deprived, trying to buy Red Bull and some dodgy sandwiches in a newsagent somewhere. So I just don't think it's a judicious use of anyone's time, including yours, sir, to be out there looking for him.'

'But his car was found,' Swift responded. 'He can't be far away from it, can he, seeing as he's on foot?'

'If you want everyone here, and anyone else you want to bring in, walking the streets, knocking on doors, then that's your prerogative,' Harry said. 'But with that, there's every chance he'll see or hear about what's happening and we'll only delay his turning himself in, because us looking for him will only panic him more.'

Swift's lips went so thin they practically disappeared. Then he took a deep breath and held it for just a little too long, before letting it out through his nose.

Harry waited for the man to say something, then waited some more. Eventually, he just gave up and said, 'My point though, sir, is that there's also the very good chance that it wasn't the husband. And if that's the case then, well, would we not be better off focusing on finding out who the killer actually is?'

Swift unfolded his arms with the deliberate slowness of a tired swan loosening its wings, but with considerably less grace and natural beauty. It was the first time since arriving back at the community centre that Harry had realised that the DSup's arms had been folded the whole time, like he was either protecting himself, or trying to stop his chest from exploding outwards.

'So, how would you advise we progress the case, then, DCI Grimm?' Swift asked.

Harry grimaced. *Progress the case?* What the hell did that

actually mean? 'I'd send everyone home now, sir,' Harry said. 'Get a good night's sleep. Get back here tomorrow, get on with the job. It's the weekend and everyone knows that pulling long, unsociable hours is part of the job, but everyone needs a break.'

Swift shook his head. 'A break? We're not soft southerners, you know?'

If the room had been quiet before, it was deathly silent now, Swift's words working like a vacuum and sucking every ounce of sound and warmth from it in a beat.

Since arriving in the dales, it had been very clear to Harry that Swift not only didn't like him, but didn't think he should be there in the first place. Despite this, and regardless of the way the man's manner towards him was always and without fail never anything less than pure disdain, Harry worked to be as professional as he could. It was one thing to not like your superior, to even disagree with them, but it was another thing entirely to express that in front of the rest of the team. So right now, with Swift's words still hanging in the air like starved crows on a powerline, Harry was fighting with everything that he had to not respond in kind.

When Harry spoke, his words were measured to the point of being so flat and distant from each other that he sounded rather like someone in a trance. 'I'm just saying that I think everyone will work better at sorting this out if they've had a rest.'

'So that's it, is it?' Swift replied, clearly not getting the message or, if he was, refusing to hear and take heed of it. 'Just send everyone home and hope it all comes together tomorrow?'

Harry decided it best to keep his mouth shut and just gave a nod.

'Well fine, then.' Swift sniffed like he'd just caught a whiff of something unpleasant in the room. 'But I fully expect everyone to be back here first thing tomorrow. Is that understood?'

'I don't think there's any question about it not being,' Harry said, after which there was a rather awkward pause where no one moved or spoke, other than Swift, who quietly gathered up his things, namely a grey jacket, a hat that Harry was pretty sure belonged to a time when everything was costed out in farthings, shillings, and crowns, and an unnecessarily colourful scarf, before leaving without another word said.

'Well, that was definitely a meeting we all had,' Matt said, standing up and stretching. 'Who's for a brew?'

Harry checked his watch. 'It's nearly six,' he said. 'The lot of you, home, now. We'll have to be in tomorrow first thing, like Swift said, and I'll want you all sharp.'

Something wet touched Harry's hand and he looked down to see Fly sitting at his feet staring up at him.

'You know, I think he'd happily come home with you,' Jim said, coming over and clipping a lead onto the dog's collar.

Harry reached down and tickled the fur under the dog's chin. 'He'd soon get bored,' he said, standing up. 'I'll be asleep as soon as I sit down and put the telly on.'

Later, when Harry was actually in front of his television, and munching his way through possibly the worst tea he'd ever prepared for himself—a feast of cold tinned mackerel on dry toast, washed down with a glass of lukewarm water thanks to him having poured it from the wrong tap and then been too tired and thus not arsed enough to get back up again and get a fresh one—he once again pulled out the bag containing the little white plastic balls found at the scene.

Staring at the bag, sipping on and grimacing at the glass of water, Harry considered everything they knew so far. Kirsty had left her husband. Whatever had happened, the evidence of the burned photos was more than enough to suggest it had been somewhat acrimonious. What they'd found on the fells above Gunnerside suggested that she'd gone away on her own, probably to celebrate her new-found freedom, a solo celebration.

Then there was Daryl, who they knew had not only put a tracker on his wife's car, had then followed her to the Lodge in Keld, left a less than friendly note on her car, and then gone looking for her in at least one local pub, according to what Matt and Jen had found out from Gary. Kirsty's night had then ended in the worst possible way. Daryl had done a runner. And, when all was said and done, and even though they'd not yet gotten anything back from the SOC team or the pathologist, it was difficult to avoid the fact that the soon-to-be-ex-husband was the prime suspect.

But it was the white plastic balls that were bothering Harry. They were, as he'd explained to Jim, something that didn't belong. Everything else at the crime scene made sense, from the tent to the burned photos to the blood. But those little plastic balls? What the hell were they and why were they there in the first place? Were they connected to what had happened? They were wrong and their very presence at the scene of the crime was working its way under Harry's skin like grit in a graze.

Harry went to finish his glass of water, decided against it, leaned back in the sofa, and closed his eyes. When he opened them again, the world outside his window was ink-black, and the channel he'd been watching had moved on from early evening family entertainment to late-night horror movie. Evening gone, Harry stood up, walked through to his bedroom, and climbed into bed. Sleep took him then, and Harry was lost to a night of moorland dreams of darkness and blood.

Outside his flat, a car pulled in and parked up. The driver kept the engine running as the passenger climbed out, walked up to Harry's door, and pushed something through the letterbox. Then he returned to the car, jumped back in, and they were gone.

CHAPTER EIGHTEEN

HARRY WAS FIRST TO ARRIVE AT THE COMMUNITY centre, but not by much, which hadn't been the plan. A restless night, and a breakfast which pretty much matched his meal the evening before when it came to being sad and depressingly unappetising, had sent him out into the morning before much of the world had woken up. He'd spotted an envelope on the carpet by the front door as he'd been leaving, but had been in no mood to check what it was, so had ignored it. Probably junk mail anyway, he'd thought, slamming the door behind himself.

A walk up the hill to Gayle, then back across the little age-worn flagstone path, which crossed dew-wet fields and followed the beck, had done nothing to clear his head. He'd done his best to drink deep of the beauty of the dales. Gazing off into the distance, his eyes had wandered up the fells, which swam deep in the colours which bathed them. The rich air, so much more alive early in the morning, crisp and bright with promise, filled his lungs. But it still hadn't been enough. He'd hoped that a bit of time alone in the office before everyone else turned up, nursing a huge mug of strong tea, might help, but the other arrival had put an end to that with the slam of a car door and a terse call of his rank and name.

'DCI Grimm.'

'Sir,' Harry nodded, as Detective Superintendent Swift stared at him from where he'd parked his car, then walked towards him with the cold, mean purpose of a vampire looking for a quick kill before having to turn in for the day. Harry checked his watch. 'It's not even eight, sir. Can't say that I expected to see you quite yet.'

'And just what are you suggesting by that?'

'Nothing,' Harry replied, searching for the office keys in a pocket. 'You've a longer journey than most, that's all.'

'I have indeed,' replied Swift. 'But I wanted to get here good and early so that I could really get things moving along.'

Harry was fairly sure that a lot more was hidden behind those words than they actually communicated, but he ignored his suspicions, opened the door into the community centre, and walked through to the offices used by himself and the rest of the team. The soft footfalls of his temporary boss followed him through, all the way up to the kettle.

'Tea, please, Grimm,' Swift instructed.

'Milk?' Harry asked, barely able to disguise his irritation at being ordered about.

'Yes, but no sugar. I bring my own sweetener.'

Doesn't seem to be working, does it? Harry thought. 'How did yesterday go?' Harry asked. 'With the parents?' Didn't get a chance to ask.'

'As terrible as can be expected,' Swift said. 'With DI Haig away, I've sourced the relevant support for them, so that's dealt with and we don't need to worry about it.'

Harry was worried about it, though, because right now he was worried about everything to do with this case. As the tea brewed, he moved over to stand in front of the board Jen had done a good job of keeping up to date with everything that had gone on the day before. Swift joined him.

'Hmmm,' Swift said, rubbing his chin. 'Is this all we have?'

'Well, it's not changed since you and I saw it yesterday,' Harry replied. 'So, yes. We can put a note on about the parents being told, and I'm assuming there was nothing suspicious there?'

Harry caught the glare from Swift at what he was suggesting.

'Suspicious?' Swift spat. 'They were her bloody parents, Grimm! Her parents!'

Harry breathed deep then relaxed into his next sentence. 'I know, sir, but we have to be sure. I've no doubt that we've both dealt with cases of filicide.'

'And why would they kill her?' Swift asked. 'What reason? There isn't one, is there, Grimm?'

'I wasn't suggesting there was,' Harry countered. 'I was simply checking that you were happy with what you found. And clearly you are, so we can move on.'

'Happy?' Swift repeated. 'No, I am not happy, as you well know. But, moving on is exactly what we are going to do! So, what about forensics?'

'First thing this morning, I should think,' Harry said, knowing that the pathologist, Rebecca Sowerby, was not the kind of person to be late with anything. 'And we'll be getting the evidence over from the crime scene as well, so we'll be able to have a look through that, see if it sparks any new lines of inquiry.'

Harry was happy with the way that sentence had ended. Using the phrase *new lines of inquiry* was one he had used on numerous occasions to hush up another officer asking too many bloody questions. And that was something Swift did, though he was never one for coming forward with a helping hand to find the answers.

'Well, hopefully, none of it will be necessary,' Swift said, moving away from the board, almost as though he had already dismissed the case as done and dusted. 'If the husband shows himself, or does the sensible thing and hands himself in, then we should be able to wrap this up nice and quickly.'

'Not if it wasn't him, though,' Harry said.

Swift twisted round to face Harry, who stepped back just enough to prevent the man from invading his personal space. Then Swift took another step forward, clearly intent on continuing with the invasion.

'You still think that, then, do you?' Swift asked.

'I'm just not jumping to any conclusions, that's all,' Harry said. 'Something isn't right here, I'm sure of it. Yes, he's buggered off, and yes what we've found so far—the burned photos, the tracking device—points to him, but even so, I don't think we should just assume this was a case of love gone sour.'

'The only thing not right here is you, Grimm,' Swift said. 'You seem to think that wherever you are, that the crime rate, the people you're dealing with, it's just the same as down south in the *city*. It's not, you know. Not by a long shot!'

Swift performed air quotes with his fingers around the word 'city'. Harry had absolutely no idea why and it made him want to reach out and snap them off at the knuckles.

'All I'm saying,' Harry explained, amazed that he was

staying so calm, 'is that we need to wait to hear from the SOC team, the pathologist, and see what's what.'

Swift sucked in a thick breath through his small nose and the sound of it was that of an aggressive vacuum cleaner with something jammed in its pipe. 'So, when are you heading home, then?' he asked, changing the subject so quickly that Harry was surprised the man didn't get whiplash.

'Not sure,' Harry shrugged. 'I'm in no rush to get back. There's plenty to do here. The team is great as well. Why do you ask? Has Firbank been in touch?'

Detective Superintendent Alice Firbank was Harry's boss back down in Bristol. It had been a few months now since she'd sent him away, somewhat indefinitely, after an operation hadn't exactly gone according to plan. The last time Harry had spoken to her had been nearly three months ago, and there had been no mention at the time of an end game to whatever it was Harry was doing up north. That conversation had focused on his brother who, despite being in prison, had been threatened by their criminal father, who neither of them had seen in decades, not since Harry had arrived home from a tour with the Paras to find Ben beaten and their mother dead.

The fleeting reminder of his father had Harry suddenly remembering the unexpected and wholly strange phone call he'd had with the man two nights ago. The memory twisted his gut with the ravaging violence of a bayonet thrust. How could that voice and its sentiment have anything to do with the man he hated?

'I'm sure it must be difficult for you though, yes?' Swift said, hooking Harry out of his thoughts. 'Being away from home. Then there's your brother, too. How is he by the way?'

'He's fine,' Harry said, not really listening. 'As far as I know.'

'Put away for dealing drugs, wasn't it?' Swift pressed.

'He's due for parole next month,' Harry said, ignoring the DSup's needling little questions.

'You really will want to be home then,' Swift said, and Harry heard the smile in each and every word, as though Harry leaving would make him the happiest man alive.

'To be honest, sir, I think living up here would do him a world of good, like it's done me.'

'What?'

'You know as well as I do, sir, that the reason offenders reoffend is because we just send them back to their homes, back to the streets they grew up on, to hang around with the very same people who helped get them in trouble and land them inside.'

Swift, Harry could see, was starting to get flustered. Good, he thought, served the nosy bastard right.

'Last place Ben should go is back home,' Harry continued, really getting into the swing of it now. 'He's got nothing there other than trouble. Here, though? Here, he's got hope, a chance, you know?'

'No, I'm not sure that I do,' Swift blustered, walking away from Harry now, clearly having had enough of the conversation, at least enough of where it was now leading.

'Remember that week I arrived?' Harry asked.

'How could I forget?' Swift replied, mouth grimacing on a razorblade smile sharp enough to draw blood.

'I met those two wild swimmers down at Semerwater,' Harry said. 'Ended up giving it a go myself, you know? Bloody cold it was.' Harry smiled at the memory of it, the sensation causing him to shiver even as he spoke. 'I mean, my testicles disappeared so far up inside that they didn't come back out for at least a week, but other than that, the experience was fantastic.'

Swift backed further away with that comment, but it only served to have Harry push on, to really hammer the point home.

'I remember thinking,' Harry continued, relishing the impact his words were having, 'as I floated in the lake, my balls gone, and my skin screeching with the pinpricks of pain from the cold, I remember thinking that it was what Ben needed, to be there, in that lake. He needed to be somewhere that wasn't where he'd always been. Somewhere that he could start again, start afresh, and be nowhere near any of that bollocks that had put him in prison in the first place.'

Swift had reached the far wall of the room and had nowhere else to go, so turned around to face Harry. 'Surely you're not serious, though?' he said. 'It wouldn't be right for him. I'm not sure he would, well, fit, if you know what I mean? We're not used to people like that around here.'

'People like what?' Harry asked.

'You know what I mean,' Swift said.

'Yes,' Harry said, pausing just long enough to allow the silence in the room to become just painful enough. 'I do.' Then, for the first time since the conversation had started, he turned up the menace in his voice, slowly moving over towards Swift and making full use of his physical presence, his messed-up face. 'But Ben's no different to anyone else, to you, to me. He got dealt a shitty hand, didn't know how to deal with it, that's all.'

'All of this is moot,' Swift said, dodging past Harry to walk back into the centre of the room. 'I'm sure you won't be here much longer, anyway. Probably have time to crack this little murder and then that'll be it, you'll be off. It's for the best.'

Right then, staring at the flustered Swift, Harry knew for the first time since arriving in the dales that he would be very happy if he was allowed to stay on permanently. It wouldn't be just to annoy Swift, but that would most definitely be the icing on the proverbial cake.

The office door swept open and Harry saw a wave of relief wash over Swift with such force the man visibly shook.

'Morning, Boss!' Matt said, strolling in, then as he saw Swift, added a rather unenthusiastic, 'es.'

Harry nodded a hello back.

'I can come back in a bit?' Matt suggested, his eyes darting from one superior officer to another. 'Not a problem.'

'No, it's fine,' Swift said, resting his mug on a table then heading to the door. 'I'm going to grab a little bit of fresh air anyway. You know, help clear my head before the day!'

And with that, the man was gone.

'He's not easy to like, is he?' Matt said, staring at the space Swift had, just a second or two ago, occupied. 'You both looked very serious. Something up?'

'Nothing to worry about,' Harry said. 'How was your evening?'

'Oh, you know, shite television, glass of wine, the usual.'

'You heard anything from Gordy at all?'

'I'm sure we'll receive a postcard,' Matt said. 'It'll be one of those recipe ones,' he added. 'Not that anyone really needs to know how to make haggis. And even if they did, I'm not sure I'd trust the recipe on a postcard where the photo is clearly from the 1920s.'

The conversation petered out then, and both men took to staring at the board or wandering around the room, apparently deep in thought. Harry, for one, was happy when the rest of the team started to turn up, particularly when the furriest and newest member of the team bounded in. Harry dropped down on his haunches and Fly raced over to jump up at him and lick his chin.

'You're going to ruin that dog for me, you know that?' Jim said, watching his pup attack Harry. 'He's going to be a working dog, you know that, right?'

Smiling, Harry stood back up, with Fly under his arm. He ruffled the hair on the dog's head, which resulted in yet more licking. 'He'll be fine, I'm sure,' he said. 'And it's a good job no one in the team is allergic, right?'

'I wouldn't be so sure about that,' said another voice, only it wasn't one Harry had been expecting to hear. Not yet, anyway, and certainly not in person. He peered around Jim and there, standing in the doorway, was Rebecca Sowerby, a briefcase in one hand. And before he knew what he was doing, he was waving at her with one of Fly's oversized paws.

CHAPTER NINETEEN

'Yours?' Rebecca asked, moving past Jim and up to Fly. She scratched the little hound's head and he scrambled from Harry's embrace to try and get to her, his tongue a weapon of slobbery affection.

Harry gestured to Rebecca, to see if she wanted to hold Fly, and to his surprise not only did she take him, she reached out for him, flipped him onto his back in her arms, and tickled his stomach, much to the dog's delight.

'Not mine, no,' Harry said, more than a little bemused. Usually, by now, both he and the pathologist had taken swipes at each other.

'He's mine, actually,' Jim said, reaching over to take the pup away from the pathologist. 'I'll go and put him out in the truck for a while.'

'Don't do that on account of me,' Rebecca said, and Harry was pretty sure he heard genuine disappointment in her voice.

'Oh, I'm not,' Jim replied. 'Everyone's daft with him

anyway, so it's probably best he has a bit of time to himself and grabs a nap. I'll fetch him back in a while.'

As Jim left, Jen arrived, face flushed red.

'You look like you ran here!' Harry said. 'I was going to do the same, you know, it's just that I wanted to get here extra early, so I'm going for a run later on.'

Jen shook her head, both in answer to Harry's question, and also in despair at Harry's poor excuse for not running. 'Is my face red?' she asked. 'It is, isn't it?'

'A little,' Harry replied. 'By which I mean, on a scale of one to ten, where one is a glass of milk and ten is a beetroot, you've pretty much bathed in the stuff.'

Jen slumped down into a chair. 'Takes me ages to cool down sometimes,' she said. 'Have you not noticed before? And has anyone got the kettle on?'

'Yes, I have.' Harry nodded. 'But I usually politely avoid mentioning it. Jim?'

Jim had just arrived back in the office from dropping Fly out to his Land Rover. 'Kettle on?'

Harry winked a 'Yes'.

'You? Polite?' Rebecca said, as the crackle and hiss of the kettle warming up joined in the conversation. 'Can't say that I'm convinced.'

'I can be polite!' Harry said, doing his best to sound wounded and failing, and also wondering if this more approachable pathologist was here to stay, or if she would soon be replaced by the considerably more spiky version now that Fly was gone.

Jen, Rebecca, and Jim just stared at him. Matt was at the board and gave no indication that he was listening, as he stood, staring, rubbing his chin thoughtfully.

'It's not that you're not polite,' Jim said. 'No, it's just that you're, well, you're straight. Yes, that's it. You get to the point. No messing around. No bullshit.'

'Yes, that's it,' Jen said. 'You're a bit blunt maybe, but not rude.'

'Blunt, that's it, on the nail,' Jim said, agreeing with Jen.

'What they're trying to say,' Matt said, turning from the board to drift across into the conversation, 'is that you don't talk bollocks, Boss. And it's appreciated.'

'See, I said I could be polite,' Harry said, as though Matt's explanation was enough.

'Polite?' Matt said. 'Oh, you're not polite! Not at all. Good God, no! You're one of the rudest blokes I've ever met! But you don't talk bollocks, and that's good. We like that. Helped you fit in right from the off, to be honest.'

'I'll take that as a win,' Harry decided. 'Now, where's Jadyn?'

'And Swift?' Matt asked.

'He's gone for a walk,' Harry said.

'I hope it's a long one,' Matt mumbled, which was a good job really as, right at that moment, Swift entered the room. He walked straight up to the pathologist, ignoring everyone else.

'Good morning, Ms Sowerby!' The man's voice dripped with simpering adulation. 'Were we to be expecting you? If so, I wasn't informed.'

The DSup glared momentarily at Harry. Harry, however, kept his face impassive, or as impassive as a face like his could look, which wasn't easy. Generally, his face gave the impression of being in a permanent rage, and that wasn't just down to the scarring, either. Harry had eyes on him which could, in a beat, give a stare that would send a wolf running.

'No, you weren't,' Rebecca said. 'But something else came in yesterday and I ended up somewhat delayed. I thought I would come over today and go through what I found, and to see if I can be of any further help.'

'Any particular reason?' Swift pressed. 'For this offer of further help, I mean?'

'I'm just doing my job,' Rebecca replied. And there it was again, Harry noticed, the edge to the woman's voice.

Harry remembered what her mother had told him in confidence about Rebecca's awful experience at university, how it had changed the direction of her life. He had little doubt that it had something to do with her being here now.

'Thank you,' Harry said before Swift had a chance to do so himself. 'It's very much appreciated.'

'I'm not making a habit of it, though,' Rebecca said.

'Of that I'm sure,' Harry said. Then realised his tone was back on the offensive, so he quickly said, 'I do have something I need to ask you though, about something found at the crime scene—'

'Later, Grimm,' Swift said, cutting Harry off with all the tact and care of a rusty scythe through a limb. 'Shall we get on?'

'That's what I was doing,' Harry said, but Swift ignored him.

'Now that everyone's here,' Swift continued, 'I think that the best way to get things started is to hear from the pathologist. Ms Sowerby?' He stepped back from where he was standing, up and in front of the team, and gestured to the space he had previously occupied, almost as though he was implying huge generosity by giving it to her.

Rebecca Sowerby stood up. 'Firstly, we've yet to find any fingerprints or other DNA from the evidence collected at the scene, other than what belongs to the victim. Which I know is not what you want to hear.'

'Not a surprise, though,' Harry said. 'The whole thing looked planned. I can't see the person responsible being careless enough to leave anything behind that could be traced back to them.'

'The blood on the tent is the victim's,' Rebecca continued. 'We found a hat at the scene, which we assume was Kirsty's. It was soaked in her blood as well, so it could be that it was used to write her name. The stab wound was from a single thrust of a bladed weapon. From the shape of the wound, it looks to be double-edged, a dagger of some sort.'

'Aren't they illegal?' Jadyn asked.

'To carry out and about, but not to own,' Harry said. 'Most knife crime involves kitchen knives, not military-style daggers.'

'Why's that, then?' Jadyn asked.

'They're cheaper, easier to get hold of, simple as that.'

'Anything from all of the camping equipment?' Jen asked.

'Nothing,' Rebecca said. 'It was all new, looked like this was the first time it had been used. Any residue on it, soil or whatever, was from the site where Kirsty had set up her tent. She was clearly there on her own.'

'What about the car?' Matt asked.

'Well, you know about the tracking device. Other than that, there's not that much really. Fingerprints are mainly the victim's. Any others we found are being checked, though most of those are the deceased's husband, which is no surprise. A mobile phone was found and the team has managed to unlock it. However, they're waiting on a request sent to Facebook to access her social media accounts.'

'But that'll take ages.' Jadyn sighed.

'Not anymore,' Rebecca replied. 'We used to have to put in a Mutual Assistance Legal request via the Government, to access any data at all, and that could take anywhere from six months to two years, which was a nightmare. Now, though, there's a Bilateral Data Sharing Agreement with the US, so it should only take a few days.'

'And you think they'll do it?' Jadyn asked. 'Hand it over, just like that? I thought social media companies were all up their own arses about invasion of privacy or whatever.'

'Last year,' Rebecca explained, 'over ninety percent of all requests resulted in the provision of data, so I think we'll be fine.'

Harry was listening intently. He knew everything the pathologist was saying to be accurate, but he was worried that any request for data would take too long. It always did. They needed all the information they could get their hands on right now, not in a few days' time or, even worse, a week or two.

'What about around the site?' Jen asked, getting everyone back to where Kirsty's body was found. 'Any signs of how the killer managed to get to Kirsty without her knowing?'

'The Corpse Road is a well-used footpath,' Rebecca explained. 'We found plenty of footprints from that day, but nothing stands out.'

'This isn't sounding very encouraging,' Swift said. 'Was there nothing at the site to link back to the husband?'

'Only the photographs,' Rebecca said. 'The burned ones. But they have nothing to do with him as such. He just happens to be in them, that's all.'

'I still think that gives us a good spotlight on motive,' Swift said.

'What about those little plastic balls?' Harry asked, pulling the evidence bag from his jacket pocket. He caught the pathologist's eye and handed it over to her.

Rebecca held the bag up for a moment, staring at the contents, before speaking again. 'When we found these at the crime scene, we hadn't the faintest idea what they were. But then, during the autopsy, something came to light.'

Harry and the team watched as Rebecca stood up and opened her briefcase. She then removed a file from it and asked for something to attach its contents to the board. Jen handed her some sticky tape.

'These,' Rebecca said, sticking a number of photos on the board, 'are bruises on the victim's body.'

Harry stared at the grim photographs, the flesh in them pale, broken only by small, round marks the same size as the plastic balls.

'That doesn't make sense,' Jim said. 'I know I said yesterday about them reminding me of toy guns I had as a kid, but no toy would do that.'

'You're right,' Rebecca said. 'No toy would. And these were not done by plastic balls shot from a toy gun. Well, not in so many ways, anyway.'

'So, how exactly did those balls make those bruises, then?' Matt asked, confusion written in the lines on his face.

Harry was starting to get an idea as to where Rebecca was going with this, but he kept quiet. He had a feeling that if she was going to say what he guessed, then with Swift in the room it was better coming from her, if only to add credibility.

Rebecca pointed at one of the photos, her finger just at the edge of a bruise. 'To cause this mark, a plastic ball like the ones found at the crime scene would have to be travelling at well over five hundred feet per second.'

'Bloody hell,' Matt huffed.

'Definitely not a toy gun, then,' Jim said.

'No,' Rebecca agreed, then held up the bag containing the plastic balls which Harry had given her. 'To fire one of these at that speed? The only way to do it is to use an airsoft gun. The legal limit is just over five hundred fps, or feet per second.'

'A what now?' Jadyn asked.

'Airsoft,' explained Rebecca. 'It's a competitive team shooting sport where opposing teams act out different wargames or battle scenarios. You eliminate opposing players by shooting them with these from replica guns.'

Jen laughed. 'You mean grown-ups running around playing war?'

'I mean exactly that,' Rebecca said and added some more photos to the board. 'These are the kind of guns we're talking about.'

'Bloody hell,' Jim said. 'They look real!'

Harry stared at the photos along with the rest of the team. He could identify a good number of the guns in the photos. Some he'd even used the true, real-life versions of, and the memories of being out in theatre were still there with him, just below the surface. But he pushed them away and focused on what was being discussed.

'They're supposed to,' Rebecca said. 'They can't be converted into real guns, and unless you like your gun to be bright blue, then you have to have a licence to own one, but yes, they do look real.'

Harry leaned forward, hands clasped, elbows on his knees, head down. 'So, you're saying that what we're dealing with here is someone who thinks they're some kind of soldier, right?'

Rebecca's expression remained impassive. 'Those balls were shot at the victim by someone using an airsoft gun, who then went on to kill her with a single thrust of a long-bladed knife through her throat. Whatever they think they are, they're a killer.'

Harry was quiet for a moment, then asked, 'What's the range of one of these guns?'

'From what we know, they can reach well over a hundred metres,' Rebecca said. 'But at a greatly reduced velocity and accuracy. The shooter would have had to have been considerably closer to cause these bruises.'

'How close?' Jim asked.

'Thirty, perhaps forty metres?' answered Rebecca.

Harry stood up and walked over to the board, his eyes on the photographs. 'The legal limit is five hundred fps, right?'

'Yes.' Rebecca nodded.

'So, what if the gun used was over the legal limit? What then?'

'How do you mean?'

'I mean,' Harry said, 'that if there's a legal limit to these things, then clearly they can be made more powerful, right? Otherwise, you wouldn't have a limit imposed. The whole point is to outlaw anything that's deemed too powerful, too dangerous.'

'It's the same with air rifles,' Jim said. 'The legal limit is twelve-foot pounds. If you want something more powerful, then the rifle is classed as a firearm and you need a firearms licence.'

'You serious?' Jadyn asked. 'Aren't air rifles just for knocking cans over in a back garden?'

Jim shook his head. 'No, they're not. And the ones I have back on the farm certainly aren't, that's for sure.'

Harry turned to Rebecca and asked, 'How far did the SOC team search around the site?'

'We searched everything that was cordoned off,' she replied. 'And we did a sweep of the wider area.'

'By how much?' Harry asked. 'How much wider exactly?'

'I'm not sure,' Rebecca answered. 'Twenty, maybe thirty metres. We didn't find anything.'

Harry faced the team. 'Meeting's over. We need to move.'

Swift sprung to his feet, confusion and irritation in his eyes. 'Why? What are you doing, Grimm? What's going on? This briefing isn't finished!'

'I think our killer was out there waiting for Kirsty,' Harry said. 'And I think they were far enough away to take potshots at her without any chance of being seen.'

'But why do that?' Swift asked. 'If our killer is playing at being a soldier, then what do you expect to find?'

'I don't think he was playing at being a soldier at all, sir,' Harry said. 'In fact, I would go so far as to say that there was no playing involved. This was serious. Deadly so.'

'And what do you mean by that?'

'I mean,' Harry said, 'that I think our killer believes he's not just a soldier, but a sniper . . .'

CHAPTER TWENTY

THE MOORS WERE NO LESS BEAUTIFUL FOR THE HORROR they'd witnessed two nights ago. And yet Harry was sure that the place where they'd found Kirsty felt sadder, almost as though some memory of it had been recorded by the natural world. And perhaps it had, he thought—an echo of her last moments, the ghost of her last breath still dancing around the drystone walls, bracken, and heather, searching for some-where to rest. Though he doubted there would be any rest, not until the killer was found.

'It's a shame Detective Superintendent Swift isn't with us,' Matt said, coming to stand alongside Harry. The day was racing on already and lunchtime had already come and gone. The rest of the team were making their way over to them after the walk up the gill from Gunnerside. Fly was with them and clearly loving every moment of being out in the hills in the fresh air.

'You don't mean that,' Harry said.

'You're right, I don't. What gave it away?'

'He's still our senior officer,' Harry said. 'So, a word to the wise, no matter how pissed off that man makes you, don't let him know, and absolutely make sure you don't let the rest of the team know. Dissent is easy to spread and hard to get rid of.'

'Fair point, boss,' Matt said. 'Apologies. Now, what are we on with?'

Harry waited for the others to join them. When they did, Jim dropped down and twisted a metal spike into the ground to which he attached Fly's lead.

'That'll keep him out of trouble while we get on,' Jim said.

Harry gestured with a nod to where Kirsty had been found, then pulled out a file which Rebecca had given him before heading off. It contained printouts of the photos taken of the scene, though the files themselves had been uploaded to the cloud. He held up one of the photos, which showed the open tent, the stove just inside.

'To answer our detective sergeant's question,' Harry began, 'we're here to catch a hunter because I think that's what we're dealing with.'

'How do you mean?' Jim asked.

'Exactly what I just said,' Harry replied. 'I think the killer approached this like a hunter, someone stalking their prey. So we're here to get into that mindset. And that means seeing it not just from the killer's perspective, but the victim's as well. His prey.'

'Not sure I quite understand,' Jim said.

'You're not alone on that one,' muttered Jen.

'Right,' Harry said, clapping his hands together. 'Looking at the photos, the tent is here and facing that way.' He pointed out into the blanket of vibrant green bracken before them 'So, by my reckoning, the only way the killer could have landed any shots at all inside the tent would be if they were lying out in that direction somewhere. So, that's where we're going to look.'

'And what are we looking for, exactly?' Jen asked.

'A scrape,' Harry said, then remembered he wasn't talking to a bunch of squaddies. 'What I mean, is that you're looking for an area that's been carefully scraped out of the ground so that a soldier can hide in it. Probably only about a foot deep.' Harry looked out to where he was telling them to look. 'There are a few thicker areas out there, so have a look in those, too. You might find that he's used a bung to block up his entrance into it. That's where you cut your way into the bush or undergrowth you want to hide in, then tie that clump together, probably with green paracord, then pull it in behind you.'

'You sound like you know what you're talking about,' Jadyn said.

'Once a Para always a Para.' Harry smiled grimly. 'Right, spread out, and let's see if we can't find at least something out there, eh?'

BACK AT THE COMMUNITY CENTRE, PCSO Liz Coates rolled her motorbike to a stop, heel kicked the stand down onto the tarmac, then swung herself off. Finding the building locked, she pulled out her set of keys and was quickly inside and through to where the team had been earlier that day. The air was still rich with the aroma of tea and she quickly got on with making herself a brew. As she did so, she stood at the board and worked her way through the evidence so far presented. She may have been away, but the others had all kept her up to date with what had happened, particularly Jim, who saw it as some kind of PCSO loyalty to be the one to share as much information as possible with his colleague.

Tea brewed, Liz went back to the board. She knew where the others were, but on Harry's instruction upon hearing she was back early, had headed into Hawes to be at the centre. That way, they could be sure to have a police presence should anything come in from Swift, such as news about the husband's whereabouts, or if something not to do with the murder investigation needed to be dealt with. And that could mean anything from the proverbial cat up a tree to a domestic disturbance or traffic incident. She was also there to receive the evidence from the crime scene, and she made sure that was all locked up good and proper in the designated temporary storage room. As she locked the door, she tried to recall the last time it had been used but couldn't. In fact, she was pretty sure that the last time it was used had been to store booze for the Christmas party last year.

A knock at the door caught Liz's attention and she glanced over to see a face she recognised standing there, waving.

'Hiya, Dave!' Liz said, opening the door. 'And what can I do for you, then?'

Dave Calvert stood in the doorway, dapperly dressed in tweed trousers and waistcoat. He'd been the first person to welcome Harry into the community centre on the day the DCI had arrived up north. When he wasn't in Hawes he was out working offshore, earning good money for being stuck on a rig in the middle of the sea.

'Is Harry around?' Dave asked. 'I've just got back and said I'd pop in and see if he was up for a pint, like.'

'Sorry,' Liz said. 'Rest of the team's out at the moment,

but I'll tell him you called.'

Dave nodded his thanks but hesitated in the doorway before leaving.

'Is there something else?' Liz asked.

'I don't know, to be honest,' Dave said, 'and I'm probably just being daft, but . . .'

'But what?' Liz pressed, picking up the concern in Dave's voice.

'Well, you see, the thing is, I went round to Harry's before coming here, like,' Dave explained. 'And I'm not usually suspicious, but I'm pretty sure . . . no, you'll think I'm daft, that I've been watching too much TV.'

'Get to the point, Dave,' Liz said. 'Come on, out with it.'

Liz could see that the big man was clearly uncomfortable, but whatever he'd seen had been enough to bring him here, so she wanted to know exactly what it was.

'Two men,' Dave said. 'In a car.'

'So?'

'So, there were two men in a car!' Dave repeated. 'Just sitting there. And I'm sure they were keeping an eye on Harry's place.'

'Why?'

'They were staring at me when I walked past and over to his door,' Dave said. 'And they were staring when I left.'

'Could be anything,' Liz said. 'Tourists just being nosy, probably.'

'They didn't look like tourists,' Dave said. 'And don't go saying something like, "*And what do tourists look like?*" because you know what I mean, right?'

Liz wasn't sure that she did, exactly, but nevertheless, she smiled at Dave and said, 'Tell you what, I'll go and have a look. How's that sound?'

Dave shook his head. 'I'm not sure.'

Liz saw the concern in the man's eyes. 'I'll be fine. It's a bright afternoon, what are they going to do?'

'Well, you just be careful,' Dave said. 'Oh, and you'll pass on my message to Harry, won't you?'

'Yes, of course, I will,' Liz said following Dave out of the community centre and locking up behind her.

Walking down through the marketplace, which being a Sunday was a little quieter than usual, Liz hoped that the team was okay. From what she'd been told, the murder had been brutal. She couldn't say that she was looking forward to getting involved, because that just sounded wrong, but she was definitely keen to be a part of the investigation.

Approaching Harry's flat, Liz looked around to see if she could spot the car Dave had mentioned. At first, nothing seemed out of the ordinary, but then, just ahead, she saw it— a non-descript saloon and its shadowy interior hiding the two occupants from view.

Liz was stuck for what to do. She had no real reason to go over and speak to them, and if they were in any way dodgy, then what she really needed to do was to speak to Harry about it, but he wasn't exactly available.

With little other choice, Liz decided that the best thing to do was to, first of all, take a walk past the car and make her way over to the front door of Harry's flat, then turn around and walk past again. If anything was up, then perhaps she would notice. It was probably nothing, but as a PCSO she knew her role was to show that the police were there for the communities they served, and right there and then, that's exactly what she was doing. And if a few folks saw her around, then that was all for the better, wasn't it?

As Liz walked towards the car, her mind decided to race

ahead with all kinds of calamitous happenings, from her being jumped and thrown into the boot and taken hostage, to the two men jumping out, all guns blazing, riddling her with bullets. Passing the car, she had to work hard to make sure she didn't speed up, because she thought that might just give it away that she was watching them. When she reached Harry's door, she decided a bit of amateur dramatics might add to the whole thing, so she quickly rapped a knuckle against the door, waited, did it again, then walked away, working hard to look disappointed.

Leaving Harry's flat behind, Liz walked back the way she'd come. She had the car's number plate now, so that was something that she could check on later. Then, just when she thought everything was fine, she cast a look over to the car and caught both men staring at her.

She froze, her eyes locked on the two faces glaring at her from inside the car. Then, as she made to move away, she heard the car's engine kick into life, and watched as the driver swung the vehicle out from where it was parked and onto the road. Slowly, he drove it in a wide circle around her, all the while never taking his eyes off her. Then, when he was facing the opposite way, he moved off. And far too slowly, Liz thought, deliberately almost. She was sure that she could still feel his eyes on her, even as the car disappeared out of sight.

Back at the community centre, Liz took out her notebook, jotted down what she'd seen, including the number plate, the car model, and the number of occupants. She then tried to ring Harry, but there was no answer, so she left a message. She then let out a breath that she hadn't even realised she'd been holding.

When a knock came at the office door, she screamed.

CHAPTER TWENTY-ONE

'So what exactly are we looking at here, then?' Matt asked. 'Because right now I'm seeing nowt, if I'm honest. And by nowt, what I actually mean is bugger all.'

Afternoon had turned its head to early evening and Harry had kept the team out longer than he should have. They'd stuck at it despite getting a little bit grumpy, but that was fair enough, and it had paid off in the end. He just needed to show them how, exactly, and to get them thinking as a team. There was also a message on his phone from Liz, but he would check that in a bit. It obviously wasn't that important, he thought, or she would have called again or phoned one of the others.

'This,' Harry explained, crouching on the ground and pointing just in front of him, 'is a scrape.'

'You mentioned that earlier,' Jim said. 'But what's a scrape when it's at home? Can't say it looks like much from here.'

With the team gathered around, they stared down at

where he was pointing, which was a shallow hole, probably no longer than eight foot in length.

'As you can see,' Harry explained, 'it's just long enough for someone to hide in, with whatever gear they're carrying. Anyone who happened to be walking close by wouldn't spot them. Not unless they got close enough to pretty much trip over them, that is.' He looked closer at the shallow trench. 'This one's been used a fair bit as well,' he said. 'You can tell by the dead bracken in the bottom of it, the way the edges are all worn smooth.'

'What does that mean?' Jen asked.

'It means that whoever made this didn't just use it on Friday night,' Harry explained. 'They've been coming up here a lot, and for a good while, I'd say. Recceing the area, getting to know it.'

The scrape was further hidden by the heather which surrounded it, purple and bright under the increasingly low sun, almost as though it was leading the way back home and trying to get there first.

'So, you think that our killer was right here?' Jen asked. 'Lying in wait for Kirsty?'

'That I do,' Harry said, then laid himself down in it. 'See? Fits me easily. Something like this you can stay out of sight, get eyes on your target. It's not exactly comfortable, but soldiering isn't supposed to be.'

'Soldiering?' Jadyn said. 'You think that's what we're dealing with here, a professional soldier?'

Harry twisted his head up to answer Jadyn's question. 'Now that, I don't know. But what we've got is evidence that whoever did it, is certainly going about this like someone who is.'

'Wait,' Jim said, staring at his boss, concern in his eyes.

'What about evidence? Isn't this part of the crime scene? And if so, aren't you damaging it?'

Harry rolled onto his side to look up at Jim. 'Yes, it is, and if there's one thing we've learned so far it's that our killer has left sod all for us to find. They're good, they know what they're doing, and they've made pretty damned sure there's no contamination from them anywhere at all.'

'So, what are you doing, then?' Matt asked, staring down at the DCI.

'Trying to get into his head,' Harry explained. 'In fact . . .' He climbed out of the scrape. 'Matt?'

'What?'

'Get in.'

'You mean get down there on the ground?'

'Yes,' Harry said. 'I want everyone to see this from the perspective of both the killer and the victim, or should I say the hunter and the prey. We need to think about what must have been going through their minds, what preparation the killer must have done to even get to this point. And what it was like for Kirsty.'

'I can do that standing up,' Matt said, resisting Harry's request. 'I don't need to climb into a hole.'

'It wasn't a request,' Harry advised, his expression steely-eyed. Then he jabbed a fat thumb at the scrape. 'So, you'll be doing it lying down. Get in. Now.'

Grumbling a little, Matt eased himself down to his knees, then slowly slid himself into the hole.

'You're making some brilliant old man sounds,' Jim said.

'And you'll make some brilliant young man ones when I get up out of here and give you a slap,' Matt replied, stretching out as Harry had done earlier. 'Now what?'

'Now,' Harry instructed, 'I want you to look over to

where Kirsty had pitched her tent. The rest of you? Follow me.'

Leaving Matt in the scrape, Harry led the rest of the team away from Matt, who he could hear muttering and grumbling to himself as they walked away. When they got to the campsite, Harry gathered them around, facing him. 'Right, what you're going to do now, is to turn around and try to spot Matt, okay? Simple as that. Ready?'

Everyone gave a collective nod.

'Good,' Harry said. 'Then, turn around.'

Harry watched as the team stared out into the moors, eyes scanning for Matt's not inconsiderable bulk. At first, it was clear to Harry that they had all thought it would be an easy task, but soon their cocky smiles faded to frowns.

While they were all staring, Harry's own eyes wandered along the route of the old Corpse Road, thinking again about the question Matt had asked, about whether Kirsty had been killed up here because of the name of the place. His eyes caught on something, a huge rock, someway over to their left, at the edge of the footpath.

'That's the old Coffin Stone,' Jim said.

'What is?'

'That massive rock you're staring at.'

'Coffin stone? Good God, is everything up here creepy as hell?'

'It's worth a look if you get a moment. Folk used to rest their dead on it when they were travelling the road. You can still see crosses and the initials of the dead inscribed on it if you look closely.'

'Maybe not today, eh?' Harry said. Then he turned to the team and asked, 'Anyone spot him, yet?'

The only response he got was the shaking of heads.

'You're sure of that?'

More head shaking.

'Right, then,' Harry said, then shouted out, 'Matt?'

'Boss!'

'Can you stand up, please? But stay where you are for a mo'?'

'Righto, will do!'

Harry watched as from the undergrowth Matt emerged, slowly and a little stiffly, looking rather like an ageing gorilla stirring from its nest. He waved.

'Bloody hell,' Jadyn said, his voice a whisper.

'What is it?' Harry asked. 'What are you thinking?'

'Just that I thought he'd be easy to spot,' Jadyn said. 'He's not even camouflaged or anything and none of us could see him.'

'Exactly,' Harry said. 'So, what does this tell us?'

Silence first, then Jen said, 'The killer knew exactly where Kirsty was going to pitch her tent.'

'Which means what?'

'That he'd been here before?' Jim said.

'I think there's more to it than that,' Harry said. 'The killer came out here and did a bit of a recce, right? Then dug out that scrape so that it would give them a clear line of fire to Kirsty's tent at the same time as making sure she wouldn't see them. And my guess is that our killer was probably camouflaged as well. Possibly in a ghillie suit.'

'A what?' Jadyn asked.

'Sniper suit, right?' Jim said, receiving a confirming smile from Harry. 'Named after the Gaelic word for gamekeeper. Wear one of those and no one's going to see you.'

'Yeah, but how did they know where she would be?' Jadyn asked. 'It doesn't make sense.'

Matt had by now wandered over to re-join the team. 'It does,' he said, leaning into the conversation, 'if whoever the killer is actually set the whole thing up from the off.'

Harry gave Matt a nod of approval. 'The killer knew the route Kirsty was going to take, agreed? They knew where she would pitch her tent, where they would need to dig that scrape. They knew every part of what went down on Friday night. And if you throw in the fact that all of Kirsty's kit was brand new, implying that this was a first for her, then—'

'Jesus . . .' said Jen, cutting Matt off.

'As our good Lord and Saviour is nowhere to be seen right now,' Harry said, 'I'm assuming a thought has just bubbled to the surface?'

'They knew each other,' Jen said, her words hesitant. 'Or the killer knew Kirsty, anyway. Otherwise, how would they have known where a newbie camper like her was going to be on Friday night, right? They would've had to know every bit of what she planned to do, when she would be here, everything!'

'Bit of a jump, though, isn't it?' Jadyn said.

'I don't think any of this is random,' Harry said. 'Yes, there's a chance that whoever it is, they came out here night after night in the hope of someone camping right here. But that's not exactly boxing clever, is it?'

'Here's another thought,' Matt offered. 'What if the only reason Kirsty camped here at all was because the killer actually suggested it? Somehow gave her the idea so that they could be all set up, have the place scoped out, be sure where Kirsty would be, everything really.'

The rest of the team turned their attention to the detective sergeant.

'Think about it,' Matt continued. 'None of this is random. We've a woman camping solo, for the first time in her life it seems, and she's out here in Swaledale of all places, and on the Corpse Road. That in itself seems a bit weird, right? At the same time, we've a killer who knows where Kirsty was going to camp, the route, where to observe, where to shoot those little white balls at her from.'

'The question, though, is how,' Harry said. 'And that's what this has all been about. Finding a murderer isn't just about discovering everything you can about who they are, their motives, their lives. You have to turn it on its head and not just think about what it was like for the victim, but to become them.'

'Explain,' Matt said.

'We now know that the killer, the hunter, was out there, right? They were either waiting for Kirsty to arrive, or came up after, but what matters is, they had the whole thing scoped out. So now think about it as the victim, the hunter's prey.'

'You mean how is it that Kirsty ended up here at all?' Jim said.

'Exactly that.' Harry smiled. 'She had no interest in camping until recently, and yet here she is, loads of new kit, on a very specific route, and she's been murdered by someone who clearly knew where she was going to be. So, someone got her here, didn't they? Guided her right to this very spot to have her killed. It's not random. Not one bit of it.'

'But how the hell did the killer know how to do any of this?' Matt asked, frustration in his voice. 'And more to the point, why?'

'Think like the victim, the prey,' Harry suggested. 'Where would Kirsty have got any of the ideas that would eventually see her ending up here?'

'We start with friends, family, work, social groups,' Jadyn said.

'Social media,' suggested Jen. 'If Kirsty's on Facebook or Instagram or whatever—and who isn't, right?—then there might be something there.'

'Like the pathologist said, we've already got a request in with Facebook,' Harry said.

'But that could take days,' Jen replied.

Harry couldn't argue with her voiced concern.

'And those little ball things,' Jim said. 'We need to have a look at what this Airsoft is all about, don't we? Might give us a bit more background. You said it's a team thing so maybe there's somewhere close by that does it.'

'We don't know that the killer is local, though,' Jadyn said.

'Maybe there have been other incidents?' Matt said. 'Folk getting pinged at by those balls? It's a long shot, but you never know, right? There are reports every year of kids taking potshots at people with air rifles from tower blocks.'

'Bit of an exaggeration,' Harry said. 'But, yes, definitely worth looking into.' He stepped back from the team. 'Looks like we've a busy day tomorrow,' he said. 'What say we all get home?'

Matt checked his watch. 'Just in time for *Antiques Road-show* as well.'

When Harry arrived back at his flat, the afternoon was long gone and the sky was a dark blue dotted with the brightest stars. He pushed through his front door, phone to his ear, returning Liz's call from earlier. As he waited for her to answer, he saw the envelope again, the one he'd spotted on the doormat that morning, so he picked it up and opened it.

'Liz,' Harry said. 'Just returning your call.'

'It's probably nothing,' Liz replied. 'Dave Calvert was around and said he'd seen them, you see, so I thought I'd go and have a look myself, just in case. And it's good for folk to see us out and about, isn't it? Police presence and all that.'

'What are you talking about, Liz?' Harry asked, slipping the contents out of the envelope. 'A look at what?'

'Two blokes,' Liz explained. 'Dave saw them when he went round to your flat to ask if you were up for a pint as he's back from work for a week or two. I saw them as well. They nearly ran me over, the pillocks!'

But Harry wasn't listening. Instead, he was staring at what he'd pulled from the envelope—a collection of photographs which turned his blood to ice.

'Boss?' Liz said, sensing the pause at the other end of the line. 'You still there? What do you think they were doing? Those men, I mean? What do you think they were after? They're not linked to something back home, are they? Something in Bristol?'

'Did you get the number plate?' Harry asked, ignoring Liz's questions, his voice almost catching in his throat.

Liz read it down the phone. 'You know them, then, do you?'

'No,' Harry said, his voice gruff and hard-edged. 'No, I don't. But they seem to know me.'

Liz fell quiet for a moment, then asked, 'You okay? Is there anything I can do?'

'No, honestly, I'm fine,' Harry said, though he knew the tone of his voice said the exact opposite. 'I'll see you in the morning, right? And thanks for passing on the message. I'll give Dave a call in the week.'

Hanging up, Harry carried the photographs through to the lounge and splayed them out on the coffee table, sitting himself down on the sofa. From the photos, his brother stared back at him, from the inside of a prison, oblivious to the fact that his photograph had been taken.

CHAPTER TWENTY-TWO

'IF YOU DON'T MIND ME SAYING SO, BOSS, AND I HOPE you take this as my considered, professional opinion, but you look like utter shite.'

Harry knew that Matt had a point, but it was hardly one he needed hammering home right there and then. But behind the jokey façade, he caught the concern in the man's voice, and that stopped him from biting back at the DS too hard. 'Thanks for pointing that out, Detective Sergeant. Very kind.'

Harry had arrived at the community centre that morning after a night of very little sleep and an awful lot of worry. As Matt was office manager, Harry had given him the responsibility of running through the morning briefing, and now, with that behind them, everyone was on with the rest of the day.

'This is what you need,' Matt said, handing over to Harry the pint mug he'd bought him a couple of months ago.

Harry took the steaming mug and sat down, rubbing his eyes in a weak attempt to push the weariness away.

'And this.'

The other thing in Matt's hand was a white paper bag, grease already staining the surface.

'That doesn't look like a bacon butty,' Harry said.

'It isn't,' Matt said. 'It's a breakfast pie!'

'A what?'

'Imagine it,' Matt said, taking a seat next to Harry as though he was about to bestow upon him the greatest knowledge known to humankind, 'and I mean really imagine it—a whole breakfast! In a pie!'

Harry leaned away from the DS's offering. 'That sounds completely horrific.'

'It's heaven in a pastry!' Matt said, offering his superior the paper-wrapped pie.

'But breakfast?' Harry said. 'In a pie? Does it come with a topping of Crunchy Nut Cornflakes, as well?'

Matt looked thoughtful for a second or two, almost as though he was considering Harry's suggestion as an idea to put to the baker. 'It's got sausage, black pudding, beans, and scrambled eggs in it,' Matt said. 'Trust me, once you've experienced it, you'll never forget it.'

'That's what's worrying me,' Harry said, but despite his misgivings, he took the kindly offered gift and took a bite.

'Well?' Matt said, staring at Harry expectantly. 'What do you think? Fantastic, isn't it? Cockett's has a winner here, I reckon. Bloody wonderful stuff!'

'The amazing thing about it,' Harry said, having survived his first mouthful, 'is that I'm pretty sure I can actually hear my arteries clogging up with each bite.'

'Ah, get away with you,' Matt said. 'That there is a work of genius!'

Harry settled back and continued to munch his way through the pie, washing it down with hot tea.

'Bad night, then?' Matt asked.

'Yeah,' Harry nodded, wiping his mouth of pastry crumbs. 'You could say that.'

'Anything I can help with?'

Harry shook his head. 'No, I don't think so. Personal stuff, that's all. The pie was much appreciated though, thank you.'

'There's a pie for every occasion, I'm sure,' Matt said. 'And it's my personal mission to find them all.'

Harry didn't doubt it.

Matt leaned back in his chair. 'Family then, I'm guessing, right? Can't live with them, can't kill them. Well, you can, but it's not advisable.'

Harry, smiling at Matt's approach to showing genuine concern, looked around at the rest of the team. All things considered, they were looking pretty fresh. Liz was with them now, too, so that was good. And the evidence room was nice and full, so he'd have to go and have a look at all of that very soon.

'Look,' Matt said, and Harry noticed that the man's voice was serious now, 'if you need to head home and grab some shut-eye or whatever, we've got everything covered here, I'm sure. Did anything come up from that number plate Liz gave you?'

Harry shook his head. He'd hoped to catch Liz that morning before she'd had a chance to talk to any of the others about the men in the car, but that hadn't happened and now everyone knew. The important thing was, though, that Swift didn't, not yet anyway, and they'd all promised Harry to keep it to themselves. Not that there was actually that much to know, Harry thought, taking a final long glug from his mug to drain it dry, but still, he didn't really want his private life spilling over into the day job. Not professional. Now, however, seemingly unavoidable.

Harry called Liz over. 'Who was it you said called at the office?' he asked. 'Not Dave, I mean later, after you'd been out?'

'Oh, that,' Liz said. 'No one. By which I mean, it was some tourist, bit worse for wear he was. Thought this was the hostel he was staying at! I put him right, not least because he couldn't have been more wrong.'

Harry smiled at what, to him, summed up being in the police. One minute you were dealing with a murder, next you were making sure that a pisshead got into the right bed. One thing the job certainly didn't lack, was variety.

Jim called from the door and gave a wave. 'Best I go see what all this Airsoft is about then, right?' he said, while Fly, who was wriggling like mad in his arms, stretched up to try and lick his chin.

'Don't come back all *Rambo*, now,' Matt said.

With Jim gone, next to follow was Jadyn, who was heading off to see if he could discover more about Kirsty's wider life beyond what they already knew, which wasn't really that much. He had the contact details for some friends, thanks to her parents, and there was her workplace to check out as well, and the gym she used. He'd be gone for the rest of the day and Harry could see that the lad was happy to be getting out and on with the job.

'You heading off now as well?' Harry asked Matt, finishing his tea.

'Well, there's a fair few doors to knock,' Matt said. 'But

I've got a couple of uniform joining me over in Keld to help me out, like, so we should be able to get around the places we need to. You know, Keld itself, Gunnerside, Reeth, Fremington, Grinton. And I'm going to just pop in and see Mr Harker.'

'Who?' Harry asked.

'Gary and Adam's next-door neighbour. Just crossing the t's, dotting the i's, as it were.'

'I know it's a ball ache,' Harry said, 'but it's always worth checking. Our killer left the hills before the rescue team showed up so someone might have seen something, heard something. You never know.'

Matt stood to leave as a knock sounded from the door. Looking over, Harry saw Liz answer it to reveal a young man with short, dark scruffy hair standing there more than a little awkwardly. It reminded Harry of a kid being sent to see the headteacher.

'Yes?' Liz said, as Matt pushed past and strode off into the day.

'Oh, hi, yes,' the young man replied. 'I'm looking for . . . actually, I've forgotten her name, and . . . I . . . er . . .'

Jen peered around the door. 'Gary?'

'Hello!' the young man said, seeing Jen. Harry watched as his face broke into an awkward smile, embarrassed almost. 'Sorry, are you busy?'

'Yes, I am,' Jen answered. 'We all are. Why? Have you remembered something?'

Harry could see that Gary was starting to feel a bit awkward, but he was fairly sure that Jen had it all in hand so continued to observe from a distance.

'No, I mean, it was just torchlight,' Gary explained. 'That was all.'

'Oh, okay then,' Jen said, a little bit of confusion squeezing into her voice. 'So, there's something else, is there? Has something happened?'

Gary shuffled his feet a little. 'No, I mean, I was just driving through, like. Picking something up from Mike at the garage? And I thought, you know, that I'd just pop in to see if you wanted a quick spin in the car, that's all.'

'Well, that's very kind,' Jen began, glancing back over to Liz and Harry, her eyes wide.

'You said you liked it,' Gary explained. 'Remember? And I was in the area, so I just thought . . . I mean, I don't meet many people who like the car, but no bother, not if you're busy.'

Even from where he was sitting, Harry could see the hint of red spreading across Gary's cheeks.

'Well, yes, I am busy,' Jen said. 'But, honestly, thank you. That's very kind.'

'Sorry,' Gary stuttered, backing away a little and out of the door, 'I didn't mean to . . . Look, I'll go.'

'Perhaps some other time, yeah?' Jen said, as Gary moved to leave. 'Mondays are never good, really. Start of a new week, catch up from the weekend, that kind of thing.'

'No, of course, I get it,' Gary said. 'I'll give you a call later in the week, maybe?'

'Yes, do that,' Jen said. 'Much better, I think. And thanks again. It really is a great car!'

Gary gave a short nod, then was gone.

'Well, that was awkward,' Jen said, wiping her brow in mock relief.

'He's obviously a bit smitten, that's all,' Liz said. 'Got to admire him for coming over. Takes brass, that.'

Harry got to his feet and stretched, his back cracking and

popping as he did so. Jen waved goodbye and was then gone
out of the door, clearly desperate to get out and make herself
busier than she'd looked when Gary had knocked.

'You need to take up yoga,' Liz advised, looking over to
Harry.

'And you need to stop giving orders to senior officers,'
Harry retorted, smiling. 'I don't need you having a go at me
as well. It's bad enough with Jen keeping at me about the
running.' He put his mug down by the sink and threw the
bag from the breakfast pie in the bin. 'You got the keys for the
evidence room?'

Liz handed them over, then swung herself round to the
single laptop used by the team.

'Right, then,' she said, flexing her fingers. 'Time for a bit
of social media snooping . . .'

'Has Facebook sent the data in, then?' Harry asked,
wondering if he'd missed something vital, or just not been
told, probably by Swift.

Liz shook her head. 'We can't be waiting around for that,
right? But if I can find out what groups she was in, that kind
of thing, I might be able to get a bit closer to how she ended
up in Swaledale.'

Harry was very pleased not to have anything to do with
it. He'd been horrified by all that social media represented
from the moment it all began, with Friends Reunited, and
MySpace, and whatever else had come and gone over the
years. Now though, with Facebook, Instagram, Twitter,
SnapChat, and whatever the hell else was going on now, he'd
moved from horrified to truly terrified. To Harry, the thought
of having his life displayed for all to see, seemed to be not
just astonishingly nihilistic, but also dangerous. And perhaps
Liz would find something that proved his concern to be

correctly placed. So, leaving Liz to it, he slipped out of the office and made his way through the community centre to the designated temporary evidence storage room. He wasn't really sure what he was going to find, if anything, but sometimes you just didn't know until you started looking.

CHAPTER TWENTY-THREE

JADYN, HAVING GOT NOWHERE AT ALL WITH EITHER Kirsty's gym or her place of work, was beginning to think the day was a total loss. It was already closing in on mid-afternoon and there was no way he was going to get back to Hawes before the end of the day.

At the gym, all he'd been told was that yes, Kirsty had a membership, a joint one with her husband, and that, yes, she was a regular attendee at classes like Body Pump and Pilates, but other than that, there was nothing else the staff could tell him. The only contact details they had on record were hers and her husband's, so that was a dead end. The person at reception, a man who clearly bought clothes a touch on the small side to emphasise his physical splendour, had tried his best to persuade Jadyn to take up a free consultation, but Jadyn had got out of there sharpish. Gyms weren't his thing. Fitness was, though, and he had plenty of kit at home to keep him in shape.

As to Kirsty's place of work, everyone there had been far too busy to see him, and not one of them had looked at him

with anything other than disdain. Her line manager, Mr
Wilkinson, a man in his late fifties, who Jadyn had thought
was not so much thin as narrow, like he had been in some
unfortunate industrial accident involving an enormous
pressing machine, had not just been disinterested but also
strangely racist.

'And where are you from?' he'd asked, staring at Jadyn
through glasses that were all lens and little else.

'North Yorkshire Police,' Jadyn had answered. 'Rich-
mondshire area.'

'No, I mean originally,' Mr Wilkinson had then said,
seemingly oblivious to where the conversation was suddenly
going. 'Your name, you see? Okri. It's an interesting one,
isn't it?'

'Bradford,' Jadyn had answered. 'Can't move for Okris
down there, you know.'

Mr Wilkinson had furrowed his brow, offered little else
to Jadyn other than the limpest attempt at shock and upset
when informed about Kirsty's death, then left him in the
reception area where he'd met him.

Now though, Jadyn was standing outside an old stone
terrace house in Richmond, hoping that not only was there
going to be someone on the other side of the door he was
about to knock on, but that they were going to be rather more
useful.

Jadyn double-checked the name and address, lifted his
hand, and knocked.

The door opened as though sucked from the other side
by a vacuum to reveal a figure wearing a leather apron and a
welder's mask.

'Yes?'

'Jane Peacock?' Jadyn said, somewhat hesitantly. 'I'm Police Constable Okri. I rang earlier?'

The figure was still for a moment then reached a hand up to the welder's mask and lifted it. The woman's face beneath it was red, sweaty, and bleary-eyed, her dark hair pulled back in a ponytail.

'You're black,' the woman said.

'Yes, I am,' Jadyn said, not really sure how to respond.

'No, I mean, this is Richmond, in Yorkshire. It's not exactly the most diverse of populations. Come in, please.'

The woman stepped back from the door, inviting Jadyn to cross the threshold into her home.

'Thank you for your time,' Jadyn said, his hat removed and stowed under his arm. 'I'm sure this won't take too long.'

The woman walked ahead and down a short hall, leading Jadyn through to a kitchen diner. 'Tea?'

'No, I'm fine, thank you,' Jadyn said.

'Well, I'm having one, that's for sure,' the woman said. 'I'm parched. Please, sit down.' She then gestured to the dining table, which looked out through French windows onto a long garden, which ended with a nicely built wooden office.

Jadyn pulled a chair out and sat down at the table.

'You'll have to excuse all of this,' the woman said, gesturing to what she was wearing. 'I'm an artist, you see? I make stuff out of metal, sculptures, individual pieces, that kind of thing, garden whatevers, but I won't bore you with it all. And after the news about Kirsty, well, it was the only way I could think to cope, really. Just threw myself into a new piece, trying to make it represent her, but it's not easy, not when it's so raw.'

Jadyn wasn't given much of an opportunity to respond as the woman's words spilled out of her, a verbal torrent pinning him to his chair. Then, with a fresh mug of tea in hand, she sat down opposite him.

'So, how can I help? Jadyn, is it? Yes. Good.'

Jadyn opened his notebook.

'Oh, you still write everything on a little pad? I was expecting you to have a tablet or something, be all high tech.'

Jadyn said, 'No, it's notebooks all the way. No batteries.'

With those important points out of the way, Jadyn first of all offered his condolences. 'There's nothing I can say, I know,' he said, 'but I'm very sorry for your loss.'

Jane at last took her welder's mask off completely then scratched her head. 'I'll be fine,' she said. 'It's her poor parents I feel for, though. Bloody awful.'

'How long have you known Kirsty?' Jadyn asked. Never quite sure whether to talk about the recently deceased in the past or present tense, he went for the present, as it felt more appropriate somehow.

'Since university,' Jane said. 'Durham. She just walked into my room on the first day and introduced herself. From that point on we were best friends, really.' Jane laughed then, and it was loud and genuine and warm, but it tapered off quickly, cut sharp by the threat of tears. 'She was always there for me, you know? Well, until that bastard turned up.'

Jadyn waited for Jane to explain further rather than interrupt with a question. But she fell silent, leaving him no choice but to pry further.

'College boyfriend?'

Jane shook her head. 'Oh, there were plenty of those. It was university, after all, so there's no point settling down when there's so many choices, right?'

Jadyn remained passive, allowing Jane to continue.

'No, it wasn't a college boyfriend, which was a shame,

because one of them, Paul something-or-other, he was lovely. Fit, too, if you know what I mean. But he buggered off around the world so that was the end of that.'

Jane reached for her tea and warmed her hands on it, even though the room was warm.

'Did she stay in touch with Paul?' Jadyn asked, half thinking that maybe some long lost lover had been her end, though doubting it with pretty much every ounce of his being.

Jane laughed then, but the sound was a cold bark hard enough to shatter granite. 'Stay in touch? With Daryl calling the shots? Not a chance!'

'Her husband,' Jadyn confirmed.

'Owner, more like,' Jane sneered. 'A complete and total bastard. I never liked him, not from the moment she introduced him to the rest of us. It was a Christmas party, couple of years after the end of uni. Met him at work.'

Jadyn was beginning to think that Daryl was already sounding increasingly like the kind of person they were looking for. 'But Kirsty liked him,' he said.

'Oh, yes, but she was blind, wasn't she?' Jane replied. 'All she could see were those shockingly shiny teeth, the flash car, the rich parents! It was all so different from her own background, so exciting. She couldn't see it. Wouldn't listen.'

'And what happened?' Jadyn asked.

'How do you mean?' Jane asked.

Jadyn looked back at his notes. 'You said something about Daryl calling the shots?'

Jane finished her tea. 'It started as soon as they moved in together,' she explained. 'Suddenly, she wasn't available or was too busy. You'd call her phone and Daryl would answer. I mean, we all tried, you know? Invited her out, kept calling, did what we could, but he built this invisible wall around her and it was impossible to get through.'

'But you kept in touch?'

'Actually, no,' Jane said. 'Well, not until recently. We drifted apart years ago because of that bloody man, God I hate him, but then out of the blue she gets in touch.'

'How?'

'Facebook,' Jane said. 'Must've been over five years since I'd heard from her, then I get this message about three months ago, and it's Kirsty, and it was like we hadn't been apart a day, never mind years! It was so great to hear from her again.'

'So why did she contact you?' Jadyn asked.

'Can't you guess?' Jane asked. 'Because she'd finally decided that she'd had enough of Daryl the Dickhead, that's why!'

'She told you she was leaving him?'

'Not exactly, no,' Jane said, then leaned forward, resting her elbows on the table, her hands folded. 'I mean, she didn't say she was going to leave him, nothing so specific, but she had clearly woken up to the fact that he was a controlling bastard and that she needed to get her life back.'

Jadyn thought for a moment about what to ask next. 'Did she mention anything at all about what she was doing this weekend?'

Jane shook her head and a look of bewilderment and disbelief stretched its way across her face. 'The whole camping thing?'

Jadyn gave a short nod.

'I had no idea she was going to go this weekend, if that's what you mean. But yes, I knew she wanted to do it. And believe me when I say that it was very un-Kirsty-like, if you know what I mean.'

'Go on,' Jadyn said.

'She'd grown used to the finer things in life,' Jane explained. 'She'd spent years earning a good wage, married to someone earning even more, going to expensive restaurants, flying off on the kind of holidays people like you and I can only ever dream of! And here she is getting excited about camping? Go figure.'

'So why did she do it, then?' Jadyn asked. 'Where did the idea come from?'

'I think she saw something on Facebook,' Jane said. 'She talked about the equipment she was buying, and it was like listening to a young girl getting excited about doing something behind her parents' back, you know?'

'Are you saying that Daryl didn't know?'

'Of course, he bloody well didn't!' Jane said, her voice reaching such a high pitch that Jadyn winced a little. 'She was buying all this stuff and hiding it at home in the attic. She'd tell me every time she'd get something new. Nothing cheap either, being Kirsty. Always the best. And like I said, she was getting hints and tips from some group on Facebook.'

'You didn't mention a group,' Jadyn said.

'Didn't I? Well, it was. Wild camping or something. Don't ask me. The only stuff I follow on Facebook is anything to do with puppies being cute and artists so pretentious they make you want to puke, but only after you've given them a proper slap.'

Interesting, Jadyn thought, particularly the mention of this Facebook group Kirsty had joined. He underlined it just to make sure.

Jane stood up. 'Anyway, I need to be getting on,' she said and grabbed her welding mask.

Jadyn followed her lead and rose to his feet. 'Did she say anything after she left Daryl?' he asked. 'Perhaps about how he reacted or, well, anything really?'

Jane was thoughtful for a moment. 'You know, when she told me she'd left him two weeks ago, I think that was the last time she mentioned him. Since then? Not a dicky-bird.'

'Did he know where she was going camping?'

'Haven't the faintest idea,' Jane said, 'but I can't see how. Though he was a conniving shit of a man, to be sure, so I've no doubt he kept an eye on her.'

At the front door, Jadyn thanked Jane for her time, then made his way back to his car. From all that she'd told him, he had a better idea as to why Kirsty had left her husband, and Jane's views on the man only confirmed what Harry had shared with them all, after his and Jim's visit a couple of days ago. So it was nice colour to help them build a picture of Kirsty's life, but it didn't help them much in finding her killer. The Facebook group thing, though, Jadyn thought, now that was interesting, wasn't it? Particularly after what they'd done the day before out on the moors. Because, as Matt had suggested, if the killer had actually suggested to Kirsty where to camp, then could it be that they belonged to the same group on Facebook? Was that where this had all started?

Jadyn stopped then, chilled at the thought of someone prowling social media, looking for victims, and Kirsty falling foul of it. He pulled out his phone and called Harry.

CHAPTER TWENTY-FOUR

CLOSING THE DOOR BEHIND HIMSELF, HARRY SLIPPED into the temporary evidence storage room and flicked on the light. The energy-saving bulbs spluttered unenthusiastically to life, and with the pathetic amount of light they offered once fully lit, Harry could understand why. He also wondered if the contents of the room weren't exactly helping. It wasn't that he was in any way superstitious or religious, and he certainly didn't believe in ghosts, but he'd always sensed that the physical evidence from a violent crime scene could somehow make their immediate surroundings gloomier. As though, to be in their very presence was to allow a thin, grey veil to cover your eyes, as a creeping chill scratched its way across your skin.

Harry spotted another light clamped to a shelf and flicked it on. It certainly made the room bright, but no more inviting or welcoming.

In the centre of the room stood two tables pushed together, a couple of chairs sitting beneath them. Around three walls were sturdy metal shelves and it was on these that the evidence was resting. The fourth wall contained a window that had been bricked up.

Harry walked over to the evidence and carefully moved it from the shelves and to the tables. Everything was in transparent plastic evidence bags, tagged with dates and location information, and a brief description of the contents. He also added to the pile the evidence bag containing Kirsty's purse, and the bag with the plastic balls.

For the next five minutes or so, Harry allowed himself just some quiet time to think, to take it all in. The crime had been a terrible one. The violent taking of a woman's life, by someone who had clearly set out to kill. His mind turned to Kirsty, not because he wanted it to, but because he forced it to, because everything that he was doing was for her, and he owed her that much. She would have had no idea at all that her life would end that night. Indeed, it seemed to Harry that perhaps Kirsty had viewed that night as the start of a new life for her, a fresh beginning. She was out in the moors on her own, being adventurous, being daring, and the future had probably looked so exciting.

Harry spotted the bag with the burned photos and reached for it, holding it close. He removed the photos and carefully shuffled through them. Most of them were too damaged to make anything out clearly, but the one of her wedding day still showed Daryl's face staring back. Harry wondered what Kirsty had seen in him back then, and how those feelings had changed. What it was that had caused the marriage to turn sour? He'd met the man and could guess that Kirsty had finally realised that the man was a complete arse, but was that really enough to lead to Kirsty's death? Yes, Daryl had done a runner, but unlike Detective Superintendent Swift, that just wasn't enough for Harry, not by a country mile. And anyway, the whole thing seemed too planned, too specific in its detail, to have any link at all to the husband. But if it wasn't him, then who?

Harry placed the photos back in their bag and down on the table and moved on to what else was in front of him. The largest object caught his attention first and he pulled it towards him. The label simply described the contents as a tent, but it was so much more, wasn't it? Harry thought. It was Kirsty's last-ever home, a place she had escaped to perhaps in the hope of discovering a little bit of herself which had been crushed by her marriage. She'd eaten in it, slept in it, drunk wine in it, and then, eventually died just out of its reach. Not that it would have provided any protection.

There was little need to remove the tent from its bag so Harry simply handled it, turning it over in front of him, which was when he noticed the darker stains on the fabric.

'Stacy . . .'

He muttered the name as though reading it for the first time as he had that awful night, seeing it written in blood on the tent. It was one of the things which were still niggling at him because it just didn't fit with everything else. It wasn't her name and yet there it had been, large and awful and almost proud, the letters smudged and running as their owner lay but a few metres away staring lifeless eyes into the endless heavens. So why was it there at all? And not just there, either, but carved into her forehead? Just what the hell did the name Stacy have to do with anything? Was it a deliberate red herring left by a killer with a sick sense of humour, or was it important? Was it saying more than he, at that moment, could discern?

Harry returned the tent to the shelves then shuffled back over to what was left. He saw Kirsty's rucksack and the clothing and other items she'd taken with her, including a novel and a little teddy bear which looked older than himself. The novel, he noticed, had a bookmark shoved in between the pages, and Harry thought how it was these little things that really brought the finality of death home. The unfinished book, the promised phone call that never comes, the meals uneaten. These were the pieces of life which death swept aside and the holes left behind by their absence echoed long and deep.

Other things were there, too, from the stove Kirsty had used to cook her last meal, and the empty bottle of wine Harry was sure that she had enjoyed, to a folding toothbrush, a little first aid pouch, and a blue torch small enough to pop into a trouser pocket.

Harry stared at the torch as though to do so would provide him with the answers as to what had happened. Then he picked it up and switched it on. The beam was faint as he shone it around the room, the weak circle of light gliding across the shelves, the remnants of Kirsty's last moments like the reflection of the moon on water. He wondered at what point Kirsty had used it, whether she'd really thought that help would come. And there it was, so small a thing, so innocuous, and yet it carried with it an awful weight, because of the hope it had taken up on Kirsty's behalf, and its failure, above all, to save her.

The last two items Harry examined he already knew well. The plastic balls were the other thing that scratched at the back of his mind, refusing to let him rest. They had led them to the scrape they'd found near Kirsty's camping spot, and had Harry thinking like a soldier again.

Then, there was the purse. Harry took it out of its bag to shuffle through its contents. Not that there was much to be seen, just credit cards, a driving licence, some money, and some receipts, some of which were for the very items in front of him on the shelves. Harry took these out and read through them, imagining Kirsty buying her gear, how she must have felt, the excitement at what she was about to do. It read like a holiday shopping list, the tent and the stove and everything else all joining together with the promise of adventure which ultimately ended in tragedy.

With a deep, sorrowful sigh, Harry placed the purse and the plastic balls back on the shelves with everything else. He had no idea how long he'd been in the room, no idea how the rest of the team were getting on, and was pretty sure that right then he'd learnt nothing from going through the evidence. And yet . . .

Harry stared once again at the evidence and it seemed for a moment that something amongst it was screaming back at him, desperate to get his attention. But what the hell was it? he thought. He'd looked through everything and seen nothing new! Nothing! It was just a sad and depressing collection of a woman's last moments, her dreams and God knew what else, all stuffed inside plastic bags and hidden away in the dark. So, what was there that he wasn't seeing? What was it that he was missing?

Harry, not one to give up, reached up to take out the evidence and have another look through when his phone rang.

'Grimm . . .' he answered.

'Boss, it's Jadyn,' said the voice at the other end of the call. 'You got a minute?'

CHAPTER TWENTY-FIVE

Daryl opened his eyes only to immediately snap them shut as the world in front of him swam and he jolted forward to throw up. Except that, as his body threw itself forward, vomit rushing up his throat hot and acrid, Daryl was brought up sharp, his body straining against an as yet unseen barrier. But it didn't stop the vomit, though, as it rocketed out of him, burning his throat, the stench of it filling his nose, his eyes watering with the awful strain, and the taste of it filling his mouth.

Daryl coughed, spat, roared, but his stomach wasn't finished with him. Another heave took control of his body, and still pushed forward by the violence of the first tsunami of nausea, he strained again, veins popping, sweat beading, bile charging out of him to splatter over whatever was in front of him. Because right at that moment, he couldn't see, not just because of the bleariness of his eyes, but because of the darkness he'd found himself in.

At last, Daryl's body sagged, the ferocious storm of sickness which had dragged him so fiercely from his slumber abating just enough for his head to clear, and for his mind to grasp exactly where he was, and why it was so very, very wrong.

From what Daryl could tell in the gloom, which cloaked him as thick as any wool blanket, he was strapped into the seat of his own car by black tape. He was clipped into his seatbelt, the tape wrapped around his torso, trapping his arms to his sides and the whole of his body to the back of his seat. The tape itself was so tight that it was preventing him from taking a proper deep breath and sensing panic taking over again, Daryl closed his eyes and forced himself to calm down. Whatever was going on, whatever this was, it had to be some sick prank, a joke by one of Kirsty's friends, he thought. Revenge for what had happened to her, no doubt, because who else could have killed her, but him? Idiots!

'Whoever you are, you are in massively deep shit!' Daryl said, his vomit-spattered lips gibbering as the dashboard of his car now came into focus. 'And if you're doing this because you think I killed Kirsty, as some kind of revenge? Then you couldn't be more wrong! And when I get out of this, there's nothing I won't do to make sure you're ruined, you hear me?'

The only answer Daryl got was silence, close and heavy and suffocating, like it was somehow aware of him, and listening.

'I'm serious!' Daryl snarled. 'I don't care who you are, what you think, anything! You've had your fun, proved your point, now let me go! Please!'

Still nothing. Not a word. But someone had to be out there, Daryl thought, because why else would he be tied up?

'Did you drug me, is that it?' Daryl asked. 'And how did you find me? Not even the police knew where I was.'

'Yes, but I did, Chad.'

The voice was thin and quiet and so close to Daryl's right ear that he squealed, the sound not far off that of a scared pig, he thought, wondering how such a noise could ever be from him.

'Who are you? Where are you? Show yourself, you coward! Come on! Show yourself!'

All Daryl heard then was laughter, small and over quickly and yet so sinister that a chill hooked into him and ripped clean away whatever heat and hope he had left.

'Wait a minute,' Daryl said, his mind focused now on what the voice had just said. 'Chad? I'm not Chad! That's not me! You've got the wrong person!'

More laughter.

'I'm not Chad, I'm Daryl!' Daryl said, sniffing through his words, trying not to just lose it and become hysterical. 'I'm not Chad! I'm not! I can prove it! And then you can just let me go, right? And . . . and I won't tell anyone. I promise!'

A thin rubber-covered finger pressed against Daryl's lips shushing him.

'I know all about you,' the voice said. 'I know about your life, about how everything was just given to you, how you don't even realise how lucky you are! Just like all the others, all the Chads and Stacys. No thought to the rest of us, of what we have to endure because of you, taking it all, taking everything, like it's your birthright! Well, it isn't, and you know what, Chad? You're going to help me show people exactly that!'

Daryl's mind was racing so quickly that he couldn't hold onto a single thought, a single idea, that would help him make sense of what was happening.

'I don't understand,' he muttered. 'Chad? Stacy? You're

not making any sense! Who are these people you're talking about? Who?'

Then, from the very furthest, darkest corner of Daryl's mind, something crept forward. A visit from the police. Two men, one young, neat and tidy, the other older and with some kind of horribly messed up face. Rude, too, Daryl remembered. They'd come to visit, to tell him about Kirsty's unfortunate death, hadn't they? But as they'd been leaving, the older uglier one had asked him another question, hadn't he? Something about whether or not he knew a Stacy or something.

Daryl's mind put two and two together and came to a truly terrifying answer.

'Oh, dear God . . .'

'What is it, Chad?'

'It's you, isn't it? You killed Kirsty! It was you!'

'I was going to tell you anyway,' the voice said, 'but yes, it was me. You both had it coming. A Stacy and a Chad all wrapped up in their own perfect little world, a world I have destroyed.'

Daryl was weeping now. Tears rushed from him as though trying to escape. 'You're not making any sense! What is this about? Why did you kill Kirsty? What do you want with me? Let me go! Please!'

'I'm nice, you know?' the voice said, as Daryl felt something cold splash over him. 'Okay, so I haven't got your pecs, your perfectly shaped head, and I'm not six foot, but why should any of that mean that I'm denied what you have?'

'What? What does any of that mean? My head? What are you talking about?'

A smell was now creeping up Daryl's nose, rich and sweet and powerful enough to overcome the reek of puke.

'You're all the same,' the voice said, and Daryl heard the anger sparking in it. 'You can't even see how lucky you are and how everything about you has denied people like me what is rightfully ours!'

Daryl's head was yanked back and tape wrapped around it, pinning it in place against the headrest.

'Try not to struggle now,' the voice said. 'But this will hurt a little, I'm afraid.'

Pain lanced through Daryl's body as something cut deep into his forehead. He could hear the bone underneath his flesh being chipped and scratched as the blade cut deep, slicing and carving, carving and slicing. He opened his mouth to scream but no sound came out, the pain so bright, so vivid, that it took over his whole world, his whole being, until that's all that he was.

The cutting stopped.

Daryl, aware then that his face was wet and warm with his own blood, yelled out in primal horror at what was being done to him.

'What have you done to me?' Daryl asked, his voice barely a whimper. Then, the smell was back to him again, cutting through the vomit, pushing through the sweet iron tang of his blood. 'Petrol . . . You've covered me in petrol! Oh fuck! Oh God! Oh shit! What? Why! Why are you doing this? Please let me go! LET ME GO!'

'Shush . . .' the voice cooed.

A light flashed.

'What? Why are you taking a photo of me? What do you want?'

Another flash.

'Please, let me go,' Daryl wept. 'Please . . . please . . .'

When the voice spoke again, it was as though it had been poisoned, the edges of it curled with thorns.

'People like you are denying people like me the sex and the companionship which is as rightfully ours as it is yours!'

The voice was a snarling thing, vicious and cruel.

'Do you think it's easy for us, seeing the likes of you, your wife, every day, strutting around, rubbing our faces in it? Do you?'

'I don't understand!' Daryl cried. 'I don't know what you're talking about. Please don't kill me! Please!'

'I didn't choose to be celibate, you know that, right? I mean, who does? Why would anyone? But I've no choice, because of you, Chad! Because of all the Chads and all the Stacys! All of them! Forcing us to be involuntary celibates! It has to stop! It has to stop now and I'm going to be the one to make sure it does! Because I am the ultimate gentleman, you hear? That's me! The Ultimate Gentleman!'

Daryl saw a light then, but it wasn't a cold light, the steady beam of a torch or a lamp. No. It was a flickering thing of warmth and heat.

'Please, God no . . .'

'And you had the audacity to throw it away! Both of you! So wrapped up in your perfect Chad and Stacy world that you let it crumble! How dare you!'

Daryl heard the insanity in the voice, knew he was without hope, but still cried to be spared.

'Please . . . just let me go . . . Please . . .'

'Goodbye Chad,' the voice said. 'Say hello to Stacy for me, won't you?'

Daryl saw the warm light flicker and soar and fall. It landed in his lap, innocent and small. Then his world burst into heat and pain, and the last thing he heard, as the flames embraced him, was the sound of his own scream ripping out through his throat as he was consumed by fire.

CHAPTER TWENTY-SIX

THE CALL FROM JADYN HAD RAISED MORE QUESTIONS than provided answers, and Harry, now back at his flat for the evening, was getting a headache.

Firstly, this friend of Kirsty had informed Jadyn that there was no way Daryl would have known about his wife's camping trip. So, to Harry's mind, the only reason the man had turned up in Keld and left the message on her car was because of the tracking device. He didn't know she was going camping, just that she had gone somewhere, and he was clearly a controlling headcase who didn't like the idea of her doing stuff without his permission. That he had done a runner was still a problem, but Harry didn't think it was enough to make the man the prime suspect. He was just a panicked idiot who needed to be found, nothing more. Not that Swift would be persuaded of that yet, Harry mused.

Then there was what she had said about Kirsty getting the idea for the camping trip in the first place from Facebook. This had supported Liz's line of enquiry and Harry was pleased that they weren't just hanging around waiting for permission from the gods of social media. Which was why, right now, Harry was staring at his phone, baffled and terrified in equal measure, by something he'd never used in his life—Facebook.

After the chat with Jadyn, Harry had shared the constable's findings with Liz. She had then gone through what she'd found on Facebook and, to Harry's delight, it had been rather easy for her to at least find the place where Kirsty had gotten the wild camping bug. Then, Jen had headed off down dale to deal with something else that had come up.

'Continuing with your whole *"become the prey"* thing,' Liz said, 'This is a group on Facebook, which is, as we've discussed, how we think Kirsty got the idea in the first place to not just go camping, but to head to Swaledale.'

'Hmm, yes,' Harry nodded, not exactly sure what Liz was talking about.

'Basically, what it is, right, is you can have groups about anything, okay?' Liz said. 'You just have a shared interest and there you go!'

'And this group is all about wild camping?'

'Yep,' Liz replied.

'And that's different to normal camping how?'

'It's wild,' Liz said. 'You don't camp on a site, with loos and showers and a bar. You head off into the wilds, simple as that.'

'So, who set it up?'

'The administrators,' Liz explained. 'Basically, if you've got a hobby or an interest or whatever, you can set up a group on Facebook, and then you get to share your interest with like-minded people, chat about it, share ideas, photos, stories, that kind of thing.'

'Why?' Harry asked, trying to get his head around the

whole social media thing. 'I mean, why not just meet people for real?'

'It's not that easy,' Liz said. 'And this allows you to meet more people than you would if, for example, you had a monthly meeting in the local village hall. And it's cheaper, more convenient.'

'Hmmm,' Harry said, not really able to offer much else. 'So, what have you found out?'

Liz said, 'Well, I've set up an account in another name, with a different email to my own, used some free images to give the impression that I'm real. Then, all I had to do was find Kirsty, which was easy to be honest, because her profile is still live. And from that, I then found the groups she had commented on, and, well, here we are. Look . . .'

Liz had then shown Harry the wild camping Facebook group.

'How do you know she was looking at this?'

'Took a while,' Liz replied. 'Lots of scrolling through her posts, until I found one where she'd commented about camping, and then after a bit more digging, I was in! I had to join the group, but that was easy.'

'So now what?' Harry had asked.

This was where Liz's face had lost its excitement at what she'd discovered.

'The group has over ten thousand members,' she said, her shoulders sagging a little. 'We can't exactly get all of their phone numbers and call them.'

'So what do you suggest?' Harry asked.

For a moment, Liz had said nothing, her face serious, lips tight.

'Liz?'

She had turned to him then, no less serious. 'This is where we go back to your whole *"become the prey"* thing . . .'

After Liz had explained her idea, Harry had decided that if anyone was going to do it, then it was going to be him. It wasn't dangerous as such, but he still didn't want Liz being responsible for trying to get a bite from a murderer.

Having helped Harry download Facebook onto his phone, Liz had then given him a quick How-To on the ins and outs of social media etiquette, as well as the log-in details she'd set up. Then she had headed off home, leaving Harry not exactly sure what it was he was doing, but intrigued as to whether it would be effective. And everything was worth trying, so he'd figured he'd give it a go.

So, back in his flat, with dinner eaten, Harry had started to search through the wild camping group that Kirsty had been involved with. He'd quickly grown bored of it, baffled by how people could seemingly spend hours on something like this, just commenting on other people's comments and photos. No, it wasn't comments, was it? It was their status and postings, or something.

Dear God . . .

Harry considered what it was he was trying to do. That being, to see if he could find someone in the group who had given Kirsty the idea of camping in Swaledale. As far as he was concerned, the chances were slim, but it was better than doing nothing. And if that person was indeed the murderer, then it was worth a try.

Liz had given him a few pointers, questions to ask others, things to say, but so far he'd gotten nowhere. Well, that wasn't strictly true. He'd learned a fair amount about wood-burning camping stoves, witnessed a few arguments about land access between people who had obviously never met, and even taken part in a discussion about the best things to cook in a Dutch oven. But so far, he was no further on than when he'd started.

Harry switched his phone off and dropped it onto the coffee table in front of him. It landed next to the envelope of photos which had been pushed through his letterbox the day before, he assumed by the two men Liz had told him about.

Reaching for the envelope, Harry slipped the photos out once again and shuffled through them. Each one was of his brother, Ben, in prison, oblivious to this invasion of his privacy. Harry assumed the photos had been taken on a phone smuggled into the prison. It didn't take much, what with bent guards and now the rise in the use of drones to drop packages over prison walls.

Harry grabbed his phone again and hit a number he'd not called in a while. It went through to voicemail, which wasn't a surprise, considering it was getting on to late evening. Harry left a message and hoped that Alice Firbank, the detective superintendent who had sent him up north from Bristol in the first place, would call him back as soon as she listened to it.

Yawning, but still pretty wired, Harry decided against going to bed quite yet. His brain needed time to process, and sometimes the best way to allow it to do that was to watch some bollocks on the television and to have a mug of tea. So that's exactly what he did, making himself a brew then sitting down to watch, of all things, the darts.

Harry wasn't sure when he'd dropped off, only that the darts had been replaced by two overly tanned and enthusiastic men trying to convince him to buy a piece of fitness equipment, which appeared to comprise of little more than some elastic straps to attach to the back of an office chair, and that the reason he had woken up at all was because his phone was ringing.

Groggy from dropping off, Harry grabbed his phone and tried to pull himself together enough to talk to his superior officer, impressed that she had called him back, despite the hour. But the voice that came back to him was Matt's.

'Boss?'

'Yes, what?' Harry replied. 'I mean, what is it, Detective Sergeant? I'm assuming you know what time it is?'

'I think we've found Daryl,' Matt said.

Harry woke up as if someone had just set his feet on fire. 'Really? Where? Has he been brought in for questioning?'

There was a brief pause before Matt replied and it was enough to worry Harry.

'What is it, Matt? What's wrong?'

'Well, we won't know it's him until the fire's out,' Matt said.

'What? What fire? What are you on about?'

'His car was found half an hour ago,' Matt explained. 'Someone had set it on fire. And it looks like Daryl is still inside.'

CHAPTER TWENTY-SEVEN

By the time Harry arrived, whatever fire had been burning was long ago dead. As was the person sat in the driver's seat of the car. Daryl, he assumed, though it was pretty difficult to tell, now that he was the crispy colour of a joint of meat after a day or so in a hot oven.

Harry had headed over in his own vehicle this time, instead of being picked up by one of the team, and was rather happy with the cheap little 4x4 he'd purchased a few days ago from Mike the mechanic. It wasn't exactly luxurious, but it did the job, and that was fine by him. Posh, expensive cars made him feel uncomfortable.

The scene before him was one of quiet resolve, the fire engine now no longer in use, the fire itself fully out, but the crew still working to clear things up and make sure the road was okay.

The car, which was now little more than a burned shell, a skeletal beast showing metal ribs and the roasted remains of its insides, was parked up in a layby. The traffic officers who had been first on the scene had shut off half of the road and were standing out in the middle of it directing any drivers heading by. Not that there were many so late in the night, which was now, Harry realised, early morning. Harry saw as well that the Scene of Crime team was standing by, their vehicles parked a bit further up in the same layby. There was no way they would be able to get access to the vehicle until it was safe enough to do so. Harry could hear metal still popping with heat as it cooled, so it would be a while yet.

Climbing out of his vehicle, Harry strode over to stand with Matt, who had given him a rather awkward wave from behind the cordon tape now surrounding the scene. The air was still thick, not just with the smoke from the car fire, but the smell of it. There were notes of burned rubber and scorched grass and mud, and petrol. But behind all of that, the scent that really added the tang of horror to the scene was that of a barbeque put out by the rain, of charred meat dampened by water and still steaming. And it was.

'So where am I, exactly?' Harry asked, trying to ignore the smell.

'Hurgill Road,' Matt said. 'Makes its way over from Richmond and down on into Swaledale.'

'Swaledale?' Harry said. 'Really?'

'You're thinking the same, then?' Matt said.

'Bit of a coincidence,' Harry said, but deep down he thought that was really all that it was. 'And we think it's Daryl?'

Matt nodded over at the car. 'The number plate checks out. It's definitely his. And seeing as he buggered off in it last Saturday, I can't see it being anyone else.'

'So it's definitely him?' Harry asked. 'We're sure about that?'

Matt didn't answer directly. Instead, he led Harry under

the cordon tape and over towards the vehicle. Up close, the heat was still noticeable and the reek of what had taken place was even stronger.

'It looks like he was strapped to his seat,' Matt said, pointing through the driver's door with the bright beam from a small but surprisingly powerful torch. On the ground in front of the door lay the remains of what had once been its window, now shattered by the heat, a carpet of scattered diamonds, stars fallen from the black sky above.

Harry leaned in for a closer look and at first couldn't see anything, then his eye caught the glint of metal around the corpse in the driver's seat.

'Someone chained him in?'

'I guess so,' Matt replied. 'Which pretty much tells us he was alive when, well, you know.'

Yeah, Harry did know, and he immediately locked down his mind, keeping it from painting a lurid picture of what had happened to poor Daryl.

Some of the SOC folk have had a nosy and they reckon it wasn't just chains, either,' Matt added.

'How do you mean?'

'Look at the way the body is,' said Matt, pointing at the horrifying remains, teeth bared in a death throes grimace of absolute terror and agony. 'See how it's really pulled back in the seat? And the head, that's all pulled back as well, like it was tied to the headrest, but there's no chains there, you see?'

'So, what are you saying?'

Matt breathed long and slow, a sigh of disgust at what humans could do to each other. 'One of them told me that they think it was probably Gorilla tape or something. The chains would've held him to the seat, no doubt about that, but they think that he was strapped in with tape as well, around his body, around his head. To stop him wriggling about, like.'

'Wriggling about?' Harry said, repeating Matt's choice of words. 'Why the hell would someone want to stop him doing that? It's not exactly like he's going to do anything else, chained into his own car and smelling the petrol that he probably knew was about to be lit!'

Matt allowed the beam of the torch to move up the body to the head. 'So that whoever did this could do that,' he said, then his voice fell almost to a whisper. 'Look at his forehead, Boss.'

It took a moment for Harry's eyes to actually see what Matt was referring to, but when he did, his eyes widened in shock.

'Shitting Hell . . .'

Harry was staring at scratch marks carved into the charred forehead of what he assumed to be the body of the man he had spoken to only a couple of days before. He couldn't make out what they were, exactly, but they were deep and clear and he dared not think about the pain that Daryl would have felt as they'd been cut and chiselled into him.

'Yeah,' Matt said. 'That. Pretty awful, right? I mean, who the hell does that? And why, boss?'

'Any idea what they are, exactly?' Harry asked. 'I think I can make out a letter or two. Is that a C on the left side?'

'Can't work out what it says, if anything at all,' Matt answered. 'But it does look like it could be a word or a name. Frankly, I'm still just having trouble dealing with the fact that it was done at all.'

Harry stepped back to try and take it all in. 'So, if it is Daryl, Kirsty's husband,' Harry said, 'and I think we can pretty much assume that it is, then odds are that whoever did this has to be the same person who killed Kirsty.'

'Agreed,' Matt said. 'Why, though? That's what's getting me right now. Why would they do what they did to Kirsty and then do this to her husband? What the hell are we dealing with here? And just what kind of enemies had they made to end up like this? This is Wensleydale, for God's sake! This kind of shit belongs in Mexico with those mentalist drug cartels, not here!'

There was nothing that Harry could say to make any of it better. They had another corpse, someone killed in a truly horrifying fashion, and they were still no closer to finding who was responsible for Kirsty's death.

Harry moved away from the grisly scene and headed back under the cordon tape and over to his vehicle. He stared out over the view in front of him. To his left, he saw the lights of Richmond flickering and blinking in the darkness like the distant lamps of ships on a black sea. To his right, the dale was darker, stretching off towards the low, hulking shapes of the Swaledale fells, which stood as silent watchers to the lives which came and went at their feet.

'What time is it?' Harry asked as Matt came to stand at his side.

'Getting on for four,' Matt answered. 'And dark, too, if you don't mind me saying. Too dark. Sun'll be coming up soon. Needs to hurry up.'

'You okay here?'

'Of course,' Matt said. 'You heading off?'

'Not exactly, no,' Harry said. 'Thought I'd take a drive down to Swaledale, do some thinking, have a mooch around Gunnerside.'

'Well, if you go up onto the fells again, you make sure

you've a torch with you and a fully charged phone. I don't want to be having you snapping an ankle then dying of exposure.'

'The torch on my phone will have to do,' Harry said.

'Well, it won't, not if I've got anything to say about it,' Matt said, then held out his hand. 'Here, take this.'

Harry saw that Matt was handing him his small torch.

'Sure you don't need it?'

Matt shook his head. 'Two is one, one is none, if you know what I mean.'

Harry did, thanks to his old Paratrooper days. 'You've a spare, then?'

Matt gave a nod. 'Three is better, so I've another in my jacket and one in the car.'

Harry took the torch. 'How did yesterday go, by the way?'

'We knocked on doors, learned bugger all,' Matt said. 'No one saw anything, and no one's been shot at with those little plastic balls, either.'

'What about that Mr Harker you mentioned?' Harry asked. 'Gary's story check out?'

Matt gave a nod. 'Yeah, all good. Lovely old bloke, too. Insisted on making us a pot of tea and some sandwiches. By the end of it, he'd managed to persuade us to take his rubbish out, get his television tuned in properly, and have a go at fixing the clock in his lounge!'

Harry smiled briefly, but his eyes were still on the terrible visage of Daryl, welded to his car by the searing heat which had killed him, and the smile faded. 'And you can fix clocks, can you?'

'I say fix, but it just needed winding up, is all,' Matt said. 'Turns out it's the only clock the old lad has in the house, and he's just a bit forgetful and doesn't always remember to wind it up. It was running a few hours fast. Easy to sort out.'

Harry opened the door to his car. 'Give my regards to the surgeon and pathologist, won't you?'

Then he was gone, pulling away from the nightmare of Daryl's last moments, and heading back towards the place where the dead man's wife had hers.

CHAPTER TWENTY-EIGHT

THE ULTIMATE GENTLEMAN, NOW WASHED CLEAN OF the acts he had committed just over an hour ago, was once again bathing in the glory of what he was doing.

You rock!

Served that Chad right!

Ha! The Stacy and the Chad together in Hell! Burn, bitches!

The adoration was intoxicating, and he was drinking it in as quickly as he could, chugging it down like he was shotgunning a can of beer.

You carved him real good, Man!

Smell that Chad meat BBQ!

I love the smell of Chad in the morning!

As the praise kept on coming, and the views of his video and the photos he'd posted continued to climb, he knew then that what he was doing was good work indeed. No, it was better than good work. It was the best work. Important. Vital.

He stood up and stretched, his dressing gown sticking just a little to his still-damp body. He could still smell the faint hint of petrol on his skin, hiding behind the masculine scent from the shower gel he'd used to scrub himself clean, but he didn't really mind. If anything, he liked it, because it reminded him of what he'd done, confirmed his greatness.

He sat back down and glanced once again at his computer screen.

We're gonna get what's owed us because of you, man!

Wish I'd been there to hear that Chad scream!

Incel Rebellion is NOW!

They were right, he realised. They were all going to get what was owed to them and, yes, the rebellion was now! Not just because of him, but because of the others, his brothers before him, who had shown him the way. They had stood up and stood out, burned hot, and shown the world—humanity itself—that the status quo just wasn't fair. It needed to change. It *would* change. And from here on in, he was going to tell them how. He would show them the way.

Sitting down again, the Ultimate Gentlemen opened a word file and started to read. At the last count, it had been closing in on ten thousand words. But he had a lot to say and it all needed to be said. This was his everything, his life's work, his reason for existing at all, put down in writing.

His manifesto!

His Sermon on the Mount!

It was time! He knew that, now. Time to share his vision with the world, because his work had only just begun, and he was, right there and then, raising an army!

As he loaded up the file, ready to send it to his followers, the Ultimate Gentleman had never in his entire life felt so happy. All he needed now, was one more Stacy to really get this party started. And boy, did he have the sweetest of fruits to go and pick . . .

CHAPTER TWENTY-NINE

HAVING DRIVEN AWAY FROM THE CRIME SCENE, AND ON down the road into Swaledale, the world around him a slumbering place of shadow and night, Harry had found himself to be considerably more tired than he'd realised. Thinking he could just push on through, he'd kept going, only to find his vision starting to get shaky. So, with the road ahead of him becoming dangerously blurred, he pulled over as soon as he could, kicked his seat back so that he could stretch his legs, and then lay the back down so that he could properly rest. He'd then reached up to switch off the engine, deciding at the last minute to leave it running, so that the heater could keep him nice and toasty. And lying there in the dark, Harry's eyes fell closed all too easily, and he slipped quietly into a dreamless sleep.

When he woke, the first thing Harry saw was the huge face of a cow staring at him over the wall to the side of where he had parked up. The big brown eyes of the beast seemed to be sizing him up, analysing him.

Harry gave the creature a wave.

'Morning!' he said, sitting up. 'Don't suppose you'd be able to rustle me up a decent mug of coffee, would you?'

The cow stared back, its eyes still on Harry, who was pretty sure that so far it hadn't even blinked.

'I'll take that as a no, then,' Harry said, and opened his door to let out the foul, stale air from inside the car, and get himself a lungful or two of the considerably sweeter-smelling stuff outside.

Good God, it is beautiful, Harry thought, stepping outside to stare down the valley. He'd been asleep longer than he'd expected to be, with the time now edging up towards eight in the morning. The day was waking itself up to be one as bright and sweet as could ever be imagined.

The fells, Harry saw, were a vibrant rainbow in various shades of green, and he thought then how he had never truly appreciated just how many different types of green that there could be. Not until he'd moved north, that was.

Covering the fields and dwellings which sat beneath them, as though huddled up under those great, earth-built thrones for protection, a gossamer-thin veil of fog hung suspended, a pale white and ghostly thing, a spectral entity at rest. Cars were zipping along the wall-lined roads and lanes, dots of colour against the green and grey. The air, so rich with the scent of peat and hill and heather, was fully alive with the sound of birds on the wing catching their morning feast, and of sheep calling to each other to share the night's secrets.

After a hefty and somewhat groan-filled stretch, Harry climbed back into his car. He rubbed his face, his eyes, then fished some chewing gum from out of a pocket as a poor replacement for toothpaste and a brush. As he did so, his fingers knocked against something else and along with the chewing gum, he pulled out a small, blue torch. For a moment he had no idea where it was from or how it had got there and he clicked it on. The beam was feeble at best and then he remembered. It was Kirsty's torch. He must have put it in his pocket by accident when he'd been looking through all the evidence back at the community centre. Well, he thought, I'd best keep that to myself. Don't want it getting back to Swift that I'm taking evidence without signing it out first. Then, as refreshed as he could hope to be under such circumstances, he stuffed the torch back into his pocket, started the engine, dropped his window into the door, and drove onwards.

After a few minutes, the road stretching on like a thread stitching together the quilt of fields that surrounded him, Harry spotted a sign ahead to the village of Marrick. He recognised the name but couldn't immediately remember why. And then he had it, recalling speaking with Adam on that first and truly awful Friday when Kirsty had been found. But it wasn't Marrick that Adam had worked at, was it? No, it was a priory going by the same name, Harry recalled. A quick look on his phone and he had found it, just away and on a bit from where he was, a sharp left, and then down a single-track lane by the looks of things.

Well, Harry thought, I may as well head over there and have a chat, seeing as I'm in the area.

He wasn't really sure why, but then Adam had been first on the scene, so perhaps he'd remembered something since, as often happened in such events and goings-on.

Harry followed the road along until a signpost had him take the left turn that he'd seen on the map. The road was narrow, dropping a little to his right as he headed along. He spotted the river Swale there at the edge of the fields, flowing in the same direction that he was driving.

A mile or so on from where he had left the main road, Harry came to the priory, a building set in a dip just on his right, down from the road. A wooden barred gate blocked the way in, but there was parking just nearby so he pulled in next to an old Land Rover. The vehicle was a little different to the ones he'd seen driven around the dales. It was smaller, in phenomenal condition, the dark green paint and canvas hood so pristine he guessed it rarely, if ever, went off-road.

Walking over to the gate, Harry made his way through and down the drive. In front of him, he saw a plain bungalow to his right and directly ahead, the tower of what he assumed to be the old priory. Although, it had more of the look of a church about it than anything so grand as a priory, he thought. Gravestones were dotted about, and Harry wondered then about the stories he could well imagine the staff telling the visiting groups of school children, of ghosts walking the grounds, voices in the night.

Further down, and at the main entrance to the priory itself, Harry was able to make out stonework in the ground, peeping up through the lush grass, which he guessed formed the ruins of the building the priory had once been. It was still a grand place, and no less so by being smaller than its name suggested. Harry could almost sense the history of the place, as though it seeped from the ancient stones about him and tumbled from the tower which rose high above.

The entrance into the priory itself was formed of large windows and beyond them, Harry could see that the centre itself was abustle with children and adults hurrying on into the day ahead of them. He'd spotted on his way down the drive what he assumed to be the storage area, between the bungalow and the main building of the priory. Hanging outside it he had seen equipment ranging from buoyancy aids and helmets to bows and targets. He could well imagine the excitement on the other side of the glass at the thought of what the day held.

Harry was making his way over to the door leading into the building in the hope of finding Adam, when he heard his name being called. Turning, he saw Adam striding towards him and was once again struck by just how fit the man seemed, almost as though he oozed with every possible benefit a life lived outdoors provided.

'DCI Grimm,' Adam said, arriving a second or two later, and reaching out a hand. 'Good to see you.'

'And you,' Harry said, returning the handshake. 'Sorry to just turn up like this, but I was in the area and thought I'd just pop in. I hope it's not too much of a problem.'

'It's not a problem at all,' Adam replied. 'You manage to park at the top? If I'd known you were coming over, I'd have unlocked the gate.'

'Squeezed myself in next to a Land Rover,' Harry said. 'Not that I've ever seen one in such good condition.'

Adam beamed. 'That's mine. It's a Series One. Renovated it myself. No way I could afford to buy it now if it was up for sale!'

'You and Gary, you're both into your vehicles, then?'

'We are that,' Adam said. 'He's more into speed, though. That old thing doesn't really accelerate as such, it just sort of gains momentum.'

'I can see you're busy,' Harry said, gesturing to the children milling about inside the building. 'I can come back another time.'

'That's all taken care of,' Adam explained. 'They're all

busy making their lunches, so unless you want to get all covered in margarine and Marmite, I reckon you're safer out here.'

'Then, here's where I'll stay,' Harry said.

'So, how can I help?' Adam asked, leading Harry away from the entrance to sit on a low wall overlooking the fields which ran their way down to the river Swale below.

Harry was quiet for a moment, gathering his thoughts. 'I'll be honest, I'm not exactly sure,' he said at last. 'It's just that, well, after last night . . .'

'Has something happened?' Adam asked.

'You could say that, yes,' Harry said. 'Kirsty's husband was found on the road between here and Richmond.'

'Found? What was it, a car accident? Roads around here are a nightmare. Too many accidents. People treat them like it's a race track.'

'Nothing so simple as that,' Harry replied. 'I'll spare you the details, but let's just say it's looking very suspicious.'

'Well, I'm sorry to hear that,' Adam said. 'Can't say I envy you your job at all.'

Harry stayed quiet.

'Do you know what happened?' Adam asked.

Harry shook his head. 'Can't say that I do. All I know is that we've now got two deaths and no answers as to what the hell actually happened.'

'Sounds like you could do with a coffee,' Adam suggested. 'Interested?'

'I don't think I need to answer that, do I?'

Following Adam into the priory, Harry was guided around to a small office with a couple of desks, a few too many filing cabinets, and walls covered in maps and noticeboards, as well as certificates and photographs. The former professing the qualifications of the staff to instruct people in numerous and potentially dangerous pursuits, the latter comprising dozens of shots of people having the time of their lives in those self-same pursuits. He spotted a climbing harness hanging from a hook on the back of the door, walking boots stuffed under one of the desks, rucksacks, and a comprehensive-looking first aid kit.

'Must be a fun place to work,' Harry said, as Adam joined him in the office and handed over a large mug of steaming coffee. As he drank down the hot liquid, willing the caffeine to kick in as soon as possible, his eyes continued to explore the room, taking in even more detail.

'It's brilliant,' Adam replied. 'Best job in the world. The pay sucks, like, but you can't have everything, right?'

Harry sipped his coffee, the liquid burning his lips. The maps, he noticed, were of the whole of Swaledale, and on closer inspection, he saw one covering the area around Crackpot, and another the mines above Gunnerside. Then his eyes were drawn to something else entirely, a strange-looking schematic of what he assumed to be caverns.

'That's the map of Crackpot,' Adam explained. 'The cave we take the kids down. It's a nice little adventure.'

'I'll take your word for it,' Harry said, eyes still wandering, across the walls, down onto the desks.

'Not your kind of thing, then?'

Harry shook his head. 'The closest you'll ever get me to caving is reaching under the bed for a lost sock.'

Adam laughed, Harry sipped, and then his mind seemed to snag on something. He wasn't sure what, but it was something that he'd seen, but not really processed. But what was it? And where?

Adam was talking and Harry dialled back into what he was saying.

'. . . almost impossible. I mean, it's the easiest of caves to do, which is why we do it with kids, but you try getting someone out of it if they're in a stretcher? Not fun at all!'

'So how do you do it, then?' Harry asked, still trying to find the thing that his mind had become snagged on. 'Get someone out of the cave, I mean?'

'There's one bit, called Kneewrecker Passage, or as some of us call it, Fat Man's Agony, where you have to crawl for a bit on all this scalloped rock. Really does your knees in if you're not careful. To get someone out through that? Well, we all had to lie on our backs, head to toe, and pass them over the top of us. And the person we were trying to get out wasn't exactly a lightweight either.'

'Sounds fun,' Harry said, his eyes now gliding over the windowsill behind one of the desks.

'Definitely worth a visit,' Adam said.

'Matt's said the same,' Harry mumbled, almost to himself, and he was about to continue talking when his eyes fell on the thing which had caught his mind like a fishhook in the reeds.

Shuffling across the floor, Harry reached over to the windowsill and lifted the thing for a closer look.

'Anything I can help with?' Adam asked.

But Harry wasn't listening. He couldn't. Because there, in his hands, was a clear plastic tub. And it was filled to the brim with small, plastic balls.

Harry turned to face Adam, holding the container up in the air for them both to see clearly.

'Can you tell me what this is?' Harry asked. He was

working hard to keep his face passive, to not give anything away, not yet, anyway. His eyes wandered across the office walls again and fell on the map of the mines above Gunnerside.

'Of course, I can,' Adam said. 'They're plastic BBs. Why do you ask?'

'And what are they for?' Harry pressed.

'You wouldn't believe me if I told you.'

'Try me,' Harry said, as he flipped open the lid of the container and tipped some of the BBs into the palm of his hand. The small, white balls sat there, inert and innocent, and yet all his mind was filled with right then were the images that the pathologist had shown them, the photographs of the bruises on Kirsty's body.

'Well, do you remember playing army at school?' Adam asked.

Harry nodded, as he pushed the balls around in the palm of his hand with a finger.

'We used to do this thing called Join On For Army,' Adam said, laughing then. 'We'd join up in a line, arms over each other's shoulders, then walk around the playground shouting *Join on for army! Join on for army!* If anyone wanted to join on, then that's what they did! More often than not, we'd end up with a massive line of lads and then the bell would go!'

'And what's that got to do with these?' Harry asked, holding out the hand with the BBs.

'Imagine those army games we all played as kids, with cap guns, only played as adults, with life-size replicas, where you get to shoot your opponents for real!'

'I was in the Paras,' Harry said. 'I've done it for real. Can't say I really need to pretend.'

'You should give it a go, though,' Adam said. 'Loads of ex-forces lads do it. It's great fun! It's called Airsoft or Skirmishing.'

'So, you do this, then, do you? Skirmishing?' Harry asked, tipping the BBs from his palm back into the tub and clicking it shut.

'I've got all the gear,' Adam admitted then. 'It's pretty expensive stuff, but I don't mind. I mean, it's outdoors for a start. And it can be pretty knackering, running around shooting the other team. You should give it a go.'

'And where do you do it?' Harry asked. 'This skirmishing?'

'Over Richmond way,' Adam said. 'There's a site there. It's excellent. Loads of scenarios, too.'

Harry remembered that Jim had headed off to a skirmish site in Richmond the day before. He'd been meaning to catch up with him later on. Perhaps now he didn't need to.

'When was the last time you did it?' Harry asked.

Adam shrugged. 'Couple of weeks ago, perhaps? Work's been pretty full-on, and we've had a member of staff sick.'

'What about last week?' Harry asked.

'Last week?' Adam said, repeating Harry's words.

'Friday, for example,' said Harry.

'No, I was here,' Adam said. 'Like I told you, remember?'

'Yes, I do, actually,' Harry said. 'You were observing your staff, I think, yes?'

'That's right.'

'And would they have known that you were there?'

Adam shrugged. 'I don't know. I mean, they knew I was there, but I doubt they saw me, which was the point, like I said. Give them space.'

'Could you have just headed home instead?' Harry asked. 'Left them to it? Would they have known?'

'I could, yes,' Adam said, and Harry saw a flicker of concern spark in the man's eyes. 'Why? What are you suggesting?'

Harry paused for a moment, trying to gather his thoughts into some sort of order. Right there and then, what he knew was that Adam had been first on the scene. He now also knew that Adam was into skirmishing courtesy of the little plastic BBs he'd just found in the man's office. There was the map of the moors above Gunnerside on the office wall, suggesting Adam knew the area very well. And it looked as though his alibi for Friday evening wasn't exactly watertight. Considering how fit the man was, and the short distance from the priory to Gunnerside, Harry figured that getting from one to the other, then up on the moors, wouldn't exactly take very long. But what he didn't have was any specific link from Adam to Kirsty or Daryl. But he certainly had enough to be concerned.

'I'd like you to come with me to Hawes,' Harry said. 'Routine questions, that's all. Important though, as I'm sure you can imagine.'

'Well, I'm a bit busy right now,' Adam said. 'Can I come by later?'

Harry shook his head. 'I'm afraid it needs to be now. Your staff can cover for you.'

'Yes, but still . . .' Adam began, but Harry cut him off.

'I need you to come with me now, Mr Bright,' Harry said, his voice quiet, calm, firm. 'Please.'

'Mr Bright?' Adam said, repeating his own name. 'That all sounds very formal.' Then his expression changed, confusion falling from his face, tumbling away to reveal another one entirely. And in it, Harry saw the white-hot light of fear.

CHAPTER THIRTY

HARRY WAITED AT THE TOP OF THE DRIVE OF THE priory, phone at his ear. Matt was on the other end of the call.

'Adam Bright? You can't be serious!'

'Look, I'm bringing him in for questioning,' Harry explained. 'I'm not arresting him. I can't, because we haven't got anything, really, have we?'

'Not really, no,' Matt replied. 'But you're sure? You think it could be him?'

Harry didn't know what he was thinking. But what he did know was that a lot of things had all come together at once and they were pointing at Adam. And his job dictated that he explore every possibility. And if it was Adam, then there was no way he could just walk away now, was there? No. He had to get the man in, keep him relaxed so as not to spook him, and see if anything came from a few questions.

'All I'm saying is that I'm bringing him in,' Harry said. 'He'll be with me. If it comes to nothing, we can drop him back later. Any news on your end?'

Matt said, 'Well, we've got a postcard in from Gordy. Want me to read it to you?'

'Yes, could you?' Harry said.

'Dear team,' Matt began, but Harry cut him off.

'I was taking the piss!'

'Oh, right, yes, of course,' Matt said, stumbling over his words. 'You can see it when you get in. See you in a bit, boss.'

Harry stuffed his phone back in his pocket and watched Adam making his way up towards him from the priory. He was walking with purpose, Harry noticed, but right then Harry couldn't really put his finger on what that purpose was. Whether it was a man ready to prove his innocence, or a guilty man planning on not giving anything away, only time would tell.

'So, where are we going then?' Adam asked.

'Just back to Hawes,' Harry replied. 'Everything sorted with your staff?'

'They're a bit concerned,' Adam said. 'Didn't really know what to tell them.'

Harry didn't offer an answer. 'We've a room at the community centre we can have a chat in.'

Adam opened the passenger door. 'You sure that's all that this is? A chat?'

Harry gave a firm nod. 'Yes, just a chat. So we can clear a few things up, go over some details, that kind of thing. It's normal police procedure. Nothing to worry about.' That last bit's potentially a massive lie, Harry thought, because if this went south then there was quite a lot to worry about indeed.

Adam didn't reply and instead just slumped down into Harry's car, so Harry joined him, dropping himself into his seat, and starting the engine.

'I've only just bought this,' Harry said, working hard to

make conversation and to sound relaxed. 'So I've no CDs or anything yet. Just the radio. Hope that's okay?'

There was no answer from Adam and Harry saw that the man was staring out of the passenger window. He seemed smaller somehow, Harry thought. Deflated. Whether that was a good sign or not, he hadn't the faintest idea. So he knocked the car into reverse, turned around, and headed away from the priory.

AT THE COMMUNITY CENTRE, Harry asked Matt to take Adam through to one of the other rooms, which Matt did quietly and professionally, and asked Jim to follow on with some tea and biscuits. Fly was curled up at Liz's feet under the desk. Harry then made his way through to the main room.

'Morning, all.'

The three faces that turned to acknowledge his presence were all serious. Liz walked over and handed something to Harry.

'It's the postcard from Gordy,' she said. 'Sounds like she's having a great time up in Scotland with the family.'

'Could do with her here, though,' Harry muttered to himself, taking the postcard. He then scanned what Gordy had to say, noted that she'd mainly written about how beautiful the Highlands were and that, 'Yorkshire has no right to call its hills *hills*,' not when you compared it to, 'Glencoe, the most hauntingly beautiful place on Earth,' then he mooched over to the kettle.

'How are you doing, then?' Jen asked, coming over to stand next to Harry. 'Matt told us you were bringing Adam in for a chat. You don't think . . .?'

'I don't know what I think right now, if I'm honest,' Harry said, reaching for the enormous mug of his, dropping in two teabags, then filling it up with boiling water. His mind wasn't just on the murders, but on the contents of the envelope he'd found back at the flat, what Liz had told him about the two men she'd seen, and the fact that, as yet, he'd not had a return call from his old DSup. 'Hopefully a chat with him will clear things up, though, eh?'

Harry's attempt at a smile felt awkward and he knew that his eyes weren't in on it.

'Boss?'

Harry glanced over to see Jadyn sitting next to Liz. On the table in front of them, the laptop was open. Leaving his tea to brew, he made his way over.

'What's up?'

'Remember that profile we set up yesterday?' Liz said. 'Facebook?'

Harry shuddered. 'Yeah, I remember alright. Can't say that I'm any the wiser as to why people think it's a good idea to have it in their lives.'

'Yes, but you were on it last night anyway, weren't you?' Jadyn said.

'That I was,' Harry said. 'For a while, anyway. As long as I could bear. Why?'

Jadyn pointed at the screen in front of Liz. 'Best you have a look for yourself.'

Harry turned his attention to the screen to see the Facebook monster staring back at him. 'So what am I looking at exactly?'

'Firstly, this,' Liz said, and opened a drop-down menu on the right of the screen. 'Remember I told you what this little bell symbol was? Notifications? Well, you've got a few. Look.'

Harry leaned over for a look but was none the wiser. 'And?'

'And,' Jadyn said, 'these are all notifications to tell you that someone has either reacted to your posts or commented on them.'

Liz clicked one of the notifications, the screen changed, and Harry was looking at something he'd posted from the night before. Underneath the posting were symbols comprising hearts and thumbs-up. There were comments, too.

'So, some people I've never met in my life commented or liked something I put up on Facebook,' Harry said. 'Whoopee-doo. How is that important?'

'We've been through all your comments,' Liz said. 'Quite a few more responses than I expected, if I'm honest, so this is obviously quite a lively little group. The thing is though that one name seems to have been commenting more than the others. Look.'

Liz scrolled down, and sure enough, someone had indeed commented more than the others.

'It's like this on all of your posts, and the ones that I did, too,' Liz said.

'And there's a message,' Jadyn said. 'Check it out.'

Liz clicked on the icon next to the bell, the one shaped like a speech bubble with a bolt of lightning in it. Harry had wondered what that was.

'So, what does it say?' Harry asked.

'It's not much, really,' Jadyn said. 'Just an offer of help.'

'So why am I looking at it, then?' Harry said.

'Because,' Liz said, 'this is someone reaching out to you. No one else has. This is someone making personal contact with you from the same group that Kirsty joined. And they're not just reaching out, either. They're offering to help you find somewhere good to go and enjoy your first solo camp.'

'But I don't want to,' Harry said, a little shocked at the suggestion. 'I've got literally no intention at all of going solo camping anywhere! I got my fill of sleeping under the stars when I was in the Paras. Do you think I want to be heading off and doing all of that again?'

'Well of course you haven't!' Liz said, and Harry noticed the hint of exasperation in her voice. 'This isn't you, is it? It's a profile we set up to see if we could get a response. And we have!'

'So, I don't have to go solo camping?'

'No, you don't!'

'Well, that's a relief,' Harry said. 'So, now what?'

Liz was back to her screen, made a few quick clicks. 'This is the profile of the person who contacted you.'

Harry looked over the PCSO's shoulder. 'All I'm seeing is a few pictures of hills and tents,' he said.

'Exactly,' agreed Jadyn.

'Exactly what?'

'Whoever this is,' Jadyn continued, 'well, they're not exactly being open about who they are, are they? That profile photo isn't of them, is it? It's just a random view of some hills.'

'Well, at least we thought it was random at first, but now we don't think it is.'

'Can you get to the point, please?' Harry said. 'Before I lose consciousness?'

Liz tapped a finger on the screen over the profile photo. 'That, right there, is Swaledale,' she said. 'The rest of the photos are a mix of stuff pulled from the internet and other photos, probably the profile owner's own. But there's nothing here that openly says who this person is, what they're about. Basically, it gives you the impression that they're real, but to my mind, someone is hiding behind this.'

'You think it could be Kirsty's killer?'

'It's a possibility, isn't it?' Liz said.

Harry straightened himself up and heard his back creak and pop a little too loudly. Perhaps sleeping in his car hadn't been such a great idea after all.

'So, is there anything there yet that's of any use?' Harry asked. 'Bearing in mind that I'm about to go in and question someone.'

'No, not yet,' Liz said. 'But if we respond, we might get something. It's worth a try, right?'

'And you think this is what happened to Kirsty?'

'Could be,' Jadyn said. 'If we act in the same way, convince whoever this person is that we're genuine, they might let something slip.'

'You're setting yourself up as bait,' Harry observed.

'We're doing exactly what you said to do,' Liz stated. 'To become like the hunter's prey, remember? And this isn't us. It's a profile on social media. It's worth a try. And we've already had a bite, haven't we?'

'Could this all have been posted by Adam?' Harry asked.

'It could have been posted by anyone,' Jadyn replied. 'There's nothing on here other than the fact that we think the profile photo is of Swaledale that can link it to someone local. And even that's tenuous, to say the least.'

'Well, I'll leave you to it, then, shall I?' Harry said, leaving Liz and Jadyn to collect his now very brewed tea. As he made to leave the room, Jen was heading out as well, and clearly in a bit of a rush.

'Anything important?' Harry asked.

'Just some old bloke gone for a walkabout,' she said. 'Gary's neighbour. Gary just rang to see if one of us could go and give him a hand in finding him.'

'Best you get off then,' Harry said. 'But don't mention that we've got his brother in, okay?'

Watching Jen bounce off into the day, Harry took a gulp of tea and headed off to have a chat with Adam Bright.

CHAPTER THIRTY-ONE

Harry was just about to head into the room to talk to Adam when his phone rang.

'Grimm?' he answered.

'It's Rebecca Sowerby.'

'Good news or bad?' Harry asked.

'I'm not sure my job is about good or bad news,' Rebecca replied. 'Facts though? That I can do.'

Harry leaned back against a wall and took another glug of tea. 'Fire away, then.'

'Obviously, we've not got all the details together yet,' Rebecca said, 'but I wanted to get a few things to you as soon as possible.'

'Like what?'

'For a start, there's what was carved into the man's head. And by carved, I mean exactly that. Whoever did this wanted the word read after the fire went out, and that wasn't going to happen unless he hit bone. So he must have really gone for it to hack down that deep.'

'So, you're not sure if it's Daryl yet?'

Harry tried not to think about someone chiselling a word into another person's head, but it was hard not to. Sometimes he wondered if his imagination had it in for him, his mind immediately filling with its own lurid version of what had happened. The blood, the screaming, the unbearable agony, it just didn't bear thinking about.

'You saw the body,' Rebecca said. 'It's going to be DNA only, but we should have a confirmation either way before the end of the day.'

'So what was carved into his head, then?' Harry asked.

'It's another name,' Rebecca said.

'What do you mean, another name?'

'Well,' Rebecca said, 'Kirsty had Stacy, didn't she? This time we've got . . .' She paused, breathed. 'We've got Chad.'

'Chad?'

'Yes, Chad.'

'Who the hell is Chad?'

'Don't shout at me! I haven't the faintest idea!'

'I'm not shouting at you!' Harry said, his voice still raised. 'I'm shouting at this whole bloody case! Stacy? Chad? What the hell is going on?'

'It was carved in the same place as the name Stacy on Kirsty. Deeper, though, like I said. They really went for it. Doesn't bear thinking about.'

'And it doesn't make sense.'

'On that, we can absolutely agree.'

Harry rubbed his head with his warm mug in an attempt at getting some comfort from something because he certainly wasn't getting it from the phone call.

'Stacy and Chad.' Harry sighed. 'Who the holy hell are Stacy and Chad? What in the name of all things shite does any of it mean other than bugger all? Why use those names? It has to mean something.'

'I haven't the faintest idea,' Rebecca said.

'Anything else?' Harry was pretty sure he was getting a headache now.

'Yes,' Rebecca said. 'His head was taped to the car head-rest, at a guess to allow whoever did this to carve that name into his skull. And that's no easy task, either, to cut through skin and muscle and then to scratch and chip bone.'

'God almighty.' Harry sighed. 'And the poor bastard was alive through the whole thing?'

'That's the only reason he would've been chained and taped into his seat,' Rebecca said. 'To make sure he couldn't move. If he'd been dead or unconscious, there would've been no need. And a preliminary examination of the body shows evidence that he struggled, not just from the cutting but the . . .'

Rebecca didn't finish.

'He was burned alive?'

'Yes,' Rebecca said. 'Evidence of an accelerant was found, petrol no doubt. The centre of the fire was the driver's seat. It spread outwards from there . . . from him. And there was a tracking device under the car.'

For the briefest moment, Harry's mind was back to what he had seen the night before, only his imagination had kicked in as well. The car was alight, an inferno of twisted, screeching metal, melting plastic and rubber. The roar of the flames filled the air, but above it rose the horrifying, agonised screams of the man trapped inside, his body thrashing uselessly against the chains and tape which held him fast, pinning him to the death which came as a mercy.

'Well, thanks for calling,' Harry said. 'I think.'

'Not a problem,' Rebecca replied. 'It's a nasty one, this. You need all the help you can get.'

'You're not wrong,' Harry muttered, then hung up, turned back to the door in front of him, and pushed on through.

In the room, Harry found Adam, Matt, and Jim waiting for him in awkward silence, sitting on opposite sides of a small table. In front of them, their tea had been drunk, and whatever biscuits there had been were now gone.

Jim stood up to leave and Harry followed him through the door.

'You heading off anywhere?' Harry asked.

'Nothing urgent,' Jim said. 'Why? You got something for me to do?'

'Yes,' Harry said and relayed what the pathologist had told him.

'Chad?' Jim said. 'Who the hell is Chad?'

'Exactly,' said Harry. 'But the names must mean something, right? Stacy and Chad? So, can you go see what you can dig up?'

'On the names Stacy and Chad?'

'Look, I know it sounds daft, but for all we know that's key to this whole thing. Just see what you can find, okay?'

'Of course, no worries, boss.'

Harry patted Jim on his shoulder to say thanks, then turned back into the room, closing the door behind him. He then sat down and rested his mug to his right, between himself and Matt. Adam was opposite.

'Thanks for coming in,' Harry said. 'It's much appreciated.'

'Not sure I had much choice,' Adam said.

Harry pulled out his notebook. Matt did the same. Then he took down a few details, including the time and date.

'Look, I'm sure there's been a misunderstanding here,' Adam said.

'We just want to go over a few things, that's all,' Harry said. 'So, some of this will feel like you're repeating yourself or going over something you've already told us, but other details might come out. Is that okay?'

'Am I under arrest?' Adam asked, the tone of his voice hard, abrupt.

'No, you're not,' Harry said, and it was the truth. There wasn't sufficient reason to force him to stay.

'I can leave at any time, then?'

'Yes, that's entirely up to you,' Harry said. 'But hopefully, you can see that it's best to get things cleared up.'

Adam sucked in a deep breath, gave a resigned nod.

'So, perhaps you could go right back to last Friday for us,' Harry suggested.

'But you know all of that,' Adam replied.

'We do, yes,' Harry agreed, 'but if you could, it would be very helpful.'

Adam leaned forward, his hands clenched together, and Harry could see that they were hard hands, toughened up from a life outdoors.

'I was coming back from work—'

'What time was that?' Harry asked.

'I don't know exactly. Gone eleven, I guess?'

'Working late, then,' Matt said.

'Yes, I was,' Adam replied. 'It's an accepted part of the job, like yours.'

'So, you were heading home and Gary called?'

'Yes,' Adam said.

'To tell you he'd seen lights on the hills above Gunnerside.'

'Exactly,' Adam replied. 'He'd been to the pub for a drink and was heading back home. He usually heads down there most Fridays.'

'Was there anything about the light he saw that made Gary think it was suspicious?' Harry asked. 'I mean, it could've been anything, right? Just someone walking along the tops, a farmer maybe.'

'No, he didn't,' Adam said. 'But I wasn't going to just ignore it, just in case.'

Harry glanced at Matt. 'How far is it from Marrick Priory to Gunnerside, Detective Sergeant?'

Matt did a very good impression of looking thoughtful.

'About eight miles?'

'And how long would that take to drive?'

'Twenty minutes at a guess,' Matt said.

'How is that relevant?' Adam asked. 'To anything at all? I was at work and then I drove home.'

'Did anyone see you leave?' Harry asked.

'No. I mean, well, I'm not sure,' Adam replied, a frown settling in for the duration. 'I didn't announce my departure, if that's what you mean.'

'So, you could have left at any time?' Harry suggested. 'During this Night Owl activity that you mentioned, for example.'

'But I didn't,' Adam countered. 'Why would I? I was keeping an eye on my staff. That's my job.'

'Do the names Stacy and Chad mean anything to you?' Harry asked.

'Stacy and Chad? No! Why?'

'So, you don't know anyone called Stacy or Chad? The names mean nothing to you at all?'

'Not a thing,' Adam said.

Harry pulled a small bag from his pocket and placed it between himself and Adam.

'Can you tell me what these are?' he asked.

Adam picked up the bag to examine its contents.

'It's a bag of plastic BBs,' he said. 'Like the ones you saw in my office.'

'You mean these?' Harry asked, then from his other pocket removed the container he'd spotted at the priory.

Adam and Matt stared at the BBs.

'I didn't find those ones in your office though,' Harry said, pointing at the evidence bag that Adam was still holding.

'Where are they from, then?' Adam asked, the frown turning to confusion.

'The crime scene,' Matt said. 'Most of them were in the victim's tent, the rest were dotted about in the grass nearby.'

'And what's that got to do with me?' Adam demanded, sitting up in his chair. 'Just what the hell are you implying?'

Harry ignored Adam's rising indignation and changed subjects. 'You said it was just a short run from Gunnerside up to where the crime scene was. How short?'

'What?'

'How long would it take you to run up the gill to where Kirsty had set up camp?'

'Twenty minutes I suppose.'

'Bloody hell,' Matt said under his breath. 'That's proper quick, that is.'

'Not really,' Adam shrugged. 'I run a lot, that's all.' Then he turned his attention back to Harry, his eyes piercing. 'You think I did it, don't you?'

'We're just asking questions, that's all,' Harry said. 'Just trying to get a few details straight, like I said.'

'Like the fact that I don't actually have an alibi to prove I was at work all Friday evening, right? Because no one saw me leave?'

'You can see the problem though, can't you?' Harry said. 'You were first on the scene, answering an emergency call of sorts.'

'Of sorts? What the hell do you mean by that?'

'We've only got your word for it,' Harry said.

'And Gary's!' Adam spat back. 'He called me, remember?'

'Yes, I remember,' Harry said and pulled something else from one of his pockets.

The small blue torch sat on the table and held the attention of the three men almost as though they half-expected it to grow legs and scuttle away from them at any moment.

'Do you recognise this?' Harry asked.

'Should I?'

'This was the torch that Kirsty used to signal for help.'

'That torch?'

Harry noticed an odd change of tone in Adam's voice. It was still angry, still indignant, but there was a mocking note in there now as well.

'Yes,' Harry nodded, dropping a pointed finger onto the object in question. 'This very torch. The one Kirsty used to signal for help. The one your brother spotted on his way home.'

Adam let out a small laugh laced with contempt. 'You're serious, aren't you?'

'He's rarely anything else,' Matt interjected.

'You just mentioned that you knew your brother would

be at the pub,' Harry said, 'because he goes there every Friday night, right?'

'Yes, but—' Adam began, but Harry's question had been rhetorical, and he wasn't done speaking.

'You knew where he would be. And, as we've established, you had more than enough time to leave work, run up the gill, kill Kirsty, then use this torch to get Gary's attention.'

Adam was on his feet. 'You're not listening to me!'

Harry continued with his line of thought but didn't get to his feet, instead following Adam's eyes with his own. 'And you knew that he would call you, because his big brother is in the mountain rescue, so who else is he going to call, right?'

'No!' Adam roared, and his voice crashed around the room, a tiger let loose and filled with rage.

'No?' Harry said. 'You're saying you didn't do it?'

Harry had a fleeting worry that Adam was about to do a runner, but the man sat down.

'Yes,' Adam said, his voice quieter as he worked to get himself under control. 'But I wasn't talking about any of that. I was talking about the torch. *That* torch.'

'I don't understand,' Harry said.

'You really don't, do you?'

Adam reached over and picked up the torch.

'So, this is the torch Gary saw, right? The one Kirsty used?'

Harry nodded a yes, then said, 'What's your point?'

'This is my point,' Adam said and switched the torch on.

Harry and Matt stared at the light struggling to escape the lens.

'Not quite sure I'm getting what you're on about,' Harry said.

'Nor me,' agreed Matt.

'There's no way this is the one found at the crime scene,' Adam said. 'It just can't be.'

'And why's that?' Harry asked.

Adam shone the torch beam directly into Harry's eyes.

'Because,' he said, his voice growing loud once more, 'I wouldn't use this to find the end of my own sodding nose, never mind to signal for help, because it's absolutely bloody useless!'

Harry and Matt stared at the torch, the light from it barely enough to have them turn away from it.

'So, how did your brother see it, then?' Harry asked. 'Answer me that.'

'I . . . I can't,' Adam said.

And Harry was sure that the room had suddenly become very, very cold.

CHAPTER THIRTY-TWO

HARRY RACED OUT OF THE ROOM, LEAVING MATT AND Adam more than a little bemused behind him, and crashed through into the main office. Three very confused faces looked up at him. Fly stood up and gave a half-arsed attempt at a bark before crashing back down onto the floor.

'What's happened?' Jim asked, standing up to meet Harry halfway across the floor. 'You okay?'

'Where's Jen?' Harry asked, his mind racing now, desperate to prevent all the bad things happening which were now painting themselves across the inside of his skull. 'Where is she? Where's Jen?'

'She's out,' Jim said. 'Oh, and about those names, Stacy and Chad—'

Harry cut in over Jim, his voice sharp and desperate. 'Has anyone spoken to her? Did she tell you exactly where she was going? Do we know where she is?'

Harry knew that his words were tumbling over each other, but he didn't care. They needed to find Jen. They needed to get her safe.

'She was just popping over to Swaledale, that's all,' Liz said. 'Helping that Gary lad find his old next-door neighbour.'

'She's not back then?'

'She's only been gone an hour,' Jadyn said.

'Shit!'

Matt scuttled into the room behind Harry.

'What's going on, Boss? What's wrong? You raced out of there like your arse was on fire!'

'Gary!' Harry said. 'That's what I'm thinking! Gary! We need to find him! Now!'

Matt looked confused. 'You mean Adam's brother? That Gary? Why?'

Harry ignored Matt. 'Liz, call her now! Call Jen. Get her on the phone! I need to know she's okay!'

Jim tried to get Harry's attention, but Harry wasn't taking any notice, his focus still on Liz.

'And when you're done with that, I want you to keep Adam here, okay? Just look after him, feed him if you need to, but don't let him leave. Arrest him if you have to. But right now, I don't want him getting in on any part of this.'

Harry had no idea how Adam would react to his new train of thought, but he knew that what he didn't need was an older brother wading in and trying to help. If he was right, then what they were dealing with was someone who had already murdered two people in cold blood and was moving on to more. The why of it all, now that was what was bugging him, but he'd get to that soon enough. He'd have to. But first things first.

'No problem,' Liz replied, phone to her ear now. 'What's happening? Where are you all going?'

Harry turned to the rest of the team. 'I suggest we take two cars,' he said. 'Just in case.'

'Just in case of what?' Matt asked.

'Right now, I've not got the faintest idea,' Harry said. 'But two is one, one is none, remember?'

That got a solid nod from Matt, remembering their conversation the night before.

'Come on then,' Harry said. 'We need to get over to Swaledale right now. And Liz?'

'Yes, Boss?'

'You keep trying Jen, okay?'

'There's no answer yet—'

'Well, you just keep on trying until there is!' Harry bit back. 'And as soon as you do, you let me know!'

'Of course—' Liz began, but Harry cut her off once again.

'I mean it, Liz! You don't stop calling until you get through, okay? She's in danger! And as soon as you get her you tell her that we're on our way and that she needs to get the hell away from Gary sharpish. Understand?'

'Of course!'

'I don't want any heroics from her, nor from any of you lot either!' Harry glared fiery eyes at Matt, Jim, and Jadyn. They stared back, faces stern. 'If what I think is true—and right now, even though I haven't connected everything together, I think it bloody well is—then Gary is a hell of a lot more dangerous than he looks, or wants any of us to think. Now let's move it!'

Outside, Harry raced over to where the patrol cars were parked, the footsteps of the other three chasing after him, their urgency clear for anyone who saw them.

'Jim, you're with me. Matt, you know where we're going, right?'

'I'm guessing Adam and Gary's place? Jen and me, we were over there on Monday, and I was back there yesterday to have a chat with Mr Harker.'

'We'll follow you, then,' Harry said. 'And don't drive like a complete idiot. We want to arrive alive.'

Jim opened the other patrol car and Harry joined him.

'You sure you're okay driving this?' Harry asked, clipping his seatbelt in. 'I mean, it's not a Land Rover, is it? And I'm pretty sure you were born in one of those, right?'

'Best you hold on then,' Jim said, and started the engine. 'Blues and twos?'

'Too bloody right!' Harry said. 'If I had access to a police helicopter right now, then we'd be in that for sure.'

Jim hit a switch and the siren blared out at the same time as the lights on the roof started to flash. The faces of pedestrians turned to stare at them with the bewildered, wide-eyed looks of hungry vultures, the lights strobing across them.

Harry saw and heard Matt do the same and then both cars were on the main road and heading down through town and out towards the Buttertubs Pass.

Once out of Hawes, both drivers accelerated. Harry was immediately impressed with Jim's driving skills. He was young, and just a PCSO, but there was no denying that he could drive. He'd not checked how much additional training the lad had done, but there was reason enough to believe he took his driving skills seriously. Corners came and went, smooth and careful, but with such speed that Harry barely had time to register them. Around them, the deep, vibrant greens of the fells blurred as the fields sped past, bleeding into each other through the gaps in the walls separating them. High above, the tops stayed steady, staring silently down. Harry wasn't sure if there was sorrow in the shadows cast down by the great mounds, but it certainly felt like it, almost as though they were following on behind, mourners to the funeral he was desperate to prevent. Because there was no way that he was going to lose an officer. No way in hell.

JEN WASN'T EXACTLY sure where she was or what had happened. She remembered arriving at Gary's little cottage and giving the door a knock. She remembered him coming to the door, thanking her for coming over. He'd seemed more confident than the last time she'd seen him when he'd popped into the community centre to offer her a ride in his car. Cocky, almost. And then she remembered entering the house to wait for him while he went to grab his coat. But that was it. So what had happened since? And where on earth was she?

Jen went to stand up but couldn't. She tried to move her arms, but she couldn't do that either. And why couldn't she see? What the hell was going on?

Jen struggled, realising that she was not only bound to something and lying down, but that she was blindfolded as well. And she was cold, not just from the wind she could now feel against her skin, but whatever she was lying on.

Panic crashed into her, a gut-punch of terror that sent a choked scream out of her throat.

'You're awake then. That's good. It's right that you are because there's a lot we have to get through now.'

'Gary?'

'Don't try to move. Not that you can. I made sure of that. Made it easier for me to carry you. Like they used to in the old days, when they brought their dead along here. Can you imagine that? Having to carry your dead mum or dad, brother or sister, hell even your own kids, to church to bury them?'

Jen wasn't listening. She could feel panic roiling up in her stomach, reaching tendrils of cold dread through her body, thin wires of electric fear. 'Gary, whatever it is you're doing, you need to let me go. Now.'

Gary laughed and the sound was childlike, excited, but edged with meanness. 'But I don't want to. Do you want to know why? Do you? I'll tell you. I didn't tell the others, but you're different. You're more important.'

'If I'm important, then you need to help me understand and to help,' Jen said, fighting with everything she had to not just lose it, to instead try and do something, anything, to get out of whatever situation she was now in.

'I'm sorry it's not very comfortable,' Gary said, and this time his voice was closer, and Jen felt his warm breath across her face. 'But then it was never meant for that, you know. The dead don't really need something to lie on, do they? To keep the cold out. Because it's already there.'

Jen wanted to cry. It was all she could do to just hold onto that part of her which was strong enough still to keep her tied to what little sanity she had left.

'I don't understand,' she said. 'What are you doing? What do you want with me? What is this about?'

For a moment, there was no response from Gary, just the sound of him scuffling about.

'We've not got long you know,' he said. 'Someone might come along and see what's happening, but I think we'll be okay. I think there's enough time. But if someone does, I'll be able to deal with them. It won't be a problem. You don't need to worry.'

'Worry?' Jen said, her voice catching in her throat. 'I'm

bloody terrified, Gary! What the hell is this? What are you doing? What do you want with me? WHAT?'

'It didn't have to be like this. You know that, don't you?' Gary said. 'All you had to do was say yes. When I came over, remember? To see if you wanted to have a bit of a spin in my car? I thought you were different, then, thought we had a connection. But you're just like the others. All of you, looking down at people like me, not seeing us for what we are.'

Jen was confused as well as scared now.

'Others? What others? What on earth are you talking about, Gary? Let me go! LET ME GO!'

'I'm a gentleman, you know that, right?' Gary whispered, the closeness of his voice to her ear causing her to flinch. 'The ultimate gentleman, actually. Not that the world gives a shit. Because it's all about you, isn't it? You perfect little bitches and your perfect lives and perfect boyfriends!'

Tears came then and Jen couldn't stop them. Her mind was crashing, fear shooting her body with adrenaline and causing it to shake. She wrenched hard against the ropes that held her, a scream scorching her throat as she roared out to be let free.

'Let me go, Gary! LET ME GO!'

'You had your chance,' Gary said, his voice further away now, floating somewhere above her. 'But I see you now for what you are. You're a Stacy, Jen. And that means you have to die.'

Then something hammered into Jen's cheek, the pain like a nail being driven into her flesh, and she screamed.

CHAPTER THIRTY-THREE

HARRY WAS OUT OF THE CAR BEFORE JIM HAD PULLED IT up to a dead stop, feet hitting grit on the run.

'Which is Gary's house?' he shouted, as Matt, Jim, and Jadyn jumped out of the cars. 'Which one?'

'That one!' Matt said, pointing at the small cottage at the end of the row. 'Mr Harker's next door. Gary's car's gone, though.'

'Could be at the garage,' Harry said. 'He was over there on Monday.'

'Yeah, actually, that was weird, thinking about it,' Matt said. 'I didn't really think anything of it at the time, but there's a garage in Reeth as well. So, why did he say he was over at Mike's?'

'There might be something inside that tells us where he's gone,' Harry said. 'Matt, Jadyn, you take Gary's. Jim, you and me are in here.'

Harry was up at the door, fist hammering hard. 'Police! Open the door! OPEN THE DOOR!'

Just a few metres away, Matt's voice joined in.

'Jadyn, Jim! Go round the back! See if you can get in!'

Jadyn and Jim headed off round to the left, disappearing round the corner of Gary and Adam's cottage.

'Open the door! OPEN THE DOOR!' Harry's fist was hurting, but he didn't care. 'OPEN TH—'

The door opened and there, standing in front of him, was a very confused old man.

'Mr Harker?'

'Yes? I was having a nap. Think I had rather too much for breakfast! Can I help?'

Harry pushed past and into the old man's cosy little lounge. 'We're looking for Gary. Have you seen him?'

'Gary? Yes, he was here last Friday. Lovely lad. Comes round to keep me company sometimes, play a game of draughts. Is everything okay?'

Harry raced through from the lounge to the kitchen, thought about heading upstairs, but he knew there was no point. Gary wasn't there. Neither was Jen. He remembered then why Matt had been round the day before—to check up on Gary's whereabouts that fateful Friday night. He ran back into the lounge.

'About last Friday,' Harry asked quickly, Mr Harker still standing over by the door. 'You told my detective sergeant that Gary was here all evening.'

'Oh, yes, I remember him visiting. How is he? Got my clock going for me again. Very kind. It stops rather a lot, you see. That one there. Only one I have. I do love the sound of it ticking on, you know.'

'Are you sure Gary was with you all night?'

'Why wouldn't he be?'

Jim was at the door, with Jadyn and Matt. 'Managed to get in round the back, but there's no one there.'

'Mr Harker,' Harry asked again, 'are you sure Gary was with you the whole time?'

'He came round late afternoon I think. He's such a lovely lad, you know.'

'And he was with you all evening?'

'Well, I dozed off for a while, but he was here when I woke up. And I checked the time. He popped off to go to the pub then, you know, because it was late. Last orders he said. I'd have gone with him, but I was rather tired. I do like a pint now and again.'

Harry snapped round to look at Matt. 'Didn't you say that this clock here had been running fast?'

'Yes,' Matt said. 'By about three hours, I think.'

'Three hours . . .' Harry repeated, his voice quiet as he took a second to think. 'Jim?'

'Boss?'

'How long would it take to get from here to that scrape up on the hill?'

'Three-quarters of an hour max,' Jim replied. 'Quicker if you took the lane partway up over the moors, the one the rescue team used.'

'Bastard . . .' Harry hissed. 'He changed the clock!'

Realisation at what Harry had said, and what it implied, tumbled into the room.

'Is there a problem?' Mr Harker said. 'Is Gary in a bit of trouble? What that young man needs is a good woman, if you ask me.'

Harry thanked Mr Harker for his time and went outside. 'So, where the hell is he, then? Where has he taken Jen?'

'When we were up on the hill, on Sunday,' Jadyn said. 'Remember you said how that scrape was all worn, like it had been used loads?'

Harry turned to Jadyn. 'It wasn't freshly dug. Gary must've been going up there regularly.'

'So maybe he's there again,' Jadyn suggested. 'Maybe that's where he likes to go to . . .'

The police constable's voice faded.

'Doesn't explain the other killing though,' Matt said.

'No, it doesn't,' said Harry. 'But right now, it's all we've got.'

'We'll take the track up to the top,' Jim said, jumping in.

Harry followed suit, slamming the door behind him.

'What do we do if he's not there?' Jim asked, starting the engine.

'Just hope that he is, Jim,' Harry said. 'Just hope that he is. Now move it!'

BRIGHT LIGHT TORE through into Jen's brain as her blindfold was pulled up and off. The light was painful, a boxing glove pin cushion to the face. Above her, she saw Gary. In his right hand was his phone, which he was pointing down at her. And he was talking, not to her, Jen realised, but to the phone, narrating what he was doing. His left hand was hanging loose by his side and held casually in its grip was a pistol.

'. . . just another Stacy, just like all the others. Sad, I know, right? But that's the truth of it, isn't it? The world is full of them, these Stacys and their Chads, all hanging out together, rejecting us, pushing us to one side. But no more! It stops now because we're rising up! The rebellion is here! It is HERE!'

Gary laughed then and turned his gaze from his phone down to Jen and pointed at her with the barrel of the pistol. 'I hope you're not too comfortable down there, Stacy. Wouldn't want that, now, would we?'

'What the hell are you talking about?' Jen replied. 'Stacy? That's not my name! It wasn't Kirsty's name! Why did you kill her, Gary? What the hell do you want? WHAT? And where the hell did you get a pistol?'

Pain lanced through Jen as something slammed into her face, just below her eye, the searing sting of it lighting her head with bright lights and fury.

'Hurts, doesn't it?' Gary said. 'I've only shot you twice, but I'll bet you don't want me to do it again, do you?'

'You shot me?'

Gary held the pistol up with obvious pride. 'I'm afraid it only shoots BBs, but it still looks cool, don't you think? It's Adam's, if you're wondering. You need a licence, you see, and I don't have one. So I took a couple of the ones he never uses and, well, you know, customised them a bit.'

'I've no idea what you're talking about,' Jen said.

'They're more powerful,' continued Gary. 'Illegal, now, actually. Had to be done, though. Improved range, that kind of thing. I'll be able to hunt more now that I've tested it all. Once I'm past what I have planned for you.'

Gary turned away from Jen and was back to talking into his phone. 'I've not got long now, need to wrap this up pretty soon. But this won't be my last video. No way! There's going to be more! Yeah, you heard that right! I'm not going out in a blaze of glory because I've got work to do and a life to live! No point doing this if I don't get to enjoy what is rightly mine, right? And more of these Stacys and Chads are gonna fall because of me! And they need to, to make the world sit up and take notice of us!'

'Shut up, Gary! Shut UP!' Jen screamed, her voice

breaking and cracking with every word. Her face was sore from the impact of the two BBs Gary had shot at her. 'Just shut up and LET ME GO! Untie me, you mad bastard! Untie me!'

Jen looked around then and recognised where she was, the Corpse Road, up above Gunnerside, the place where Kirsty had been murdered. Then Jen remembered the BBs that the SOC team had found.

Gary crouched down, the movement so fast and cat-like that Jen flinched.

'It's easy for people like you,' he said, his hand reaching out, still holding the pistol, to stroke Jen's face gently. 'You don't know the meaning of loneliness, of rejection. You never give a thought to people like me. But you will now. And so will everyone else!'

Jen pulled away from Gary's hand, his skin horribly warm against her cheek, the pain from the BBs easing just a little.

'Loneliness?' she said. 'Is that what this is about? Seriously? That's why you've tied me up and shot me with your toy gun?'

'It's not a toy!'

'It shoots plastic BBs, Gary,' Jen said. 'It's absolutely a toy.'

Gary clenched his jaw, his lips thin, then cracked Jen hard on the top of her head with the pistol's barrel.

'Does that feel like a toy to you? Does it? No, it doesn't! So shut up!'

Jen's eyes watered with the pain and she decided to stay quiet for a moment, to gather her thoughts, work out if there was any way at all of getting out of this.

'I'm a virgin, you know,' Gary said, changing the subject

on a pin. 'Not like my brother, Mr Outdoors, with his perfect everything. I've had to live with that, have it rubbed in my face, through school, through university, my big brother with all his looks and his girls. And me, with what I've got.'

'You're not making sense,' Jen said. 'Can you not hear yourself? It's insane!'

'I'm making perfect sense!' Gary howled back at Jen, spit flying from his mouth with the rage which had suddenly taken hold of him. 'Can you imagine it? A virgin at my age! Who goes to uni and doesn't get laid? Who, Stacy? Nobody, that's who. And that's what you and all the other Stacys and Chads think I am, isn't it? A nobody? Well, I'm not! And I've proved it!'

Jen wanted to say so much right then, but she had to get a hold of herself, work out a way to get Gary onside, to talk him down. She had to. Because if what he had done to Kirsty was anything to go by, then it was pretty clear where this was leading.

'But you're not alone,' Jen said. 'And there's nothing wrong with being a virgin! That's not something you just give away, you know? It's precious!' She was struggling for words, struggling to sound sincere. 'You have to look after it. Give it to someone who deserves it. Deserves you.'

Jen didn't really know what she was saying. She was just talking, saying anything to keep Gary as far away as possible from whatever the end game was.

Gary shook his head in clear disbelief, turning away from Jen, scratching his head with the end of the pistol's barrel.

'Can you hear yourself?' he said, turning back. 'It's all so easy for you to say, though, isn't it? You're not the one who has spent so long being mocked, being ignored, being rejected and . . . and living with your unfulfilled desires!'

'Everyone gets rejected, Gary!' Jen said, unable to stop herself raising her voice. 'Everyone gets lonely. That's just life. It's normal!'

Gary was back down at Jen's side again and she saw a wildness in his eyes then, almost as though she could hear the faint sound of the locks binding him to what sanity he had left slowly giving way and snapping in two.

'Girls gave their affection, their sex, their love, their touch, and their everything to other men, to Chads, but never to me. Never to me! And it's not fair! Do you think I chose to be celibate? Do you really think I go about life like this, no sex at all, not a goddamn thing, because I want to? Well, you're wrong, Stacy! This is involuntary, all of it, and it's because of you and everyone like you! It's your fault!'

Despite where she was and what was happening, Jen nearly laughed. What the hell had happened to turn him into whatever this was in front of her now? She couldn't understand it, couldn't fathom the kind of crazy that had so obviously twisted Gary up and sent him down such a dark, terrible road. And what the hell was all that stuff about celibacy? Did he really think he was entitled to sex? That was . . . well, it was crazy! It was the kind of insanity you only ever heard about on the news!

And then Jen realised exactly what she was dealing with.

'Jesus . . .'

'What about him?' Gary asked suddenly. 'He's not listening, by the way. I know. I've asked for his help. And he's never given it. And you know why? Because I bet he never felt like this. So he couldn't help, could he? Why else did Mary hang around with him, hm? Even the holy Son of God got some, but me? Nothing! Not a goddamn thing! And it's not fair! It's NOT FAIR!'

'You're an incel,' Jen said, snapping back at Gary, her only plan now to keep him talking, to give her time to think of something, perhaps enough time for someone to come along the Corpse Road, a walker, a runner, a farmer. 'That's what all this is, isn't it? You're like those other sad bastards who think they're entitled to sex, to relationships, and go on about how it's everyone else's fault but theirs!'

'I'm not a bad person,' Gary said. 'I'm really not. But no one has ever been able to find that out because they've never given me a chance. You didn't, did you?'

'And that's why we're here now, is it?' Jen asked. 'Why you killed Kirsty? And you killed her husband as well, didn't you?'

'Yes, I did,' Gary said. Then, as he spoke, it was as though he was reliving what had happened, pacing out his actions, miming what he had done. 'Kirsty was my first! She was so easy to catch. Found her on Facebook. Went fishing and there she was. Such an easy catch!' He put a finger in his mouth and pulled at his cheek like a hook was caught in it. 'So entitled, so rich, so perfect! So easy. I was only going to scare her, you know? That was the plan. Go up there, spy on her, use the rifle to shoot at her, really terrify her! But then, when I was there, in the moment, I saw her for what she was. A Stacy. So, I had to do it, don't you see that? I had to make an example of her! To show the world that I, and everyone like me, that we won't take it anymore! We won't be ignored! We deserve what's rightfully ours as much as you do!'

As Gary raged on, half talking to her, half to his phone, Jen searched deep down for some grain of hope, for some idea, some solution, that would get her out of the shit she was in now. But she couldn't find anything. Then she thought about the rest of the team. They knew where she had headed off to, but that wasn't where she was now. They knew that she was with Gary, but only she knew *what* Gary was! They had no idea, no idea at all! And hadn't Harry brought in Adam, Gary's brother? They had the wrong man! They were interviewing the wrong bloody man!

Gary had stopped talking.

'You've . . . you've made your point,' Jen said. 'People will listen. I'm sure they will. I'll tell them. I'll . . . I'll help you.'

Gary's lips curled into a smile cold and hard.

'Yes, I know you will,' he said and pulled out a knife.

CHAPTER THIRTY-FOUR

HARRY BRACED HIMSELF AS JIM SWUNG THE PATROL CAR off the main road and onto a gravel track, which led up to the moors above Gunnerside. Ahead, Matt was kicking up grit and dust, the car dancing along the track.

'She has to be up here, right?' Jim asked, his eyes dead ahead. 'She has to be!'

'It's our best guess,' Harry said, 'and right now it's all we've got.' He remembered something Jim had been saying before they'd left the community centre. 'Stacy and Chad, then? You were going to say something about those names, just before we left. What was it?'

Jim hooked the car round a sharp bend, down a dip, and then back up the other side.

'You wouldn't believe me if I told you.'

'Try me,' Harry said.

'You've heard of incels, right?'

'Yes,' Harry said. 'But not much.'

'Basically, they're men who blame women for the fact that they don't have sex.'

'Involuntary celibates,' Harry said.

'Yeah, that's them. Proper crazy they are, like. You wouldn't believe some of the stuff they believe. They seem to think they have a right to have sex and they blame Stacys and Chads for the fact that they're not getting any.'

'And the Stacys and Chads are?' Harry asked.

'Everyone else, I guess,' Jim said. 'But it's generally attractive, successful people. Incels see themselves as genetically disadvantaged. It's pretty messed up stuff.'

Another corner came up and the rear of the car slid out, but Jim had it controlled and used the whip of the car's tail to help them onwards after Matt.

'I've a feeling my face means I'm no way a Chad,' Harry said. 'Sounds like he carved Stacy and Chad onto the faces of his victims because he was making an example of them.'

'I guess,' Jim said.

Ahead, Matt's car skidded to a halt. Jim threw his car in alongside. Harry jumped out.

'Where's the Corpse Road?' he asked. 'How the hell do we get to where we were on Sunday? To that bloody scrape the mad bastard carved out.'

Matt pointed ahead. 'Just up that way.'

'How far?'

'Half a kilometre, at a guess,' Matt replied.

'Then shift it!' Harry roared, and he didn't even wait for the others as he set off at a pace which, just a few months ago, would have had him upchucking his guts in seconds.

JEN WAS ON HER SIDE, her whole weight on her right hand, her hip. Her eyes were on the knife in Gary's hand. The pain coursing through her body from how she was lying didn't matter. It had gone, faded into nothing when faced with the knife. That was what mattered now—the knife. Only the knife. Just that awful blade in front of her, the glint of it, the cold effectiveness of the sweep of the dagger's edge down to its deadly point.

'You stay away from me!' she screamed, squirming on the ground. 'Stay the hell away!'

Gary smiled, moved closer, his footsteps small and slow. 'You can't escape,' he said, lifting his phone to film her once more, his pistol stowed down the front of his jeans. 'This has to happen now, because of what you did.'

'I didn't do anything!' Jen yelled back. 'You're insane!'

'Exactly, you didn't do anything,' Gary said. 'But if you had done something, if you'd just come with me in the car, got to know me, then we wouldn't be here now, would we? Surely you can see that? So, I have to punish you. I have to punish all of you. Every Stacy. Every Chad.'

Jen didn't want to cry. She didn't want to show any weakness, but she couldn't help herself. Tears were flowing now, racing down her face.

'Please,' she said. 'Just . . . just don't do it, Gary. You don't have to.'

'I do have to,' Gary said, then stepped forward.

In desperation, Jen twisted her body violently, swinging her legs out as hard as she could to keep Gary away, her voice crying out with this last chance attempt at staying alive. They connected and Gary, taken by surprise at the sudden movement, tripped over his own feet.

'Bitch!'

Gary fell forward, landing hard on top of Jen, the weight of his body winding her, his phone and knife knocked from his hands.

'You're going to pay for that!' Gary hissed, struggling to get up from Jen as she wriggled beneath him. Then, realising his face was so close, she leaned in and bit down hard.

Gary roared and screamed at the same time, rage and pain and shock twisting his cry into a hyena's howl.

Gary was on all fours now, but Jen was holding on, her teeth sinking deeper, and then warm liquid was in her mouth and she knew it was his blood.

Gary tried to shake her off, then back-handed her so hard that her skull ricocheted off the stone beneath her. But the damage had been done and Gary lifted a hand to his face, felt the wetness seeping out of it, then the stinging pain of the wound as his fingers poked it.

Jen was dazed, her mouth filled with the foul taste of hot iron. Some of the blood was in her eyes, mixing with her tears, blinding her. She tried to crawl away from where she could hear Gary crying out, but she could barely move now. The sudden movements of the last minute, the impact of Gary's body, the slap, all of it was piling in on her now, freezing her muscles solid.

Gary was on his feet.

'You're going to pay for that,' he said, then dropped down to one knee and picked up his knife. 'You're going to pay for that like you wouldn't believe, Stacy. Like you wouldn't believe . . .'

HARRY'S LUNGS WERE, he was sure, right up in the back of his throat, but he didn't care. If Jen was up here, he was going to find her. If she wasn't . . . Harry pushed that thought away. She had to be up here. It's the only place that made any sense.

Behind him, Harry could hear the others, the path too narrow for them to pass.

A cry rang out.

'You hear that?' Jim called to Harry.

'Too bloody right I did!' Harry roared. 'Come on! Shift it!'

Harry wasn't sure how much longer he could last, running at the pace he was going, he just knew that he had to, no matter what.

Another cry, this one deeper, a sound of pain-filled rage.

Harry was starting to see stars, his vision blurring just a little at the edges. His lungs felt like they were filled with broken glass and his legs were on fire. But those screams, he knew, were Jen and Gary. They had to be. He willed them to be. And pushed on.

JEN WRIGGLED BACK, but could wriggle no further, the coffin stone behind her stopping her dead.

'There's nowhere to go, Stacy,' Gary said, lifting the knife up in front of him. 'It's just you and me. And I'm afraid that this is going to hurt you a lot more than it's going to hurt me.'

As Gary moved in for the kill, Jen saw a great black shape loom up behind him. Was this it? she thought. Had Death come for her?

Jen went to close her eyes as the black shape crashed into Gary and she was sure, with the sounds that Gary and the terrible dark shadow made as they connected, that this was her end. There would be no more. Death had claimed her.

. . .

HARRY CRASHED into Gary as much out of relief at being able to stop running as it was to stop the maniac doing what he was about to do to Jen with his knife. They tumbled to the ground and Harry just caught sight of Jen, tied up, bruised, her face red with tears as they fell.

Hitting the ground hard, Harry took full advantage of his additional weight, and kept himself on top of Gary as he felt him try to squirm out from beneath him.

'You're not going anywhere,' Harry hissed. 'It's over, Gary. You're done!'

Gary struggled against Harry's weight, pushed up on his arms, kicked and flailed, but it did nothing. Harry wasn't going anywhere.

Jim was next to Harry then, and Jadyn, both dropping down at his side to take the strain. Matt fell in behind, dropping onto Gary's legs.

'We've got him, Boss,' Jim said. 'You go sort Jen.'

Harry rolled off Gary's back, ignoring the groans of pain from him as he did so. Then he was over to Jen on his hands and knees.

'Jen? Jen! It's Harry! We're here! You're okay! You're safe!'

For a moment, Jen didn't move, didn't open her eyes, her body jammed up hard against the stone.

'Jen,' Harry said again, and reached out a hand to rest on her shoulder. 'It's Harry.'

When she opened her eyes, Jen stared back at Harry and in that look, he saw the reflection of the hell that she'd been through.

'You're okay,' he said, his voice gentle. 'You're safe now.'

Then, it all came crashing in and Jen cried out.

Harry reached over for her and pulled her close. Then, as her body shook with long, racking sobs, he reached out to where Gary's knife had fallen, took hold of it, and started to cut her free.

CHAPTER THIRTY-FIVE

HARRY CLASPED HIS MUG WITH BOTH HANDS AND LIFTED it to his mouth. Everywhere hurt. His legs, his chest, his arms. His knuckles were scraped and bleeding. There were scratches on his face. Hell, even his eyelids hurt, though he had no idea how that was even possible. It had been quite a day, quite a week, actually. The job was more than enough, for sure, and his brother's problems certainly added to it. But this new stuff from his dad? What the hell was that all about? He didn't know and, in many ways right then, he wasn't sure that he cared. All that mattered at that moment was the fact that Jen was okay, they'd got there in time. 'But only just,' Harry muttered to himself, 'only just . . .'

'Tea'll help, I promise you,' Liz said, as Harry moved to slump down into one of the chairs in the team room at the community centre. 'It always does. And it'll stop you talking to yourself, anyway.'

Harry's time in the Paras had taught him many things, from jumping out of aircraft to tying snares, but of all the things he'd learned, it was that the healing properties of a good brew were not to be sniffed at.

'Yeah, sorry about that,' Harry said. 'Rather a lot on my mind.'

'Not a surprise, is it?' Liz said.

'How you doing, boss?' Matt asked, leaning himself against a table.

Harry didn't answer. He was too busy with his tea.

'What about yourself?' Liz asked, looking over at Matt.

'Oh, I'm fine,' Matt said. 'Fit as pins, me.'

'That'll be why you limped in here like you'd lost your crutches, then,' Liz said.

Harry looked up at Matt. 'Jim and Jadyn will be at Harrogate by now, right?'

Matt checked his watch. 'Another fifteen minutes I should think. You sure you don't want to follow on?'

Harry shook his head. 'No, they're young, let them have this one, I think. It'll do them both good. And I need to stay here and keep an eye on that daft dog of his.'

Harry looked over at Fly who was on his back, paws in the air, fast asleep.

'Yeah, he's a right bother, that one,' Matt laughed. 'You were the arresting officer though. By rights, it should be you.'

'Was I, though?' Harry countered. 'All I did was slam into Gary and squash him. No, they can have it. Anyway, like I said, I'm busy with this mug of tea.'

Matt sat down. 'And all that dog-watching. So, what now?' he asked.

'Well, I doubt a holiday to the south of France is on the cards,' Harry said. 'Can't imagine Swift approving of that, can you?'

'He's on his way over, by the way,' Liz said. 'To Harrogate, I mean. I rang him, like you said. Can't say I'm sure if he sounded pleased with the arrest or annoyed at being woken up from a nap.'

'Probably both,' Matt said.

'Oh, and did you get anywhere with finding anything out about those two blokes being suspicious?'

Harry shook his head. 'No, not yet,' he said. He didn't have the energy to say anymore. Perhaps later.

Harry leaned into his chair and stretched his back, the sound of the bones cracking and popping bouncing around the room. 'I tell you, I've dealt with some crazy mad nonsense in my time, but this stuff with Gary?' He rubbed his eyes, weary already, and it wasn't even mid-afternoon. 'Incels? Stacys and Chads? What the hell is wrong with people?'

'Buggered if I know,' Matt said.

Harry spotted Gordy's postcard pinned to one of the noticeboards. 'Picked a right week to be away, didn't she?' he said. Then he looked over to Liz. 'How was Adam?' he asked. 'When you told him what had happened?'

'All I told him was that Gary had been arrested, like you said. I didn't say anything about the whys and the wherefores.'

'And?'

'And he fair looked like the ship with no wind in its sails,' Liz said. 'Like, he almost shrunk in front of me.'

'Do you think he knew?' Matt asked.

Harry shook his head. 'No, I don't think he had the faintest idea of what was going on. How could he? Gary hid it from everyone. He's clearly been living this online world of incel conspiracy bollocks for years.'

'But to allow it to come to this?' Matt said. 'It's proper madness, that, if you ask me. Kid's a loon.'

'He's screwed up, that's for sure,' Harry said. 'Believing all that shite about involuntary celibacy or whatever, then doing what he did? Like I said, I've seen some crazy stuff in my time, but this? It's up there.' Harry lifted his left hand to the top of an imaginary pile of crazy things he'd encountered in his life. 'By which I mean, right up there.'

'It's jealousy gone mad,' Liz said, shaking her head.

'It's not just jealousy,' Harry said, but didn't go any further. 'I tell you though, it's not convinced me that I should be getting myself on Facebook anytime soon, that's for sure.'

'I'm with you on that,' Matt agreed. 'Right load of old bollocks.'

Harry finished his tea, then pulled out his phone to check as he'd not looked at it since early that morning. There was one missed call. And it was from Detective Superintendent Alice Firbank. He really didn't have the energy, but he also knew that he had to speak to her.

'There's a call I need to make,' he said, standing up, despite the aches. 'Won't be a mo'.'

As Harry made to leave, a knock at the door had him look over to see it open and a head pop around and into the room an inch.

'Now then,' said Dave. 'I see you're in.'

Harry was about to tell him about the call he had to make when Dave pushed the door open further and stepped in. He was a large man, built rather like a bull, Harry thought. Or a rhino. Perhaps a strange mix of the two. Either way, the man's bulk was blocking Harry's route out pretty surely, so he switched off his phone and smiled.

'Hi, Dave,' he said. 'I've been meaning to give you a call.'

'No bother,' Dave said. 'You've been busy.' He then cast his eye up and down Harry, taking in the full dishevelled nature of what was in front of him, a man cut and bruised, his clothing scuffed, torn, and covered in grass stains and mud. 'Though with what, I'm not sure I want to know right now, if that's okay with you.'

'Anything we can help you with?' Matt asked, making to stand.

Dave raised a hand to stop him halfway. 'No, there's nowt going on. Just popped in as someone had said they'd seen you lot tearing out of the marketplace earlier. And judging by how you look, wherever it was you were going, you got there just in the nick of time.'

'We did,' Harry said, then asked if Dave fancied a tea. 'I'm having another myself,' Harry said. 'We all need another.'

'I will, yes,' Dave said. 'Which reminds me . . .'

Harry watched as Dave revealed a small paper bag he'd been carrying.

'And what's that?' Harry asked.

'Something to go with the tea,' Dave said. 'When I heard that you'd all rushed off to something obviously important, I thought I'd bring something round, like. You know, just in case.'

'Just in case of what?' Harry asked.

'Well, just in case you didn't have anything in. And we can't have that, now, can we?'

'No, we can't,' Matt agreed. 'Nowt worse than not having something in.'

Harry was tired and was sensing that he was starting to lose the point of whatever it was Dave was trying to communicate.

'So, what's in the bag, Dave?'

Dave stepped over to a table and opened the bag. 'First,

there's this,' he said. 'Cake, obviously. From Cockett's as well, because I see no point in buying it from anywhere else and then being disappointed, do you?'

Harry stared at the cake, then back at Dave's bag. He could see that there was something else inside it and he was pretty sure that he didn't want to ask what it was, but he couldn't help himself.

'And second?' he asked.

Dave reached into the bag and pulled out a small block of something wrapped in wax paper. 'Wensleydale cheese,' he grinned.

'Brilliant!' Matt cheered. 'Cheese and cake! Get the kettle on, Liz!'

Harry stared at the two items on the table. After the days they'd all just lived through he was more in the mood for beer and fish and chips. Later maybe, he thought. After the call he needed to make.

Dave rested one of his massive, hefty hands onto Harry's shoulder.

'I think it's time you gave it a go,' he said. 'You can't go putting it off forever, you know.'

Harry looked at Dave, then at the cheese and cake, then at Dave once more.

'Cheese though, Dave. I mean, it's wrong, isn't it?'

Dave's hand squeezed just enough to let Harry know that he could probably keep on squeezing and crush his shoulder to mush.

Harry took a deep breath. 'Matt?'

'Yes, Boss?'

'Get me a knife, will you?'

IF YOU ENJOYED CORPSE ROAD, then you're going to love Shooting Season

---

JOIN THE VIP CLUB!

WANT to find out where it all began, and how Harry decided to join the police? Sign up to my newsletter today to get your exclusive copy of the short origin story, 'Homecoming', and to join the DCI Harry Grimm VIP Club. You'll receive regular updates on the series, plus VIP access to a photo gallery of locations from the books, and the chance to win amazing frce stuff in some fantastic competitions.

You can also connect with other fans of DCI Grimm and his team by joining The Official DCI Harry Grimm Reader Group.

Enjoyed this book? Then please tell others!

The best thing about reviews is they help people like you: other readers. So, if you can spare a few seconds and leave a review, that would be fantastic. I love hearing what readers think about my books, so you can also email me the link to your review at dciharrygrimm@hotmail.com.

AUTHOR'S NOTE

Swaledale is a very special place, not just in general terms, but to me personally. I lived in Wensleydale till I was thirteen, but the dales have always called me back. When I was eighteen, and having finished my A-Levels, I took a year out before heading off to university. And that year I spent in Swaledale itself, working at (yes, you've guessed it!) Marrick Priory! I was an assistant instructor, taking groups out doing various outdoor activities, from caving down Crackpot to abseiling, raft-building, and orienteering. I honestly wasn't expecting Marrick to play a part in this story at all, but that's the way things work out sometimes; the story takes on a life of its own and you just have to be brave—and mad—enough to go with it! Marrick may well turn up again at some point, not least, because it has its own little ghost story to tell and one that I've experienced myself.

Reeth, mentioned briefly in this story, but more so in *Best Served Cold*, is a wonderful little place. The pub Harry visits in that story is well worth a visit, as is the King's Head mentioned in *Corpse Road*. In fact, if you want a lovely day out, and you just so happen to be in the area, get yourself up to Gunnerside and head up the Gill. It's a smashing little walk, interesting too, with the ruins of mines giving plenty to look at as you stroll along. There's a magic to the place, almost as though, if you're just quiet enough, you may well meet those miners of old, or just hear the distant whispers of their long-ago conversations still dancing on the breeze.

The corpse road itself fascinated me as an idea, though I have to admit here that I have used a bit of poetic licence to describe it and its surroundings, but that's my job, right? The coffin stone I've lifted from a corpse road elsewhere in the country, but I just couldn't resist dropping it up there on the top of the fells!

The band I mention, Fourum, is real! When we lived in the dales, my dad as the Methodist minister would always be armed with his twelve-string guitar for services in the chapels which dot the dales. The chapels themselves were proper community centres and music was a big thing. Dad would perform various folk tunes, and some were by Fourum. And I can still remember them, particularly one about the river Swale, and another about Gunnerside Gill. The song about the Swale is all about loving the place, the dale, the river, and just staying there, probably forever. And in some ways, I think I did. It was a formative year, leaving home, that step into adulthood. Living there changed me, and it is wonderful to be revisiting it as I am now. As for the song about Gunnerside Gill, well I actually tip my hat to it at one point early on. Back when Harry is leaving the first crime scene, he feels as though every step is taking him back in time, which is how the song describes walking up the Gill.

Swaledale is a hauntingly beautiful place and it stays with you. And in some small way, I hope you've walked it a little in these pages. Who knows, perhaps you'll take a trip there yourself one day. I know I'll be going back. And soon.

Dave

ABOUT DAVID J. GATWARD

David had his first book published when he was 18 and has written extensively for children and young adults. *Corpse Road* is his third crime novel.

Visit David's website to find out more about him and the DCI Harry Grimm books.

 facebook.com/davidjgatwardauthor

ALSO BY DAVID J. GATWARD

THE DCI HARRY GRIMM SERIES

Grimm Up North

Best Served Cold

Shooting Season

Restless Dead

Death's Requiem

Blood Sport

Cold Sanctuary

One Bad Turn

Blood Trail

Fair Game

Unquiet Bones

The Dark Hours

Silent Ruin

Made in the USA
Monee, IL
25 July 2023